SPECIMEN

SPECIMEN

STORIES

IRINA KOVALYOVA

Copyright © 2015 Irina Kovalyova

Published in Canada in 2015 by House of Anansi Press Inc.
www.houseofanansi.com

House of Anansi Press is committed to protecting our natural environment.
As part of our efforts, the interior of this book is printed on paper that
contains 100% post-consumer recycled fibres, is acid-free, and is processed
chlorine-free.

20 19 18 17 16   2 3 4 5 6

Library and Archives Canada Cataloguing in Publication

Kovalyova, Irina, 1974–, author
Specimen : stories / by Irina Kovalyova.

Issued in print and electronic formats.
ISBN 978-1-77089-817-2 (pbk.).—ISBN 978-1-77089-818-9 (html)

I. Title.

PS8621.O9734S64 2015   C813'.6   C2015-902913-9
                                           C2015-902914-7

Book design: Alysia Shewchuk

*We acknowledge for their financial support of our publishing program
the Canada Council for the Arts, the Ontario Arts Council, and the Government of
Canada through the Canada Book Fund.*

Printed and bound in Canada

For mamochka

CONTENTS

MAMOCHKA

MARIA IVANOVNA, the chief archivist at the Institute of Physics in Minsk, remained at her desk during the lunch break. She waited until her colleagues went out to the cafeteria, then took a boiled potato out of her purse, poured a cup of hot water over a used bag of black tea, and began to write an email to her daughter in Canada. She struck the ancient keyboard with two index fingers because writing in English was not her forte. She'd learned English on her own after falling in love at the age of ten with Professor Higgins in the Hollywood film *My Fair Lady*. It had been difficult to get books in English in the Soviet Union, but Maria Ivanovna had found a way.

How are you, my dear girls? she wrote. *Lydia, how are you holding? I've been meaning to ask you something for several months now, but I begin with my news.*

Maria Ivanovna paused and looked at the stain spreading on the wallpaper under the window. The rainstorm had been raging with fury for seven days. Water poured down the basements, surged into the drainpipes, groaned, bubbled, and swelled in foaming waves on the streets. She thought of the city inspector—a grim, skeletal man in a leather coat—who had said last night on the news, "We need to lay six kilometres of new canalization pipes. At the moment we have six hundred metres in place. Therefore, in the coming days, citizens may expect further surprises." In the low-lying centre of Minsk, where the nearest hospital was located, people had to be rescued from flooded trolley buses by boat.

Maria Ivanovna did not have much news. Every time the doctor prescribed her "treatments," her days turned into some kind of—she held her two fingers above the keyboard—*thickening porridge*, she wrote, *and I have to resort to a daily planner. Not just to use it, you see, but I can't let go of it; otherwise, I forget what and when I have to do. Maybe my age is the reason. I am no longer a, how do you say it, a summer chicken?*

Maria Ivanovna bit a piece of the potato, looked at the photograph of Lydia kissing baby Hui-fang, and inserted a smiley face on the screen. She sighed and thought of her trip to Vancouver six months ago. She remembered the beautiful people with very white teeth who wore expensive clothes and bought papaya smoothies at a grocery store named Whole Foods. Lydia's husband—a short, stocky Chinese man with spiky black hair named Dingxing who insisted Maria Ivanovna call him Just Donald—took her there one day to buy artichoke pizza. Maria Ivanovna recalled how, while standing at the checkout counter holding a hot box of pizza, she'd felt as if she were an unknown object, an asteroid crashing on this *terra incognita* of abundance and wealth. She'd eaten neither papayas nor artichokes in her fifty-five years on Earth, but it wasn't important. What was important was that she'd endured. She'd endured low wages, cold winters, potholes in the streets, uniforms, flags, parades, and breadlines. She endured with humour because humour seemed to Maria Ivanovna to be the glue that held the edges of life together. In any case, she could not see what was wrong with eating potatoes.

People in Whole Foods, however, had not cared about Maria Ivanovna's humour or the richness of her inner life. Or about the fact that she was a kind, resourceful person who could quote entire pages from Tolstoy and sing solo arias in the Women's Community Choir in Minsk. All those people saw, if they had looked at Maria Ivanovna at all, was a plain, pudgy woman in black slacks, with a face lashed by the rapids of time and crowned by Afro-permed hair.

She brought the tea glass to her lips by its silver filigree holder and took a scalding sip of weak tea. Her eyes, behind large round spectacles rimmed with pink frames, zoomed in on Lydia's plump face that, with its rounded chin of a cabbage perogy, bow-shaped mouth, and button nose, so resembled Maria Ivanovna's own.

Dingxing Cheng and Lydia had met in graduate school in Ontario two years ago and, before Maria Ivanovna could say "rice cracker," married and moved to Vancouver for postgraduate work. In response to Maria Ivanovna's email in which she had questioned Lydia's wisdom in getting married so quickly to Mr. Cheng, and in which she'd suggested that perhaps Lydia didn't have as much in common with him as she thought, Lydia had written the following two terrible sentences in the subject line of an empty email: *Mother, we have all the commonality we can possibly have. We are going to have a baby.*

Oh, how Maria Ivanovna had suffered! She was hardly an enthusiast of mixed races where other people were concerned, but to think, my good God, *Bozhe moi*, to think that her only child should willingly mix her Russian blood with blood from China! It was beyond endurance for Maria Ivanovna to think that she had no say, no say whatsoever, in what was to happen to one-half of her genes.

"My *dorogaia* daughter," Maria Ivanovna had attempted to reason with Lydia over the phone, a month before the wedding to Just Donald. "Each person carries a message from their ancestors in every cell. Ciphers from the deep past are encoded in our genes. DNA neither crumbles like parchment nor does it rust away like a nail. It is history dust that lives inside us!"

"Mamochka, please calm down," Lydia replied. "Dust schmust, honestly. Would you listen to yourself? The atoms that make up human beings were actually forged in the stars."

It *was* possible, after all, that she was a little bit racist, Maria Ivanovna had to admit, but who wasn't, in Russia? Or, come to think of it, anywhere else? She had neither the training nor the knowledge in science that Lydia had, but she didn't need science to tell her that some things were immutable and that was that.

And so, on her way to Vancouver, stuffed like a herring in the steel barrel of a Lufthansa plane, Maria Ivanovna had worried about her racism and about not being able to pronounce her granddaughter's name. She'd gone to the cramped washroom at least twenty times and stood there, in front of the mirror, stretching and twisting her lips in strange ways, spelling out each individual letter of her granddaughter's name in Russian, in English, in French, finally sounding the whole thing out using Universal Phonetic notation.

"Hwah," she tried. "No. Hweh," she corrected herself. "Hweh-fang," she tried again. "Hweh-fahng. That's it — Hweh-fahng." She smiled and stretched the corners of her eyes to make herself look Asian. She'd waved at herself in the mirror and tried to sound cheerful. "Who is *this*? Is this Hweh-fahng? Is *this* my darling little doll, my *kukolka*, Hweh-fahng?"

Maria Ivanovna burst into laughter. How silly she'd been!

SHE HEARD THE sound of someone clearing their throat behind her and turned to see the head of Professor Chernov stick out from behind the door.

"Tea?" he asked, and smacked his lips. His head had a prominent flattened plateau on the top, but the rest of it looked very much like an egg.

Professor Chernov was Maria Ivanovna's favourite scientist in the Institute. Indeed, she considered him to be a friend, or in any case much more than a mere co-worker whose scientific reports she filed away. Sometimes they had lunches together, during which Professor Chernov would discuss his remarkable breakthroughs.

"Despite the perplexity of stellar corpses, I remain convinced of the existence of white dwarfs," he'd told her on one occasion. On another, he'd asked her triumphantly, "Do you realize that I'm proving the case against the black holes as we speak?"

Only once in the past had Maria Ivanovna caught a twinkle of romance in Professor Chernov's clever eyes. They'd gone to hear a jazz quartet from Moscow and to dance in the Hall of the People afterward. It was there, amid glistening faces and tall colonnades, that Professor Chernov had tried to kiss her. He circled suggestively Maria Ivanovna's waist with a soft arm and pulled her toward him. She saw a piece of green onion stuck in his beard. And for a moment, for the briefest of moments, it seemed to Maria Ivanovna that she could let go of her solitude and fall under his dwarfish spell. But—no, it was not possible. She had disengaged herself from his awkward embrace, feigned a migraine, and taken a tram home. They had neither spoken of that episode nor gone out anywhere since, and she was glad, after all, that they'd remained on good terms.

Maria Ivanovna said, "Not today, my dear professor. I'm trying to catch up on my correspondence."

The rain muffled the sound of Professor Chernov's retreating footsteps and continued to strain the cesspools of Minsk. Maria Ivanovna glanced at her watch and leaned back in her chair. Her back felt like a wood plank from the long hours of sitting. She stood up, unhooked her bra, and performed a series of exercises—arm stretches, back bends, small lunges, and push-ups. As she did so, Lydia's left breast swam abruptly into her mind's eye: it was swollen with milk and installed in the pink mouth of baby Hui-fang. Hui-fang's eyes, like Maria Ivanovna's, were set wide apart, almond-shaped, Mongolian, a remarkable aberration of green. The kind of green one could find on a vast, windswept Asian steppe, in a blade of grass licked by the tongue of a wild horse.

Maria Ivanovna let out a sob. It was all too much for her, too much. The truth was that she missed her grand-daughter so much that sometimes in the middle of songs she'd burst out in tears. She worried too about Lydia's mental health.

"Mama," Lydia had said in a Starbucks in Vancouver, "there are so many unwanted babies in this world."

Maria Ivanovna stopped licking whipped cream off her mocha.

"I look at Hui-fang every day," Lydia continued, "and I ask myself if we shouldn't do more for other children. Because we can, you know. We have the means."

Lydia went on to reveal to Maria Ivanovna that she'd made plans to go to Africa to adopt a baby.

"Well, okay, if you want to," Maria Ivanovna forced her-self to say. But what she really wanted to say was, "Are you out of your mind?"

"Some of them may have HIV," Lydia said. "It may come as a shock to you, but we really want to do this."

We — which meant Just Donald was in agreement. Despite her initial reservations, Maria Ivanovna liked her son-in-law. She liked his easy manner and his organiza-tional skills. Still, he worked in his lab every day, and Lydia juggled her work *and* the baby. Could it be that Lydia's unhappiness in her marriage led her to dream up these crazy things? No, no. Not for all the tea in China should Lydia adopt an African baby.

Lydia, Maria Ivanovna went on typing, *you mentioned a "shrink" in your last email. I confess that I had to ask Mr. Google about this word. Frankly speaking, I find it weird that you'd think that a stranger would help you unpack your "emotional" load. First and always, one should help oneself. In any case, we will speak of this "shrink" when I see you again. In the meantime, don't do anything I know you'll regret. My beloved Hui-fang is one year old already, and I think frequently about life being so short and so on, about how everyone seems to be always running to get somewhere. Why?*

Maria Ivanovna heard a door slam in the corridor and sped up the striking of keys.

I now arrive to what I wanted to ask you about for a long time. I hate it so that we are apart, Lydia dear. Is it possible that this summer you will let my darling Hui-fang stay with me in Minsk in the summer?

Maria Ivanovna pressed the Send button quickly before she could change her mind, and dabbed her eyes with a tissue. She took a small square mirror out of her purse and began reapplying pink lipstick when Olga Pavlova, a girl who worked on the third floor and whom Maria Ivanovna tutored in English on Mondays, threw the door open and cried from the threshold, "Maria Ivanovna, *dorogaia*, you must come at once, please! It's Nina."

"What is it? What's the matter?" Maria Ivanovna said calmly. She prided herself on being a buoy in the tempest of the Institute's plot.

"It's Nina!" cried Olga again. Her eyes were dark brown and wide, like saucers of gravy. "She's having a baby!"

Olga pulled at Maria Ivanovna's sleeve.

Maria Ivanovna was fond of Nina Petrova and had been worried about her for the last several months. Nina was a part-time research assistant; a shy, bookish girl from Smolensk, whose recent changes in appearance and demeanour had not escaped Maria Ivanovna's notice. Indeed, she'd written about it in her daily planner. *Nina seems distressed, distant, very unfriendly with me and ill disposed toward the others. She shows no interest at all in my anecdotes. She listens to me reluctantly and behaves as if she holds a grudge against the whole world.*

Maria Ivanovna followed Olga quickly through the hallway, down one set of stairs, and into a women's bathroom on the third floor. In the corner, gripping a black pipe under a cracked sink, squatted Nina Petrova.

Maria Ivanovna washed her hands at the sink and wiped them on her blouse. She took a moment to reflect on her remarkable luck. Shortly before Lydia went into labour, Maria Ivanovna had sent an e-file to Just Donald titled *How to Deliver a Baby in an Emergency*, for, as Maria Ivanovna put it, "due preparation for the big event." *The time may come*, she recalled its instructions now with absolute clarity, *when you have to deliver a baby with no doctor or midwife nearby. Birth is totally natural and you need to use common sense.* Maria Ivanovna was glad that she'd archived this information on one of the shelves in her brain.

"Nina," she said, and reached to lift Nina's skirt. "May I see what is happening, please? Do you feel like you need to go on the toilet?"

Nina screwed up her face and pushed Maria Ivanovna's hand away. "Mama, mamochka!" she shrieked, tearing the membranes of Maria Ivanovna's eardrums. "Mamochka!"

Maria Ivanovna waited. The contraction was over in less than a minute. Nina stopped screaming and loosened her hold on the pipe.

Maria Ivanovna turned to Olga, who stood shivering in the doorway.

"Run to Professor Chernov at once," she said, "and get me his vodka."

She scanned the bathroom cubicles with her eyes, thinking.

"And bring scissors," she added. She knew that because of the flood it would be a while yet before any medical help arrived. "Also, I need shirts and towels and strings. If you can't find strings, shoelaces will do." She motioned impatiently to Olga to execute her commands, then turned her attention back to Nina.

"Nina," she said gently. "I'm going to help you. I know what to do."

She took off her blouse and spread it on the floor.

"Okay, dear, lie down. That's it." She wedged herself between Nina's legs and lifted the edge of Nina's skirt. "I can already see the top of the baby's head. When the pain stops for a bit, begin pushing." She brushed Nina's hair away from her forehead. "And scream."

Nina screamed, pushed, screamed, pushed, screamed, pushed, pushed, screamed and pushed.

Maria Ivanovna heard the bathroom door open and close.

"What the hell, Nina?" Olga cried, when she saw a brown-skinned head emerge from between Nina's legs.

"Shut up!" Maria Ivanovna said.

Olga froze on the spot and pressed a pale hand over her mouth. In her other hand she held a half-drunk bottle of Stolichnaya wrapped in a man's flannel shirt.

Maria Ivanovna pushed the baby's head toward Nina's stomach, then grabbed and pulled out a slippery shoulder. The rest of the small, puffy body came out quickly on a rapid of reddish water.

"Shirt," Maria Ivanovna said, and stretched out her arm behind her toward Olga.

Once the baby was wrapped in the shirt, Maria Ivanova turned its face down, and began to rub its back. Nina stopped screaming. The baby gagged and did not make a sound.

Olga said, "*Bozhe moi!*"

Maria Ivanovna wiped the fluid from the baby's mouth and nose with the shirt, flicked the soles of its feet with her fingers, and slapped its brown bottom with the flat of her hand.

Everything became very quiet. The rain played a fugue on the roof.

The baby burst out crying in the classic bel canto of the newborn. Its tiny body tried to wriggle out of Maria Ivanovna's grip. As its pink palms stretched toward her, she recalled the words of Professor Chernov: "Birth is undulation. A new star is born when its core temperature exceeds ten million degrees."

After a moment, Maria Ivanovna poured vodka over the scissors. She tied a shoelace around the umbilical cord with a double knot ten centimetres from the baby's penis, and then another knot four centimetres farther up. Then she drank a little of the vodka and cut the cord between the two knots with one snip.

Nina raised herself on her elbows and said, "I don't want it. I hate it. Take it from me!"

"Olga," Maria Ivanovna said, ignoring Nina. "In a few minutes, her placenta should start coming out. Put this tea towel under her, right before the placenta appears. There will be more blood. The cord will get longer. Have her sit up and push it out."

"Where do you think you're going?" Olga screamed. "Don't leave me here alone with her!"

"Afterward, keep her warm, clean, and comfortable," Maria Ivanovna said, and walked out of the bathroom.

She walked slowly down the hallways, in a bra stained with blood, holding the baby next to her skin.

My darling Lydia, she envisioned the green words blinking on the black screen, *you wouldn't believe what just happened to me in the toilets.*

She knew that the milk kitchen at the hospital, where women donated their excess breast milk, would remain open until eight o'clock in the evening. She had stood many times in line there to get breast milk for Lydia when her own breasts refused to lactate. She would walk, take a boat, or swim to get there. She would find a way.

She bent her head to the baby and kissed his brown cheek.

"Your mamochka," she whispered, "is here, my little chocolate. Oh, she knows so many songs."

THE ECSTASY OF EDGAR ALABASTER

1886

I SHALL DESCRIBE herein the remarkable case of Edgar Alabaster, who was the subject of a mesmeric experiment conducted by myself and Doctor Rydberg on the night of Wednesday, the thirteenth of December.

At seven o'clock that fateful evening, as I was finishing my supper, I received a note from Rydberg, requesting my immediate presence in Alabaster's residence. By the time of which I write, the lurid details of Edgar's involvement with the eldest daughter of Reverend P—— had made their way into society, branding him, in effect, deranged.

I should mention that Edgar was the son of Sir Harald Alabaster, an amateur botanist and insect collector. The family, of old and noble stock, included three sisters and resided principally in Dorset, in a grand old mansion named Horsley Hall, but Sir Harald also kept a townhouse in Chelsea, in which Edgar had secluded himself since the scandal. About a month before our experiment, Rydberg had been summoned to Edgar's bedside, expecting to deal with a mild case of influenza, but what he had found instead was an advanced state of pulmonary phthisis (a form of consumption). Indeed, the ossification of both lungs in the patient was complete, prompting Rydberg to declare Edgar's dissolution imminent.

I had been for some time involved with mesmeric investigations into the limits of human perception, particularly as it related to the time just before death. Rydberg shared my interest in the unconscious mind, and through the years we'd conducted several experiments with lunatics, aiming to deduce the causes of their disease with logical inquiry. In particular, Rydberg investigated the roots of physical violence, whereas dysfunctions of a sexual nature excited my curiosity. And so, upon discovering from my learned friend (the reader may know Rydberg as the author of "Investigations into Germanic Mythology") the identity of his recent patient, I proposed to him that we take advantage of the circumstance, hoping that a series of well-considered questions directed to Alabaster under hypnosis would provide important clues as to the basis of his abnormality. In my experience, individuals of volatile temperament, which I had no doubt Alabaster possessed, exhibited exalted self-cognizance under magnetic influence. To ensure Alabaster's co-operation, I recommended we present ourselves to him as the advocates of the new science of eugenics. I had met Alabaster some years ago at a public lecture given by Doctor Francis Galton, and learned that he shared many of Galton's ideas.

As I anticipated, Alabaster consented to our request eagerly, and as I entered the invalid's room that evening,

he greeted me with the following diatribe directed at Rydberg: "No matter how much the fool tries to deny it, I
know I shall die tonight. Oh, but how vile, how unjust life
is that my noble blood should be soiled with the bacilli of
the vulgar!"

I was appalled, not only by the venomous outburst, but
also by the profound change in his appearance. Although
I had met him only briefly, I recalled Alabaster as a man
of remarkable physical beauty. He had been big and muscular, and carried his elegant frame with apparent viril-
ity. His hair had been blond and wavy, and his dark eyes
sparkled with the unmistakable vigour of life. It was easy
to understand why women (and some men, I will admit
here) found him attractive. But the body that lay before
me that evening, on a vast bed strewn with soiled sheets,
had become frighteningly altered. His face was emaciated
to the bone and wore a pale greenish hue. His eyes were
filmy yellow and rolled wildly in their sockets. Cracked
lips, partially opened, revealed a swollen tongue tinted
blue. He was breathing with great difficulty and appeared
to be in a state of agitation. And his hair, which had been
so lush once, had lost its lustre entirely, and clung in greasy
clumps to his cadaverous forehead.

He was propped up in the bed by pillows.

After taking my coat, Rydberg said, "Shall we begin? I
fear we don't have much time."

Edgar turned his face to the wall and remained silent
for several minutes.

"To hell with it," he said finally. "Do something!"

I waited two more minutes to make sure that he wasn't
going to change his mind, then, taking his hand, I asked

him to reiterate as clearly as he could his willingness to undergo the mesmeric experiment in his condition.

"Yes!" he barked, spitting blood on the floor. "I'm dying!"

I then commenced the lateral passes across his forehead, which I had found most effective with individuals in a state of nervousness, and which I suspected would work with him quite soon. As I anticipated, he was thrown into the mesmeric sleep at once. His eyes rolled up into his skull.

"Where is she?" he shrieked suddenly. "Where?"

I was terrified, as Alabaster's reaction to being put under hypnosis was unlike anything I had encountered before. I attempted to steady him with my voice.

"Who is the woman you speak of?"

"Eugenia!" he screeched in the harrowing way of a wounded animal. "She won't come to see me!"

"His sister," Rydberg whispered. He was sitting in a chair to my left, transcribing our conversation.

"Why won't she come?" I asked next. "Where is she now?"

"Horsley Hall, I reckon," Alabaster sneered, and tilted his face to one side as though to scrutinize me.

"Are you asleep?" I attempted to induce him to follow my hand, to which action he did not respond.

"No, imbecile, I'm dying." And then, unprompted, he began muttering, very quickly, as if holding a conference with himself. "Very well. If I am to die, then it's best to die early in the spring, before the hunting season. Before the dogs tear down the fields and I shall come after them on horseback to—where? Devil knows! Off to ride, ride, like all possessed. On my horse's back through the bowels of the Earth. How brave we were, once, to drive that colossal gig through narrow gaps in seven hedges. They used to say that the two of us were alike in flight: rippling with muscle and baring teeth. How I shall miss the thrill of a kill. I shall miss even the stink of horse piss in the stables. Is there anything more divine in the whole world?"

He stopped muttering and looked utterly forlorn. His breathing had become easier. I attempted another pass at his forehead.

"What do you see?"

He hesitated. "Outside?"

"Yes." As the reader may be aware, it's advisable not to question the sleepwalker's associations. "What do you see outside?"

"Butterflies. They are everywhere. She loved butterflies." He smiled to himself, and then made an impression of looking out of the window. "But no. It is winter. I'm forbidden to go outside — it is cold. The snow will come before nightfall. I can smell ice. What to do, then? Read?" He scowled in disgust. "Like my father, to brood over the meaning of *nature* after digging pitiful ants from the dirt? But to lie here, in this sour room, burning, and wait for the bloody phlegm to dry on the floor is even worse. Write, then. Yes, I must write."

He groped about him, tugging at the sheets, clearly searching for something. It had never occurred to me that a subject might wish to write something under hypnosis, and as I was pondering what to do next, Rydberg reached into his satchel and brought out a drawing pencil. I offered the pencil to Edgar, who snatched it out of my hand and began imitating the action of writing on his left palm.

I observed him silently for several minutes, and then

asked, "Mr. Alabaster, what are you writing?"

He started and turned his face up to me again. His eyelids quivered, revealing two slivers of yellowish white. His voice, when he spoke, sounded distant, as though coming out of a deep well.

"Eugenia will not come to see me. But what matter, since I no longer care if she did. My sister has become wretched and disagreeable. Her skin stretches over her face now like cracked leather. Her fingers that had pleasured me so in the past now resemble fat worms. Worms, ants, beetles, all filth. Only underbred cowards like Adamson wish to poke in the mud." He gnashed his teeth.

"Adamson?"

He frowned. "Eugenia's husband, of course! My father's protege. He came from the jungle, apparently after a shipwreck, brought my father exotic beetles, and bam!" — he clapped his hands — "married Eugenia just like that. Ah, how I wish I had killed him! How it tore me to shreds to hear her moan in his loathsome arms at night. To imagine her sharp little teeth biting his flaccid shoulder." He began hissing. "Yet it was I who planned their marriage. It was I who led him to her."

"Why, Mr. Alabaster? Why did you lead him to her?"

"Because I loved her. Because we loved each other. But we couldn't love. It's a taboo, don't you know? Incest, they call it. *Insect* with two letters switched. And I'll tell you something else. Adamson saw us in bed." His eyes darted wildly behind his eyelids. "That day he was called back to the house, under some filthy pretence — and he did nothing! Not a thing. He stood there, like a dog, with his tail curled between his legs, licked his lips, and scurried away with the governess. Gone to dance with the savages on the anthills, the pair of them. Good riddance and damn both of you to hell!"

He got hold of a bedpost and moved to the edge of the bed. "But not I. No. I shall die right here. How should I do it? Tell me right now. I cannot bear to lie here and wait. Only cowards wait for death to fetch their doom. I have always fetched what I wanted. Where is the pistol?"

Rydberg and I exchanged glances. It was imperative to calm him at once.

I said, "Mr. Alabaster, I've forgotten about Miss P——. Will you please remind me who she is?"

"A pretty girl she was. She looked like her, you know. That was why I seduced her. They all look like her. I sought them out. Some have my children. But the children are not like our own. They are half-breeds."

He spat on the floor, instilling absolute dread in me, yet I pressed on.

"You said 'our own' about the children. Do I understand you, then, to say that you and your sister have children?"

"Are you listening to me?" he cried. "Eugenia and I have three children. Adamson thought they were his, but I fathered them."

The room began spinning. I shuddered with horror and held on to the edge of the bed to steady myself. Rydberg was disturbed by Edgar's revelation in equal, if not greater, measure. His mouth hung open. He dropped the pencil on his lap. It rolled off slowly and clattered to the floor.

Meanwhile, Edgar wiped his mouth with the back of his hand and resumed imitating writing, all the while muttering, "To continue, and apropos of fetching, it's an indisputable fact that the most vigorous males are best armed for procreation. They are rendered the most attractive to females in various ways. I can attest to the truth of this universal phenomenon, for I knew many simple pusses whose little hearts beat faster when I felt for them. Their teeth parted eagerly to meet my tongue. And the maids of our Empire are in want of little fixing! They inherit the fattening quality in the flesh, but preserve no useful fat whatever in their wretched faces. How is their stock to improve, unless nobler seeds are introduced therein? Everyone knows that the best horses come from the purest lineages. It is absurd to suggest that thoroughbreds are related to drays. It is daft to propose that Arabians may be better suited to plough in the dirt than to run in the noble races. A horse breeder in Leicester has recently demonstrated that inbreeding improved desirable characteristics. Using the most advanced scientific methods, he has proven that agility and speed perpetuate themselves only in the purest of specimens."

He gazed about him with unseeing eyes, like a madman. While his ramblings provided an inward glimpse into the diseased workings of his feverish mind. I endeavoured to hasten my interrogation.

"Doctor Galton shares some of your ideas on—"

"I attended his lecture," he interposed. "His anthropometric laboratories created somewhat of a sensation in town last March. I resisted going, at first. It is unfathomable for a man of action to sit in stiff chairs with scholarly men of Adamson's ilk. But I went, my agreeable disposition undoubtedly precipitated by two bottles of excellent gin. And how glad I was to hear Galton's theories on superior races. He too thought it possible to accelerate intelligence through a selective breeding. Indeed, he encouraged attractive siblings to interbreed."

He fell silent and collapsed back on the pillows, exhausted.

Rydberg said, "He is rationalizing his relationship with his sister. It is most intriguing how absolutely he believes he did nothing wrong. Let him rest, and ring for tea."

Five minutes later, a great black hound followed by a servant girl came in through the door. The dog took his time to sniff us, released a low growl at Rydberg, and moved to the bed. He climbed on it unhurriedly, placed his head on his master's lap, and closed his eyes.

The most extraordinary scene ensued. Usually, under hypnosis, sleepwalkers do not respond to any external stimuli, being governed entirely by those who impress them. By voice, I myself had never, until that evening, heard of mesmerized individuals answering to anything in the external world while in trance. But Alabaster answered to his dog immediately. Upon sensing the dog's head on his lap, he sat up and began scratching behind the dog's ears with his fingers. Progressing to the top of the head, his hands caressed the dog's cranial bone at the apex, then moved downward to stroke the snout, and fell farther still to the lips, which he lifted to massage the gums. The tenderness between the beast and man was remarkable, and evinced undeniable kinship between them. I looked over at Rydberg and saw that he too was impressed by the evident affection between Alabaster and his dog.

After caressing the dog in this manner for ten minutes, Alabaster pushed the animal roughly away. The dog jumped off the bed then and proceeded to lick his master's blood off the floor. To our astonishment, Edgar seemed to register what the dog was doing, and commanded it to stop. He then addressed the dog as one might address the closest companion. "Have any letters come for me? Has she written?"

The dog, naturally, didn't respond, but emitted another low growl at Rydberg, trotted over to the door, and collapsed in front of it with a thump.

Rydberg turned to me and whispered, "I wonder if we shouldn't explore the butterflies. These, I think, suggest multiple meanings. Perhaps he idealizes his sister in the way one may idealize this beautiful insect. And so, when the butterfly metamorphoses into ugliness, in a reversal of the natural law, the contradictions within him float up to the surface."

It was a keenly refined observation on the part of my learned friend, but before I could respond to it, Alabaster began muttering again. This time around, however, his words were articulated distinctly and a tenderness unheard of hitherto entered his voice.

"I remember it as though it happened yesterday. One summer day, after the picnic. Eugenia was eleven. She was eating a peach. We walked through the meadow, and entered the shade of the trees. Sweet, sticky juice ran down her arm. She stopped, looked at me with those maddening eyes of blue silver, and asked if I wanted to lick her. Innocent at first. Playful, even. Until I began to desire her desperately, *knowing* that she wanted the same. I pulled her to me and slipped my arm under her dress. She stiffened but did not protest. I kissed her on the mouth and squeezed her shoulder. Yet she began to struggle, averted her face, and then started hitting me with her fists. I tripped her up and pushed her to the ground. I was forced to slap her, you understand. I might have hurt her that first time, my darling Eugenia, I do not know, but if I did, it was her fault."

His face assumed a ghostly paleness. His entire frame shivered as though from bitter cold. In the next moment, I observed a slight tremor around his lips.

Rydberg said, "He is passing away now. It is advisable not to prevent this."

It was obvious to me as well that Alabaster's death was near. I was accustomed by then to seeing patients on their deathbeds, but none had filled me with the kind of terror I experienced that dreadful night. Indeed, I sensed with horror that death had already entered the room, and was presently hovering below the ceiling, waiting for me to ask Edgar one final question. My blood curdled.

"What do you want?" I whispered.

"Absolution!" he bellowed, his body shuddering with violence as though a great earthquake was taking place within. Whereupon he collapsed on his back and stiffened completely, no longer displaying any sign of life.

"Is he gone?" I asked Rydberg.

"I'm not finished!" Alabaster groaned, sitting up in bed like a macabre marionette. "That first time — as I was pushing inside her, I saw a butterfly with white wings. It hovered enticingly in front of me. It distracted me. But as soon as I transferred my attention to it, it flew off to settle on a daffodil. I don't know whether it was basking in the sunshine or extracting nectar from its flower, but it was enjoying itself, like I was. It fluttered its wings for what seemed like eternity. At last, it became perfectly still."

He gave one last gulp, jerked upward, and expired.

From: e.a38@gmail.com
To: e.a.a.15@yahoo.com
Sent: Saturday, December 13, 2014 2:33:26 PM
Subject: New Piece
Attached: The Ecstasy of Edgar Alabaster (first_draft).
pdf (66 KB)

Dear Eugenia,

I hope you don't mind that I "borrowed" your beautiful name for this assignment. In my defence, I can only say that A.S. Byatt uses it in her novella. To explain: we've been reading *Morpho Eugenia* in my British Literature since 1945 class. The instructor is a bit of an inflated cow (her name is Phyllis) who speaks in postmodern (oh, irony!). For our term papers, she asked us to write a narrative essay from the perspective of one of the characters in the book. I chose the vile Edgar, believing (naively, as it turned out) that it would be fun to pick his dark brain.

Phyllis talks tirelessly in lectures about hybridity. Most students roll their eyes. She has proposed to us that there's no original literature, that all literature is in fact hypertexted, like the links on the Internet. Every idea can be traced to another that came before it, and every fictional character can be linked to someone else. But if this is true, I wonder what was in the beginning. What kind of person, exactly, the first writer (was there just one?) had in their mind. I bet you anything it was a villain. Because what good would the world be without the evil? How would one tell the difference?

Yesterday, I read an article about cave art they found somewhere in France. A primitive artist (why am I

convinced that it was a woman?) carved two human figures on the wall. To get to the cave, this woman had
to squeeze through two narrow tunnels, crawl under
treacherous crags, and swim through a sulphurous lake.
All for what? To chisel two human figures out of stone.
These figures, I'm thinking, must've meant a great deal
to her. And do you know something else? The figures
were holding hands. I'd like to think they're you and me.
Our original characters. Maybe once upon a time, when
we were kids.

I tried to write a narrative essay discussing Edgar's
perspective. I tried hard. But it didn't work. So I switched
to fiction. I thought you might appreciate this, knowing
how much you adore Poe. Another Edgar. His maniacal
genius seems to have been on a par with Alabaster's. The
same chromosomal imprint of the doomed. Plagiarism as
incest. Perversity made into art.

As soon as I began writing, I realized that I was writing
about myself. I am too, like my fictional Edgar, unable to
stop loving you. I too dread the day I'll have to acknowledge to myself that our love is destructive. I too am full of
regret at having done what I've done, for taking advantage
of you when you're so little, for betraying your innocence.
Yet I'm unwilling to repent our love, not now, and not
(possibly) ever. I will never apologize for it. Not ever. Even
monsters can love, remember that.

But who am I to you, after all? A dirty secret? A skel-
eton in the closet, rattling the genetic bones? They say
our kind of love is rare. I say it isn't rare if it happened to
us. Meanwhile, I'm suffused with so much love for you,
knowing as I do that our child grows inside you. But you

haven't written or called me for almost a week now. I do not want to worry.

In any case, let me know what you think of this piece. Should I submit it to Phyllis as is, or do you have any suggestions? Is there sufficient conflict? I'm not sure about that.

One more thing before I go. It seems to me that Edgar is never hypnotized, that he only pretends to be in order to tell his side of the sordid tale. Do you think it's true? And if so, what makes you think he isn't mesmerized?

The almost comical springing up of Edgar in bed at the end is deliberate on my part. Is it too much like a bad guy in a horror movie? Does the modern author slip through? Or—what?

Anyway, text me once you get this email. No, wait! Hypertext me. Something original, yes? Something clever.

Your E.

THE SIDE EFFECTS

General side effects of BOTOX COSMETIC® injections include pain, tenderness and bruising at the site of injection, weakness, and malaise (generally feeling unwell). There have been rare reports of changes in the way the heart beats, chest pain, myocardial infarction (some with fatal outcomes); skin rash; allergic reaction; shortness of breath; wheezing or difficulty breathing; swelling of the face, lips, tongue, or other parts of the body; facial paralysis; and seizures.

BOTOX COSMETIC® brochure

1st Injection

I WAS DAYDREAMING when the receptionist at the derma-tology clinic announced that the doctor was running late.

"Shouldn't be more than a few minutes," she said. "Would you like something to drink?"

I wanted to say "A dirty martini," but it wasn't an

option, so I said nothing and shook my head. No, thanks.

I'd been daydreaming about my ex-husband. We were on vacation in Tofino, paddling in a kayak. The setting was stunning. Visually arresting, my ex had said. We slipped past towering old-growth forests and tidal pools teeming with unique sea life. I should've been enjoying myself, and I was, until the two of us (we were in a double kayak) couldn't agree on which way we should be going, so we ended up being swept out to sea.

"Paula?" I heard a voice above me and looked up to see a slender woman, smiling benevolently at my forehead. "It's nice to meet you. I'm Dr. Payne."

She was wearing a silver blazer and a black pencil skirt. Her age was indiscernible: she could be thirty-five or fifty-three. She looked serious, stern even, and indestructible, like a howitzer.

"Do you speak Hungarian?" she asked me. "You have a Hungarian last name."

"No," I said, rising. "Well, not anymore. It's my husband's—" I hesitated for a moment, unsure about which part of our drama to reveal. "My *ex*-husband's name. His parents were born in Hungary and came to Canada in 1956. They settled in Nova Scotia originally, but moved to the west coast in—"

"Let me stop you right there." She held out her hand. "I can tell you love to talk. Which is wonderful. I applaud you. Don't take it the wrong way, but if we can stick to the medical issues, that would be great."

As we were walking toward her office, I began daydreaming again. "Daydreams are therapeutic," my therapist, Dr. Rankin, had told me more than once. "So, go right ahead! The subconscious is a significant evolutionary invention that has had a profound influence on human-kind." This time I daydreamed about my new boyfriend, Peter, who had told me the night before in bed, "Things will only get better from now on. I guarantee it. All this hurt has got to go." Peter was categorical about this, certain. I liked his positive outlook. But his agreeable nature made it impossible to debate serious things with him.

I met Peter at a friend's party the day after the judge granted me one-half of my son. It was strange to think that a little boy should be divided as if he were some kind of cheese, yet I understood (no matter how much it pained me) that he needed to spend time with his dad too. It was just that — well, it hadn't been easy. But my son, Thomas, was doing okay. It was amazing how flexible little kids could be when it came to divorce. I'd signed him up for grade one chess club, and in social studies he'd learned about emotional "zones." Every day now he coloured in his "feelings" circles with crayons. Blue was for sadness, green for happiness, and yellow for so-so. There was also red for anger (little kids were good at that). Thomas said he was in the yellow zone on most days. I asked him, "Why not green?" He said (in that sweet way of his) that it wasn't possible for him to be in the green zone when he wasn't with me.

Anyway, at the friend's party, Peter and I hit it off. He fetched me a dirty martini and complimented me on my shorts. We started talking about surrealism as pictorial language and somehow ended up in my bed. I didn't quite know what to make of him, really, other than he was good for me. He did everything I asked of him and agreed with me about everything. I suspected he might have a deep-rooted fear of not measuring up to people. In which case, he was like me.

Was it too soon to date again? Probably. Still, I wasn't rushing into anything. But the thing was that, lately, I hadn't been myself. I was lost in an ocean of loneliness and was dissolving in it like salt. Especially on the days I was without Thomas. Then I was in the indigo blue zone.

To make things worse, I'd broken out in a rash. Like a teenager. It was contained to my lower back at present, but I feared it might spread. I read somewhere that it wasn't uncommon for women to have rashes during middle age (apparently, my hormones were already unbalanced at thirty-seven and I had to accept my fate), but I thought my rash might be stress-related. Which was why I was here, to consult with Dr. Payne.

Who, incidentally, at that very moment was swivelling in a chair upholstered in purple plaid. Other than the chair, her office was white, like her teeth. White desk. White leather couch. White bar fridge (I noticed with approval) under a white windowsill.

The painting above her head was of a mountain. Or it might've been of a tree. I couldn't quite tell what it depicted, with its reddish swirls on pale green. Some kind of a butterfly, or a DNA helix, or a mushroom with feet.

"It is fairly obvious," Dr. Payne said, "that you are here because of your forehead, yes?"

"What?" I said, and shook my head. "No. I have a rash on my back. Here." I unbuttoned my blouse, let it slip off my shoulders, and turned to show her what I'd meant.

"Oh." She laughed. "Of course. There is a note on your

chart. I should pay more attention. The rash is okay. An allergic reaction. To clothing, I suspect. I will give you cream to resolve it. Apply a pea-size quantity once a day on the affected area and rub it in."

"That's it?" I was relieved to hear it.

"Yes. And no. Tell me, do you frown a lot?"

It seemed rather an odd question, but after a moment of reflection I said, "Yes, I suppose."

She seemed very pleased with my answer and pointed to my forehead.

"Frown for me at the maximum level," she said. "Let's see what we've got."

There was a mirror on the wall to my right and in it I watched myself scrunch up my face. A severe vertical line appeared between my eyebrows, cleaving it like the devil's foot. Even after I relaxed my face completely, a prominent version of that line remained.

Dr. Payne said, "I am continually astonished by how elastic human skin is. But time is cruel. Stress at work and on the domestic front, children, lovers, even difficult pets, all these things take their toll. Add to that years of thinking and concentrating, and you get what we call glabellar lines. Fortunately, I have a solution for you. It is called Botox. It will make you look at least ten years younger and feel like a million bucks."

Was thirty-seven really that old? Was I one of those damaged people whose unhappiness compelled them to take risks with their health? Peter didn't know where I was. And neither (not that it mattered much to me) did Mr. Sam. But I didn't want to think about Mr. Sam at that moment, I wasn't ready, and so I pushed the thoughts of him away.

I hesitated. "I don't know if I want to do Botox. It seems — well, extreme. Besides, I like looking authentic. I like being me. I like —"

"No." She cut me off brusquely. "There is no other way. If you are worried about your face looking frozen, I assure you, you will still be you. The line between your eyebrows will temporarily disappear, but everything else will remain as is. Physiologically speaking, nothing will change. Trust me."

I found the very idea quite frightening.

"Are you sure? I see women in West Vancouver who look like puffer fish all the time."

She slid to the edge of her chair and leaned across her desk toward me.

"Let me ask you a question," she said in a softer tone. "What do you do for a living?"

"I'm an architect," I said.

"Wow." She nodded her head with appreciation. "Not just a wrinkled face, then. Sorry. Bad joke. Bad, bad, bad. Please ignore it. Eastern Europeans make awful jokes. But I mean well by it. So please don't get upset. The point I am trying to make is that I am sure you know what it takes to make a building. You are a professional, yes? People trust you with their projects. You have earned their respect with your work."

I couldn't see where she was going with this, so I just said, "Sure, okay."

Privately, though, I was annoyed by her stupid eastern European humour and couldn't wait to go home.

She shook a finger at me, playfully. "I can tell you are upset a little, but that is okay. People often get upset with me before Botox. But after a couple of injections, we become good friends. So, Paula, I need you to trust me. I have a medical degree from Budapest. I have treated hundreds of patients with frown lines just like yours. I can help you, but you have to let me do what I do best. If you do not trust me, let us not waste any more of our valuable time."

She leaned back and steepled her fingers. I moved to stand up.

"But before you walk out of here," she said quickly, "I thought you might want to know that the depth of your forehead wrinkle might be in fact related to the state of your mental health. You see, there is something called emotional feedback. People's faces are manifestations of their psychological health. I watched you sit in the reception hall while you were waiting for me, and I could tell that you were thinking unhappily."

Her candour disarmed me a little. Then I recalled how the other day Thomas ran over to me (we were at the playground) and just stood there, frowning at me. I asked him what was the matter, and he said, "Mama, you look like that a lot."

I inspected my face in the mirror, turning it this way and that. What if Botox would actually make me feel better? I was tired of not being myself.

Dr. Payne began to drum her fingers impatiently on the table.

"Like many people, you might be wondering about safety," she said. "But remember: your well-being is my number one concern. Of course, pharmacology is not an exact science. If we choose to take drugs, we must accept the risks. Life itself is a risk, yes? But rest assured that the

Botox specimen I have in my office is perfectly safe. It has been approved for use in humans since 2002, with no serious side effects."

I blinked at the last words she uttered, recalling the brochure I'd flipped through while I waited for her.

"What do you mean by 'serious,' exactly? The brochure I saw in the reception describes some adverse—"

"Oh, that." She waved her hand. "Honestly, they have to write warnings like that. Legal-wise. Let me ask you another question: have you ever seen the fine print on a bottle of Tylenol? If you had seen it and believed everything it said, you would be too terrified to take a painkiller. And what would the world come to then?"

I acknowledged that she had a point, and she must've taken my nod as a green light, because before I could say anything else, she swiftly rose from her chair and crossed the room to the cart. On the cart stood a metal tray covered with a white cloth, and from under the cloth she brought out a syringe with a needle already attached on the top. Inside the syringe were thirty-five cc's of clear fluid. It was Botox.

Oh, why not, I thought then. Why not? Maybe a smooth forehead would numb my sadness. Lately I'd been numbing it in all the wrong ways anyway. I'd become restless, disorganized, anxious. After Mr. Sam left for Mongolia, I'd become unhinged. I imagined he was having a good time in Ulan Bator at the moment. I thought that's where he said he went. Or was it some other place? More rural? More authentic? Authenticity was his thing. It was possible he was riding a horse in Mongolia through a wild steppe just now. His daughter would be riding with him.

They'd throw their heads back in euphoria and laugh at the infinite sky. Afterward, they'd wash down those special dumplings he told me about with warm glasses of goat milk in a yurt.

Meanwhile, Dr. Payne picked up the syringe. Holding it like a loaded pistol, she carried it over to me.

"Did you know," she said, "that Botox is made by bacteria that live in meat cans? It is true that the original botulinum toxin is the most powerful neurotoxin known to humankind, but the Botox made for cosmetic treatment is nothing like that. It is manufactured by a reputable pharmaceutical company, in accordance with the latest safety guidelines."

She stopped talking and narrowed her eyes. "You're not pregnant, are you?"

"No," I said with a pang. I loved being pregnant with Thomas. I'd do it all over again in a heartbeat. If only one could stay pregnant forever, un-alone like that for eternity.

Post-injection

A FEW MINUTES later, I was feeling unwell. My forehead ached with a dull, throbbing pain. My whole head felt as if it had been hit with a hammer. I closed my eyes for a moment and heard Mr. Sam's voice inside my brain. *"Buuz is a type of Mongolian dumpling. It's filled with minced meat. You can flavour it with fennel seeds or oregano, but I like to use dill. A pocket of dough folds around the filling with a small opening at the top. The best part is that a chef can add a special twist to it, according to his personal taste."*

A latex glove snapped somewhere above me. I opened my eyes.

"One more thing before you go," Dr. Payne said. "There's something I think you should know. Some dermatologists think that people who've received Botox injections experience—how should I put it?—an interruption in their emotional feedback. What it means in layman's terms is that they become sort of less stressed. It's a bonus, in my opinion, to have psychological smoothness to go along with the smoothness of one's forehead."

I examined my face in the mirror. There was something distinctly robotic about my nose. My cheekbones protruded at odd angles, or was I imagining it? My eyes hurt. Meanwhile, my mind kept on ticking like a wound-up mechanical clock.

"Paula?" Dr. Payne said.

"Sorry. What did you say?"

"I asked you if you had any other questions."

I took a moment to organize my thoughts.

"Will I need re-injections?" I asked her.

"Of course. Botox is a limited-time-acting agent. As far as we know."

"How long will it last?"

"About six months. Maybe longer. Everyone has a different response."

AFTER TWO DAYS, the pain in my forehead disappeared. In fact, I stopped feeling anything up there at all. By day four, there were more physical changes. My face widened. My lips fattened. The frown line in my forehead went away.

One month after the Botox injection, I experienced

what I could only describe as bliss. A wonderful sense of calmness washed over me. I was tranquil. I was serene.

I truly felt like a new person. And I'd never looked so good in my life. My face became friendlier. Nicer. Not stupid exactly. Just innocent of thought.

My mood had improved too. A lot.

At the follow-up with Dr. Payne one week later, she was pleased by the fact that I was feeling so happy, but not too happy, she hoped. She said that some of her Botox patients who experienced extremes of happiness also suffered from something called cognitive reflex. Meaning they became less smart than they were before Botox. But she emphasized that it happened mostly to housewives. And since I was a professional woman, she was sure I'd be totally fine.

I TRIED TO explain my new reality to Dr. Rankin at my next therapy session.

He said, "Hmm. What else has changed since the last time we met?"

"Quite a lot," I admitted. "In the mornings, I actually want to get out of bed. I don't cry in my soup at lunchtime or at any other time during the day. Mr. Sam told me once that Mongolians slow-cook their traditional dishes in clay pots. Clay transfers heat well, apparently, so cooking is slow, even, and gentle in clay pots." I looked up at the ceiling to gather my thoughts. "One can say, I suppose, that lately I feel as though I've turned into a clay pot."

Dr. Rankin gave a small laugh, and for some reason his laugh reminded me of Mr. Sam.

I met Mr. Sam in a yoga class in West End, where I moved after I left my ex. It was unhealthy to sit at home and miss my son, so I signed up for a yoga class at the community centre to try to move on with my life. A round guy in a blue track suit showed up late for class one night. He had big feet and curly red hair, gathered messily into a ponytail. He entered the room boldly, made no apology to anyone, beelined right into my personal space, and uncurled his yoga mat.

I was about to take exception to his behaviour when the yoga instructor directed us to assume a "downward dog." Other, more challenging postures followed, and I was surprised to see how bendy the guy in the track suit actually was. He twisted his short legs at impossible angles and was the only one not to fall out of a half-moon pose. At the end of the class, he asked me if he could walk me home. It was getting late, he insisted. He was worried for my safety, he said. I found his concern pretty endearing, so I said, "Sure! Why not?"

We talked about our lives all the way to my apartment, while my strange attraction to him was gathering speed. I attributed it initially to my loneliness and made a special effort not to dwell on it.

It turned out that he had a daughter named Gulchitay, who went to the same school as Thomas.

"Where is your daughter now?" I asked him.

"With my mother," he said. "We help each other out a lot."

Then he told me that his late wife was a Mongolian ballerina who died tragically on a trans-Siberian train.

"When did she die?" I asked him, solemnly, trying to supress my disbelief.

"A year ago," he replied.

"Oh, I'm so sorry," I said with feeling, and meant every word.

After a long moment of silence, I told him it was okay if he didn't want to talk about it.

"Thanks," he said. "I won't."

For my part, I told him about my ex-husband, my beautiful son, and my work. It was surprisingly easy to talk to him about personal things. That was very confusing to me.

As we were approaching my building, he told me he had a master's degree in Russian Literature from UBC. It was difficult to do much with his degree in this city, so he also got a diploma from the Culinary Institute of Madrid. He worked as a sous-chef at Cardero's and wrote restaurant reviews.

"It's trendy these days to examine the issues related to food production," he told me. "I'm not indifferent either to where my food comes from. But I'm interested mainly in food consumption, in how our bodies interact with it. We're changed every day by what we eat and how we eat it. Food impacts every cell in our bodies. It's called metabolism."

He had strong, capable hands when he pulled me closer to him, and kissed me on the lips as though I were already his.

My mind made a U-turn at this point. I realized Dr. Rankin was watching me.

"Sorry," I said. "What was I saying?"

"Peter has moved in."

"Oh yes, Peter has moved in," I continued. "We've settled into a relaxed routine. We go out a lot in the evenings instead of staying in. There are many dining options around our apartment, and even when Thomas stays with us, we go out to eat. It's strange that I used to love complex flavours. Mr. Sam adored Asian food. He lived in Vietnam for a year, where he learned how to stir-fry duck legs. He also made steamed lily buds and crispy pork bellies for me. Before he went away, I mean. I loved every dish he made for me. But now I have no stomach for any of it. Spices upset me. Aromatics make me ill. It's like I've become a whole new person, on the inside as well as on the outside. My interest in existential philosophy, for example, has given way to swinging in the hammock. Peter strung one up on the balcony, and I just adore the tilting sunsets. Deep questions that used to preoccupy me no longer trouble me at all. Questions about art, life, religion. All of that nonsense has stopped. I've come to realize that the greatest art is the art of living, and I'm determined to make the most of it."

"Wonderful." Dr. Rankin frowned. "How is work?"

I sighed. "Things at work are rather strained. People are avoiding me. One person — a former friend — told me that he doesn't care for my new-found honesty. Why? Because I've started telling people what I really think about them. If I offend anyone with my directness, then it's their problem, not mine, isn't it? They say I've become bossy. And a little mean. But it's okay. My team has missed two deadlines recently and we're in danger of missing the third. I'm not worried, though. We'll make it. It's just that I look at my designs — and, well, I'm not happy. There's something disturbing about them. I don't know what it is. Nothing is wrong, exactly. But something is definitely not right."

"What do you think it might be?"

"Not sure. Curves? Maybe that's it. There are too many curves in my buildings. I'd like to go back to the plain, good, old-fashioned box."

Dr. Rankin wrote something down in his notebook.

"What about Thomas? How are things with your son?"

"Terrific." I beamed at him. "Why? Because I've taken a new approach to parenthood. I used to move through my days gripped with fear about him, but now I'm calm. A new clarity has set in. We used to read books together, but now we watch cartoons on TV. Cartoons seem better somehow, more alive, more animated, don't you think? I never thought much of bathroom humour, but Thomas has changed my mind.

"Also, he doesn't want to go to chess club anymore, and I'm okay with that. I don't blame him, really. Last week, he brought home a pile of homework. It was so hard that even I couldn't help him with it. Pawn to e2? Capture queen? It made no sense to me. It was strange, too, because I used to be pretty good at chess in high school.

"Moreover, I used to adore classical music and, as you know, forced my son to play violin. But now I've come to the conclusion that the drama of music, especially violin, might be a bit too much for him. I told him he doesn't have to practise any longer. He was so pleased.

"Also, something amazing has happened." I paused for dramatic effect.

"What's that?"

"Last week, I went to pick up Thomas from after-school care, as usual, at five o'clock. They have family photographs there, above the kids' cubbyholes. So I got there and saw a picture of Thomas, my ex, and the woman he'd met on the Internet. It turns out the teachers decided the kids should have family photos above the cubbyholes, but no one told me. I leaned in closer to inspect the picture. The three of them were beaming sunshine. My ex and his new lover had their arms around each other. Thomas was making a face. And all of a sudden I was struck by this powerful feeling that everything was okay. It's okay that my child is happy without me. It's okay that a strange woman cares for him some days. She looks like a wonderful mother. I'm sure she'll make a terrific wife. My eyes boiled with tears. I was so happy. Truly, I was in the green zone."

Dr. Rankin did not say anything for a long time. Then he coughed in his fist, stood up, pulled down a book from a shelf, and handed it to me.

It was *Buddha* by Deepak Chopra.

"As long as we speak in terms of enlightenment, we can accomplish magnificent things," Dr. Rankin said. "As long as we do not let our emotions get the better of us, we remain free. Indeed, one might compare an individual's psyche to a pendulum that swings both ways. Life displaces the pendulum sideways from its resting position. But how can we limit the pendulum's swings? The answer is that we must work constantly at steadying its wild oscillations, aiming to bring it back to its balanced state. This position is called equilibrium, and it's achieved with hard work. Meditation helps us to achieve it. I recommend it to you."

He glanced at his watch again and said he was sorry but our time was up.

"Now, Paula. I'm tremendously encouraged by the progress you've made so far. When you first came to see me, you were an emotional wreck. You wanted to kill your ex-husband. You wanted to jump off the Lions Gate Bridge. Your moods were uneven, your hormones unbalanced, and your libido, as you yourself have pointed out, was null. Except with that fellow —" He stopped abruptly and cleared his throat. "Excuse me. What was his name again? I forget."

"Mr. Sam," I said.

He helped me get up from the chair and led me to the door.

"If I were you, however," he said to me on the threshold, "I'd talk to your dermatologist about your Botox dose. She may want to adjust it a little bit. Just to be safe."

He handed me the *Buddha* book I'd left on the chair, pressed his palms together, and gave me a slight bow.

"*Namasté.*"

A MONTH LATER, I was shopping at Costco when my phone rang. It was Mr. Sam.

"Why are you calling me?" I asked.

"I'm happy to hear your voice too," he said. "How've you been? Can we meet?"

"There's no need for a meeting," I told him. "What do you want?"

There was silence.

Then he said, "I've missed you. I'm sorry you were upset with me when I went to Mongolia. But I had to go. I had to show Gulchitay where she came from. She liked the trip a lot. Her relatives are wonderful people. They taught her how to ride a horse bareback."

I didn't say anything and he began to speak faster.

"They say that Mongolian horses are short and stubby, yet they helped Genghis Khan conquer half the known world. People underestimated them. You underestimate me too, I think."

"I'm glad you had a good time in Mongolia. Say hello to Gulchitay from us. Have a nice day."

"Wait," he said. "Please. Wait, Paula. Has something happened? You sound—changed."

"Yes," I replied. "As a matter of fact, I've changed a lot. I'm with Peter now and I feel really good."

"Peter?

"Yes. I really love him. He makes things easy for me."

It's true. I loved Peter. I loved Peter a lot.

"Be that as it may," he said slowly, "life on a Mongolian steppe is pretty harsh. It made me realize that you and I have something good, something special. Let's have dinner. What do you think?"

"It's too late," I said with conviction. "I'm with Peter now. That's what I want."

"No, you don't," he said. "I know you, Paula. I understand you. You and I are alike."

"Maybe we were, but not any longer," I told him. "You're a free-roaming nomad, but I'm not like that. Things are different for me now. I've changed."

"Really? I find that hard to believe. After my wife died, I thought I'd never feel anything like what we — had."

"My therapist said that the number one thing for me right now is stability," I informed him. "The same goes for my son. Peter is great with Thomas. He really is. Maybe they don't cook together or laugh at the same jokes — Peter is not very funny — but he's here, and that's what matters a whole lot to me right now." I paused. "Peter is not going off traipsing in some godforsaken place in Mongolia to look for dumplings from outer space."

"Paula!" he shouted suddenly, his voice shaking with emotion. "I went to Mongolia to say goodbye to my wife!"

I ignored what he had just told me.

"Dr. Rankin gave me a book about Buddha," I continued. "It has changed my life."

"Buddha?" He laughed. "Give me a break, will you? To do what? Meditate yourself into nothingness until you care about not a thing in the world? We are made of organic molecules, and organic molecules react! We react to life around us. We react to love and to loss. We react because we're meant to. Because we aren't dead. To have no desire is such a load of bullshit—forgive me for being so blunt. To have no passion in one's life is a cop-out for cowards. And you are anything but."

I saw no point in speaking to him any longer. I wished him a good day and hung up. I knew exactly when he would be dropping off Gulchitay at school in the mornings, and I intended to drop off Thomas at a different time. My life with Peter was happy, I told myself. These days I agreed with him all the time.

2nd Injection

TWO MONTHS LATER, Dr. Payne's office called me for a follow-up.

"How are you feeling?" the receptionist asked.

"Good. Great, actually. What's up?"

"I'm calling to let you know that in the next little while you may begin to experience mood swings. This is normal, and simply means you're due for another injection. We're very busy this time of year, so let's schedule your appointment with Dr. Payne right now."

"Really? So soon? I thought Botox was supposed to last six months."

"Four months, typically," she said. "And you were here almost three months ago."

"My forehead is still pretty smooth," I told her. "It doesn't seem to be wearing off."

"It will. I'll have Dr. Payne give you a call."

Dr. Payne didn't call, but by the end of the month, just as the receptionist promised, my moods began to swing. I felt changeable, edgy, and guilty about missing my deadlines at work. I tried to read the *Buddha* book Dr. Rankin gave me, but it didn't interest me. Sitting under a tree to find the truth. Really? That would take incredible patience. Calmness, too. I didn't know what was suddenly happening to me, but I was tense all over again. Everything bothered me. Peter drove me up the wall. I'd watch him sitting on a beanbag chair in front of the TV eating potato chips from an oversized bag and wanted to — what? I didn't know exactly, but the word "vivisection" came to mind. Thomas was the only person who made me happy, but the court orders that spelled out my part-time parenting hours with him were making me mad again.

Then one day I looked at myself in the mirror and wondered if I'd gone colour-blind. I went out to the nearest clothing store and bought normal clothes. Then I pulled on a pair of jeans, a plain white T-shirt, laced up a pair of sneakers, and went to see Dr. Payne.

"You seem tense," she said from her purple chair. "Is everything okay?"

"No," I said. "I want to feel better. I want Botox again. More than thirty-five units this time, okay?"

She leaned over the table toward me and peered at my forehead.

"I am quite pleased with how your skin responded to it. The lines are basically gone. I would recommend less Botox, in fact, for the second round. Due to the side effects."

"What are you talking about?" I squirmed in my chair. "I'm willing to accept the risks."

"I wouldn't bet on it," she said calmly. "A clinical study came out last month describing cognitive alienation in some patients who receive Botox. Apparently, muscle par alysis delays the signal relay from the face to the brain. They even came up with a name for it — emotional blind-ness — that is how serious it is. I predict it will all blow over, but I cannot give you Botox right now."

She hesitated, sensing my agitation, then asked, "Do you want to hear a joke?"

"Is it eastern European?"

"Yes."

"Then no."

She told it to me anyway.

But I wasn't listening to her. I looked up at the paint-ing above her head instead. It was the same one I couldn't make sense of during my first visit to her office. But this time the image was clear. I was looking at Mr. Sam's face. There was no doubt about it. The face had the same round cheeks and curly hair, gathered messily into a ponytail.

And it was speaking to me.

It said, "You're a risk taker, Paula. Your passion is what I love about you. Don't blunt yourself into smoothness. You know better than that."

"But I'm lost," I tried to argue back. "I'm tired. I don't want to be in pain anymore."

"But everyone's lost, Paula," the face responded from the painting. "Do you think it was easy for me after I lost my wife? Are you the only one who has lost something? To lose is to live!"

It wasn't normal to talk to paintings. I realized it was a sign that the Botox had worn off for good. For a moment I wondered if I should mention my conversation with the painting to Dr. Payne. Then I decided that no, I should not. Because I'd already changed my mind about the Botox. Because I'd already understood that if life was the side effect of love, then I was ready for every wrinkle of it.

Postscriptum

IF THERE WAS one thing I did know, however, it was that I didn't know what to do about Mr. Sam. I was too proud to call him or text him. I wished I wasn't, but I was. I decided that sooner or later I'd run into him at the school. But to expedite matters, I began to strategize, aiming to run into him there in the morning, right after dropping Thomas off. Since he didn't work until late afternoon, I figured he might ask me to go for a walk. Or to have coffee. Or something. One thing would lead to another and we'd end up in bed.

Two weeks went by and I didn't see him. I missed him every day.

Then one Sunday morning, when the sky looked foreboding, I decided to go for a run. In the past, before Botox, exercise always made me feel better about myself. It was early, and the seawall was deserted. The clouds smudged the low sky. A man in a trench coat was skating toward me in bright orange roller skates. I narrowed my eyes because there was something very familiar about his figure.

My stomach convulsed.

"Hi," Mr. Sam said, stopping beside me.

"Those are lovely skates," I said. "Did you get them in Mongolia?"

"No," he said.

My heart was pounding in my ears. I saw circles dancing behind my eyelids.

"Peter moved out," I blurted. "I suppose you'd expected that."

"I hadn't. But I'm glad to hear it nonetheless. All this time I've been wondering when you might go for a run again."

"Have you been following me?"

He shrugged his shoulders. "More like waiting. And I hoped it wouldn't be too long."

It was awkward. I ended up apologizing to him. I said I wasn't myself when we last spoke.

Then I told him about the Botox.

Then I told him about losing my job.

Then I told him that I'd missed him like crazy and asked him if we could please go for a walk.

The seagulls were screeching above us. The wind was picking up.

He told me about his trip to Mongolia. It had been a big success. He ended up doing a piece for the *New Yorker* about those special dumplings called *buuz*. His editor was very pleased and sending him now to China to profile trends in architecture in Shanghai.

"Listen," he said. "I need an assistant. Do you think you can come with me?"

I looked at my feet because something was suddenly caught in my eyes.

At the Lumberman's Arch, we heard the floatplane approaching before we saw its fuselage above Stanley Park. The plane pointed its blunt nose downward and wiggled its wings. The pilot might've been testing the steering. Or she might've been signalling to someone that she was finally coming home. The plane dove down, landed on the water, and thrust its engine into reverse.

GDAŃSK

1. When they crossed the Soviet border on November 9,
    1989, Katya peered through the grimy train window,
    anticipating the world.

2. The terrain, however, looked the same—flat, dull, and
    marshy, broken up infrequently by stooping hills.

3. Anton, who liked to think of himself as Katya's boy-
    friend, asked if anyone had seen the iron curtain. He
    was sure he'd missed it, he said.

4. Their teacher, Comrade Filipova, who had been select-
    ed by the regional Party committee to accompany ten
    Young Communists on a four-day cultural exchange
    to the West, told him brusquely to hold his tongue
    behind his teeth.

5. Anton tossed his blond head sideways in a gesture of
    teenage defiance and asked Comrade Filipova if she
    hadn't gotten the memo that the Soviet Union was

now a democratic country. *Ergo*, he could say whatever he wanted.

6. Comrade Filipova remained unimpressed and reminded everyone that the real world wasn't anyone's oyster.

7. Most students in Katya's school were the children of the Party's apparatchiks. She was admitted there only because her mother had bribed the principal (an old English teacher of hers) with two bottles of Swedish vodka and a box of French chocolates filled with cognac.

8. Katya's school number was 54, because schools, like everything else in her country, were numbered: foodstuffs in the grocery stores, shoes in the factory outlets, even panties in the women's department of the Central Univermart.

9. As the train chugged through the outskirts of Warsaw, Katya thought of her mother's words, which were (verbatim): "The Revolution began in 1917 with the promise of love to all people but stripped every single one of us of it for more than seventy years."

10. The curriculum in Katya's school featured the familiar subjects of history, literature, mathematics, and so on, but the most useful education in Katya's mother's opinion took place on the playground, where from

an early age Katya was taught the basic survival skills based on pragmatic morality.

11. i.e., might is right.

12. Maybe Katya didn't grow up drinking Coca-Cola or watching Disney movies (there was a difference between growing up in a dictatorship and in a democracy, okay?), but the propaganda was free and it shaped her.

13. When they finally arrived in Gdańsk, each of them was matched with a Polish counterpart with whose family they'd live during their visit.

14. The names were assigned alphabetically and entered as numbers in Comrade Filipova's oversized logbook.

15. Katya was matched with Polina, who was wearing blue Levi's jeans.

16. Anton (see #3) was matched with a boy named Marion, who introduced himself to everyone as Marlon Brando and in fact looked a little bit like him, Katya thought.

17. Marlon, for his part, stole a few glances at Katya while telling everyone loudly something about Kabbalah or some such.

18. Polina shook Katya's hand, picked up Katya's suitcase, and they walked together to the parking lot, where

Polina's grandmother, a.k.a. Babcha Wacława, was waiting for them by the open passenger-side door of an ancient VW.

19. As Babcha sped said automobile through the darkening streets, she informed Katya in clunky Russian that Polina's mother was a nurse who worked night shifts in a cancer ward of a local hospital (nothing special about that), but that Polina's father was an engineer who worked in Canada on an important project related to computers in space.

20. Meanwhile, Polina was scribbling something in her notebook with a stub of a pencil, which, as she'd tell Katya later, was a poem dedicated to young people who died prematurely tragic deaths.

21. The next morning, sunlight flooded the kitchen table in Babcha's apartment.

22. Polina sat on Katya's left, smelling of Canadian laundry detergent.

23. Babcha poured Katya a cup of black tea and asked her if she believed in God.

24. At that point Polina stopped assembling her breakfast sandwich (bread-cheese-tomato-cheese-tomato-bread) and said quickly that she thought she'd made it clear that Babcha wasn't supposed to talk about that.

25. Babcha widened her eyes and asked Polina how she imagined that she, Wacława Kaminska, the person who had survived a Nazi concentration camp, wouldn't be able to ask their visitor from the Soviet Union the most important question of all.

26. Katya noticed the framed photographs of the Pope on the mantel and took a moment to examine the tea leaves at the bottom of her cup.

27. She could clearly see there the image of her mother, sitting at that precise moment in the kitchen of their apartment in Minsk and eating toast smeared with gooseberry jam and drinking Colombian coffee, for which she'd stood in line for six long hours last spring.

28. Silently, Katya asked her mother's opinion on the most important question of all, to which her mother in her typical fashion replied with a shrug.

29. Sometimes a shrug is not just a shrug.

30. While mulling over her options, Katya followed Polina's example and assembled her own breakfast sandwich of bread, tomato, and cheese. (When in Rome, etc.)

31. At long last, Katya told Babcha that the question of God was rather murky (as everyone well knew), and that, as a matter of fact, she was discouraged from talking about God in her school.

32. So.

33. Katya believed in science instead, although lately, with everything that'd been going on in her country, she'd begun to have a more open mind about religious things.

34. One had to believe in God to survive, Babcha said, and once again mentioned the Pope (see #26).

35. Katya agreed and proceeded to tell Babcha that last year she'd grown crystals of copper sulphate on a windowsill.

36. The thing Katya loved about crystals was that they never grew the way they were meant to grow.

37. In fact, crystals were false ideals because they were supposed to have perfect, exactly repeating patterns, but in reality they always had defects, places where their patterns went all out of whack.

38. Maybe, Polina proposed, God was a little bit like that.

39. In the following days, the teenagers from the Soviet Union visited numerous sights in the city of Gdańsk, stumbling upon a few political rallies, which were taking place in the city during that historic time.

40. Not unexpectedly, Katya and Marlon Brando (see #16) hit it off as only two teenagers could, and Polina

helped them to sneak a few moments together in the women's bathroom in the Medieval Torture Museum.

41. Subsequent to that dalliance, the air began to smell different to Katya in Gdańsk.

42. Marlon was a revolutionary male specimen, she thought.

43. Beauty wasn't everything, as far as Katya was concerned, but it certainly helped.

44. On the last evening in Poland, after dinner, the conversation once again turned to the subject of God.

45. Polina's mother, who was off duty that evening, said that God created cancer to keep things in balance for everyone.

46. Her exact words were, "To stop people from running ahead of themselves and remind them of their vulnerability."

47. Polina said that one day she wanted to write a poem about God because God shaped out the ways people moved through her life.

48. Katya, meanwhile, spoke again of science and revealed to everyone that one day she hoped to become a scientist as well as a mother. (In her dreams she'd already seen the exact kind of crystals she would grow for her children.)

49. Suddenly, Babcha said that God was an organism that lived in our stories and that she'd written a book of creative non-fiction in which she encouraged everyone to reflect on their own role in history.

50. If the majority of the population hadn't conformed to Communism or Fascism, or whatever, maybe the Communists or the Fascists, or whatever, wouldn't have come to power at all.

51. But even the scientists were in on it, she pointed out, showing everyone the number tattooed in her skin.

52. Even the scientists.

53. Polina said she didn't want to be a Communist or a Capitalist or a Scientist. She wanted to be a Poet. That was all.

54. The years that followed were disorienting for Katya and her mother.

55. The physical barrier in the centre of Berlin was gone in 1989, but the psychological wall between the East and the West remained for decades after. (It is still there.)

56. What was the most disorienting of all, however, was that in the spring of 1990, when it was time for the Polish teenagers to come to Minsk, at the train station Katya was matched not with Polina but with another girl, Agneshka, who had taken Polina's place

after Polina and her mother had been killed in a plane crash en route to Canada to visit Polina's dad.

57. It made sense that poets had premature and tragic deaths. Still.

58. Marlon Brando was also missing on that trip. Anton told Katya that Marlon had caught the flu.

59. Katya finished high school and went to Moscow, where she began to study physics, specifically the growth of crystals.

60. But one day she attended a lecture by a Canadian professor of biochemistry, who spoke of protein shapes.

61. Did Katya know, for example, that in humans, more than twelve diseases have been linked to defects in this shaping process? That misshaped proteins aggregated into crystals inside human cells and clogged them up?

62. Was it like cancer? Katya asked the Canadian.

63. Yes, he responded. And no. We are still looking for answers.

64. Katya switched her major to biochemistry.

65. Within a year, she was accepted to a graduate school in Canada, where — at the welcome reception for new

students in her department — she met Marlon Brando, who was older and more handsome than ever!

66. Marlon Brando worked on the genome of *C. elegans* (a free-living nematode, a.k.a. roundworm), hoping to send it one day into space to study its genes in zero gravity.

67. Worms in space, Katya wondered. Really?

68. Marlon Brando shrugged his shoulders. Why not?

69. It was plain to everyone concerned that there were six (or fewer) degrees of separation between all individuals in the world.

70. After a tumultuous courtship due to the psychological wall (see #55), Katya combined twenty-three of her chromosomes with the twenty-three chromosomes of Marion Brando (on at least two occasions) and they had a son and a daughter, whom they named Polina, so that one day she could write a poem about God.

71. In a Canadian elementary school, new Polina studied the familiar subjects of history, literature, mathematics, and so on, but the real education took place on the playground, where the students drew rainbows of love in the sand.

72. Twenty years later, new Polina came as an exchange student to Gdańsk.

1. When she crossed the border on November 9, 20__,
    she peered through the window, anticipating the
    world.

SPECIMEN

ON THE EVENING I found out that my father was a sperm donor, we talked about marmosets.

I said, "In my biology class today, Ms. Dawes pinched herself on the arm and said scientists could take a cell from your skin and make sperm out of it."

We were having Chinese takeout for dinner. I remember biting into an egg roll.

"Then my friend Lara said—this is funny—Lara said that biologists somewhere gave marmosets—"

"A what?" my mother laughed, cutting me off. She was drinking her third glass of wine and growing cheerful. My mother wasn't an alcoholic, but she liked to drink. She taught English literature at a university, and alcohol was her way, as she put it, of dealing with her colleagues. I didn't feel good about her drinking. Not because I thought she shouldn't be doing it, but because when she did she never let me finish my sentences.

"A marmoset is a monkey," I said. "A small monkey, okay? So, Lara said scientists gave marmosets a gene that made their feet glow green, and that one of them, one of the monkeys, I mean, passed it along to its baby."

"Wow," Dad said, and drank some fizzy water. He never drank alcohol, because it gave him headaches.

"And what did Ms. Dawes think about the fact that sperm could be made from skin cells?" My mother's face was flushed from the wine. She unbuttoned her blouse and touched her earrings. "One wonders how Mr. Huxley would feel about the fulfillment of his prophecies."

"Ms. Dawes said it was tragic." I paused for dramatic effect. "Tragic that humans had stolen reproduction from nature. It's one thing to manipulate DNA for medical reasons, to cure diseases and so on, but she said humans should quit making new DNA when there's plenty of old DNA to go around. She thinks we're doomed." I looked at my dad. "She was pretty intense about the whole thing."

His eyes slid to the pimples on my chin, which was pretty annoying.

He said, "I read an article in the *New York Times* about a biotech company in China that does DNA sequencing. Its goal is to decode DNA of tens of thousands of smart people to find out what makes them smart. They say they want to understand the genetic basis of human intelligence, so that in the future people could implant embryos with desirable traits."

Dad read a lot about science and was fond of explaining things to me. I used to like it when I was a kid, but lately I didn't care.

"So, are you, like, against it?" I asked him.

"Not against it, exactly, no. But, Joy, there're so many things we don't know. How do genes really work, for example? What happens when DNA gets rearranged, or when proteins meant to be in a skin cell get plunked into cells of the reproductive system? Are there maybe some molecules we don't yet know about that mess things up? Biotechnology moves too fast. Cloning embryos, making radiant moneys, artificial sperm —"

He glanced at my mother.

"Interesting thoughts here, Dad," I said. "Maybe I should write a term paper about it. We're supposed to choose a topic relevant to the current world. I think sperm might be it. All sorts of questions to explore there. Like what, for example, makes people donate it in the first place? Money, of course, is a good reason, but it's so trivial somehow, don't you think? Or — maybe donating organs might be a better topic. Why do people donate their organs? Especially when they're still living. Not when they're dead."

"Joy, please." My mother screwed up her face.

"I mean, I understand when those who are about to die donate pieces of their flesh. They think that doing so will make them continue in some way. Which is stupid. What?" I said to my mother. "Why are you looking at me like that?"

Dad stood up, touched my mother's shoulder, and walked across the dining room to open the French doors. It was October, and the air already smelled of snow. In the falling light, I could see oak leaves skateboarding on the porch railing.

"Let's change the subject, I beg you," my mother said. "Your dad's surgery is next week. Can we talk about something rosy? Something positive, for a change? How about cookies? I'm going to make a bunch of Dad's favourites tonight. He'll take them with him to the hospital. The

food there defies belief. The cookies will see him through,
I'm sure. Next Friday, we'll be sitting at this very table and
everything will be normal again."

She looked kind of sad just then, pensive, which was
unusual for her after three glasses of wine. She was a happy
drunk, typically, and liked to hug people as she retold the
same stories countless times. And so, in an effort to make
her less sombre, I attempted to lighten the mood.

"It's just a hip replacement, Mother. No big deal. The
good news is that Dad can't bleed to death. I may not be
willing to donate any of my body parts to him — the hip
won't fit anyway — but if he needs blood, I've got plenty
of it. So, no worries, okay?"

My little statement spread into the air between us like
some kind of gigantic Rorschach ink blot. I learned about
those in psychology last week from Ms. Dawes, who told
us that what you saw in those ink blots was supposed to
project your innermost thoughts.

In silence, Dad fished a cigar out of his pocket, lit it, and
drew the air in with his lips.

"We don't have the same blood type, Joy," he said slowly.
"We were going to wait until you turned eighteen to tell
you this, but since you've brought it up now and your birthday is only two months away, we might just as well."

The tone of his voice was icily distant and made me
look from him to my mother and back to him again.

"Tell me what, exactly?"

He didn't respond right away. When he did speak again,
it struck me how odd he was looking, more uncertain and
shakier than I'd ever seen him before.

"The truth is that when I was a child, I had an illness

that made me infertile," he said. "I can never have children of my own. So, when your mother and I decided to have you, we used a sperm donor to help us with it."

I blinked. "A sperm donor?"

"Yes. Your mother conceived you with donated sperm."

I looked around the room and the objects inside it seemed suddenly to have liquefied. It was like one of those Dali paintings with melted watches all over the place.

My toes and the tips of my fingers began to tingle. My stomach lurched.

"Was the sperm donor someone you knew?" I managed to ask my mother.

"No." She shook her head. "We used an anonymous donor with closed identity. Which means he's not open to contact with children produced by his sperm. But you can look at his information whenever you like, Joy. If it matters to you in any way."

In a daze, I went into the kitchen and put my plate into the sink. Then I leaned my back against the fridge and began to process what I'd just heard. I closed my eyes. I tried to "centre" myself like they'd taught us to do in mental wellness class. Then I wondered why the fact that I'd been conceived with a donor's sperm had upset me so much. After all, no one could choose their biological parents. What mattered was that I had been made. Yet it had upset me. It had upset me a lot. Because I felt that by omission my parents had stolen the truth from me. If my life didn't feel like a big lie, exactly, it did feel like a major fib.

Why, I thought bitterly, couldn't they have told me about it when I was, like, three? I'd know everything then and it wouldn't be a big deal. But now, here we were, and it all felt like a big mess.

Sensing tears welling up behind my eyes, I moved to the staircase.

"Joy," my mother called after me. "Do you want to see the donor's information?"

I turned to her, steadying myself.

"Sure, Mother," I said. "Maybe later. I've got a ton of homework to do."

ABOUT AN HOUR later, my mother came up to my room. I had dried my tears by then and was lying on my back, listening to music. My mother sat on my bed, reached for my earphones, and took them off my head.

"This is all very upsetting to your father," she said, looking rather intense. "Infertility is a difficult thing to talk about, and he's a sensitive man. He feels inadequate because of it in some fundamental way. Over time, he's managed to find ways to deal with it, within himself, but—" She touched my hand. "Joy, your father can't have any stress right now. Not before his surgery. So, we won't talk about it. In fact"—she gave me a sharp look—"we won't talk about it ever again."

"Yes," I said, yanking my hand from under hers.

She held my gaze for a moment, and then brought forth a blue shoebox.

"All information I have about your donor is in here," she said. "It's yours to keep."

After she closed the door behind her, I sprang up and locked it. By then, the prospect of having another father had begun to feel thrilling to me. What if, I thought, staring at the shoebox, what was inside it could explain everything? The unexplainable things in my life, mostly, like my bouts of depression, or my changeable moods, or my inability to relate to most people, or the fact that I liked girls? What part of my personality did I owe to the donor? In what ways was I like him?

He was born in 1962 and his blood type was A-positive. His height was one metre and seventy-five centimetres, weight sixty-eight kilograms, eye colour green, hair blond. He had no freckles and majored in engineering. His grade point average was 3.6. There was a photograph of him too, the kind you might see in a school yearbook. I looked at it for a long time. Everyone had always said that I looked like my mother, and for the most part it was true. But there was one outstanding difference: the dimple on the bottom of my chin.

THAT NIGHT, THERE was no hope of sleep. None whatever. I spent hours tossing in bed. Around eleven-thirty, I remembered that Lara's parents were out of town. Lara worked part-time in a vet's office and was planning to go to med school. She was pretty smart and always made me feel better about the general state of the universe. So I climbed out of the window, slid down to the porch, and ran to her house down the block.

She opened the door wearing pink pyjamas with white polka dots. Her expression was startled. It was, after all, nearly twelve o'clock.

"Dude, did you lose your phone?" she asked me.

"No," I said, "something happened."

She sighed. "It always does. Well" — she held the door open — "come in, then."

In the living room, she flopped down on the sofa and picked up a biology textbook.

"Before you say anything" — she held up her hand like a warning — "I have to finish this. If I get interrupted, I won't remember shit."

She turned to the book and read out loud: "'The main sugar in the blood is glucose. Glucose gets oxidized to pyruvate in the cytosol and then further to carbon dioxide in mitochondria. Red blood cells have no mitochondria and depend exclusively on glycolysis to meet their energy needs. But skeletal muscle can function in either presence or absence of oxygen.'" She looked up at me. "Neat."

"I just found out my dad's not really my father," I said.

She didn't say anything.

"Yeah, my mom used a sperm donor," I went on quickly. "I think I'm in shock."

In less than two minutes, I told her about my father's dimple, about the documents in the shoebox, about what happened at dinner, and about all the thoughts that had been churning inside my head ever since.

When I stopped talking, she asked me, "Do you want a joint?"

"God, yes!" I said.

We put on the adult coats in the entrance hall and went out into the backyard. The star-studded sky that night looked like another Rorschach ink blot.

"So why now, I wonder," Lara said, taking a drag. "Why did your parents wait so long to tell you about your conception."

"That's just it," I said, nodding. "I'm really mad at them about that."

Silence fell between us. Neither of us spoke for a while. Lara was gazing up at the night sky, every now and then picking flakes of weed off her tongue.

"You ever feel like life is totally meaningless?" she finally asked me. "This endless eating and drinking to just be alive. The sugar we crave gets made up into other molecules that only get broken up anyways. Some cells divide. Some cells die. Some cells become cancer and take over everything just like that. But at the end—what is there? At the end, there's dust."

"Not really," I said with conviction. "At the end, we leave children behind."

We stared at each other. Then she said, "I'm going to tell you something. There's this woman at work. Her name is Debbie. She was adopted—her real mother gave her up right after birth. So, a few years ago Debbie hired a private investigator to find her birth mother, and they met. And apparently, after a bucket of tears, things went pretty well, because now they go on Disney cruises together. Literally, sailing into the sunset."

She squinted at me through the smoke. "So what do you think?"

"What do I think about what?" I pretended not to understand her question.

"About finding your real father."

"I don't know. Mom said he was closed identity, which means he's not open to contact with me."

"Huh," she said. "But it's possible that he's changed his mind, right? Do you think that your parents would tell you if he'd done that?"

"I don't."

"Well, then," she said with satisfaction. "You have the right to know where you come from, Joy. As far as the donor goes, he should've thought about the future when he was making his donation. He should've thought about what it would mean for him too."

"But private investigators cost money," I pointed out.

"I hadn't thought about that. But wait, there's your tip jar, right? You can save up for college later. Plus, I can lend you the rest."

I shook my head, not wanting to appear too eager. "You know, my mother said we'd never talk about it again."

"More reason to suspect they're hiding something from you. Again."

I had to admit that she'd made good points, but thinking about how my parents might feel if I went behind their backs didn't make me feel good.

I was about to raise another objection when she threw her joint on the ground and said, "Show me what you've got on the donor. We'll take things from there, okay?"

Back in the house, I handed her the tube of rolled-up documents I'd brought with me. She slid the elastic band off it, unrolled them, and read everything carefully. When she came to my father's photograph, she fetched a magnifying glass from a kitchen drawer.

"Dude, what's with the tie?" She looked up at me through the glass, her right eye comically enlarged.

"It looks like a school logo," I said. "What are those called again?"

"Crests."

We searched the Internet for maybe five minutes and discovered that the crest on the tie of my biological father belonged to a certain well-known university on the west coast.

"Bingo." Lara beamed. "That's plenty to go on. We may not need a PI after all. All we have to do now is work out the approximate years he was a student there and get a hold of their yearbooks."

It was a good plan. But when I called the university's registrar the next day, I was told that they kept all their yearbooks in the main library on reserve. Which meant that the yearbooks weren't lent out and that anyone wishing to view them had to come to the library in the flesh. I couldn't jump on a plane and fly by myself across the country, never mind afford an airplane ticket in the first place. Plus, just because my biological father wore the university's tie in the photograph in his file from the sperm bank didn't necessarily mean he'd actually gone there for school. So Lara called Debbie. I didn't feel guilty about it one little bit.

I HAD TO wait two weeks to see the private investigator, during which time I avoided my parents as much as I could. My dad had had his surgery and was recovering at home. As for my mother, I hadn't spoken to her since the night of the dinner beyond "Hi," "Bye," and "School's good." She was busy at work anyway, and for my part I pretended to be busy at school. At long last, at the designated hour, I arrived at a nondescript downtown office to meet PI Francine.

She was wearing a charcoal suit, crocodile boots, and a no-nonsense expression. She agreed to take on my case right away. Five days after our meeting, she left a message for me on Lara's cellphone. When I called her back, she told me that my biological father lived in a nearby town, just three hours away. He worked for an automobile manu-facturer, doing safety research. And oh, he *had* changed his status with the sperm bank ten years ago. Yes, from closed to open identity, which meant I could contact him now.

"TOLD YOU SO," Lara said when I told her about Francine's revelations. "Maybe email him, okay? At his work address, in case he has a family. Maybe he'll want to meet you right away. If he does, I'll borrow my mother's car and drive you over there." She looked hard at me. "This is what you want?"

"Yes," I said, trying to keep my voice neutral. "Yes, you bet."

> *Hello there,*
>
> *My name is Joy. It has come to my attention that you provided a sperm specimen sometime in 1984. This specimen became me. As it happens, I may be travelling to your town (on personal business) next week. I wonder if you'd like to meet somewhere for coffee. Let me know what you think.*
>
> *Bye for now.*
>
> *Joy.*
>
> *P.S. I've attached a photograph of myself for your information.*

TWO DAYS LATER, his response arrived in my inbox. He wrote that he'd be happy to meet with me. Next week worked well for him. He taught graduate seminars at the Technical College on Wednesdays, but on Thursdays and Fridays he was free in the afternoons. If it were at all possible, he'd prefer it if I came to his office around noon. His office was located in the main engineering building, room 308. He thanked me for the photograph of myself I'd sent him and was looking forward to meeting me.

IN LARA'S MOTHER'S car the following Friday, I ran through the hypothetical small talk in my head. The words I kept coming up with seemed all wrong, though. And Lara wasn't helpful at all. She told me she was really tired and barely said a word to me, speeding like a maniac on the slippery highway, eyes firmly fixed on the road. But just before we took our exit, she said that the worst thing that could happen was that my biological father would turn out to be a dick. No pun intended, she added quickly. In which case I'd thank him for agreeing to meet with me and that would be it. But at best, well — She hesitated. At best, he could change the rest of my life.

We'd both lied at school, saying we were going to a fundraiser for an animal rights group. Lara volunteered with them, so the lie wasn't all that hard to sell. But to make things more convincing, we brought along an orange Labrador from the vet's office.

The sky looked discoloured as we pulled up next to a six-storey art deco building made out of glass.

"Well," Lara said, shutting the engine off, "I'll wait for you here." She passed me the dog's leash. "Good luck."

"Am I taking the dog with me?"

"Yes," she said. "Trust me. He'll help you to break the ice."

The dog and I went in, took the elevator, and walked down the brightly lit corridor, looking for room 308.

The door swung open before we reached it.

A man appeared on the threshold. I recognized him from the photograph in the sperm bank, except that twenty years later he'd filled out, cropped his hair, and grown a moustache.

"Hi, I'm Paul," he said, and extended his hand toward me.

"Hello," I said. "I'm Joy."

As we let go of each other, neither of us said that we were pleased to meet.

"Who is this?" He looked down at the dog.

I swallowed. The power of speech was leaving me.

"His name is Coby," I managed to say after a long moment. "We've—been in a car for a long time. I think he might be thirsty. If you could give him some water, that would be great."

He looked up at me. "Yes, I have water. Come in. Both of you."

His voice, I decided, didn't sound exactly like mine, but it resembled mine in some important keys. That fact comforted me somehow.

Everything seemed very clean in his office. Books stood in tidy rows on the shelves. On the table in one corner, piles of papers were stacked into perfect cubes. A poster entitled *3D Human Head Model—Sagittal Plane* was tidily pinned to the wall. Underneath it, a car crash test dummy leaned its plastic head awkwardly against a metal stand.

"Have a seat." Paul pointed to the chair that stood in front of his enormous desk. Like the rest of the objects in his office, the pens on it were very neatly arranged.

He crossed the room to the bar fridge and brought out a food bowl. Then, using a paper towel, he scooped leftover spaghetti into the garbage can. A half-empty water bottle stood on the fridge. He uncapped it, poured some water into the cleared bowl, and slid it on the floor toward Coby, who sniffed at it and turned his head away.

"Sorry," I said, feeling terribly self-conscious. "I guess he isn't thirsty after all."

"It's okay. I'm not offended," he said. "What's wrong with your dog's eye?"

"Oh, he doesn't have one. I mean, he was attacked by a pit bull. Basically, he had his whole face restored." I reached down to pet Coby's ear as he collapsed on my feet. "He used to be a guide dog for a blind person, but then he got old. Coby got old, I mean, not the blind person, so he could no longer do his job. The blind person didn't want to keep him, so he ended up at the SPCA." I hesitated, unwilling to lie to him, but also not wanting, for some reason, to tell him the whole truth. "He's not mine, actually. I'm watching him for a friend."

Paul nodded but didn't say anything. He just sat there, staring at me. I could hear the closing and opening of doors in the building.

"So, Joy," he said finally. "Are you in high school?"

I nodded.

"What grade?"

"Twelve."

"Are you going to college?"

I shrugged. "I'm not sure yet."

"You should go to college. Or university. Education is

very important for young people. For old people too." He leaned forward and his face assumed an earnest expression as though all of a sudden he became worried for me. "Do your parents know you're here?"

"Yes," I lied.

"Good," he said, tapping his fingertips together. "That's very good."

He seemed relieved.

There was another silence.

I pretended to look at the bookshelf.

He picked up a ballpoint pen and clicked it on and off a few times.

Coby began to snore.

That seemed to startle Paul. He put the pen down and, frowning slightly, said, "So, Joy. Why did you want to see me? Is there anything in particular you'd like to know?"

"I—I wanted to see you," I mumbled. It was now or never, I silently told myself. "Because you're my dad."

"No." He shook his head firmly. "No, I'm not. I'm the guy who donated sperm so that your parents could have you." He shook his head again. "The truth is that I was young and I needed the money. I was in dire financial straits. And the payment for sperm was very good at the time. That is the truth. I can't pretend that I did it because I wanted to help people. I'm sorry, but it just isn't true. Men who donate sperm always say that they do it because they want to help people. But that wasn't it for me."

Another silence fell between us. I didn't know what to say. I felt frozen. I just sat there and looked down at my feet.

"I wanted—" I said. "I mean, we're related. I wanted

to see if we could—" I looked up at him. "I thought that perhaps we could talk."

He held my gaze for a moment, and then leaned back.

"All right," he said. "I can tell you about my work. Do you like cars?"

"Sure," I said.

"Did you know that more people die in car accidents every year than from all diseases combined?"

"No," I said slowly. "I didn't know that."

"In my lab, we investigate the effects of blunt trauma on human bodies to predict what happens to them in car accidents. Then we make recommendations to the car designers to try and prevent fatal injuries."

I pointed to the dummy. "With those?"

"Sometimes. But dummies are often useless. Because real bodies don't behave like that."

I had to think about it for a moment.

"What do you mean?"

He picked some papers off his desk and tapped them down to make a neater bunch. Then he got up and began walking up and down behind his desk. Every now and then he stopped and looked at me.

"The living tissues are very different from plastic materials. They respond differently to stress. There are also differences in how they deform, how they tear—things like that. And since engineers like to have correct answers, we try to come up with synthetic materials that approximate real cells."

I was facing him, listening to him, and thinking that I wasn't there to talk to him about cars. Neither did I go to all the trouble nor come all the way there to talk about his research. I wanted to talk to him about his family. I wanted to find out if he had any other kids. Was he married? Was he any good at sports? What kind of things did he like to do in his spare time? What was his favourite food? For some reason, the answers to those ordinary questions seemed to be of extraordinary importance to me. I tried to come up with a good leading question that could bring me eventually to what I really wanted to know, but then I decided to just go for it, without a segue.

I took a deep breath and said, "Can I ask you something?"

"Of course."

"Do I have any siblings?"

His eyes widened at that. He stopped pacing and looked at me. I sensed that something had shifted inside him. Something had changed.

He ran his hand through his hair and then reached for a photograph in a silver frame. It stood on the bookshelf in front of a thick folder. I hadn't noticed it when I came in. It showed a pretty young woman in a white summer dress. On her lap she was holding a chubby, pink infant, who was wearing a baby bonnet.

"You had a brother," Paul said. "He died in his crib when he was five months old. It was an accident. Sudden Infant Death Syndrome. Have you heard of it? It's quite common, responsible for five point four deaths per ten thousand live births worldwide. I donated his body to science. My wife was against it, of course. But you must understand, Joy: there's an acute shortage of infant cadavers for research."

Things started to sort of swim in my head at that point. Coby was crushing my toes. It was as though suddenly every muscle in my body was running out of glucose.

I looked into his face, at his dimple, and the thing that I really wanted to know spilled out of my mouth before I could stop it. "Was that why you changed your consent with the sperm bank?"

He sat down and folded his arms across his chest.

"After my son died, things were difficult for me. I was depressed for a while. I even went into psychiatric care. To restore my mental health. You see, I suspected I had some kind of genetic glitch that got passed on to my son and made him more vulnerable to SIDS. I wasn't going to have another child after he died. No way. Because I knew that I wouldn't have made it if something bad happened again. But it became important for me to know if I had any other offspring that survived infanthood, that were healthy. I needed to know that it wasn't my fault."

His phone rang. He started, turned to it, and picked it up.

"It's for you," he said with a bewildered expression, after listening for a few seconds to the voice on the other end.

I took the receiver from him, very slowly.

"Hello," I said, feeling incredibly shaken. "Dad? What— How did you know to call here?"

"Lara told me. Joy, are you okay?"

"No," I said, looking up at Paul. "I mean, yes. I'm okay."

"Good," my dad said. "I'll see you at home."

He hung up.

"Do you see what he's doing?" Paul asked as I passed the receiver back to him. "He's putting me on notice. He's letting me know he's your real dad. That's what fathers do. That's what fathers *should* do. That's what I would've done if I were him."

I knew then that the meeting was over. He didn't look angry, yet there was a finality in his tone that told me it was time to go. I stood up. Coby stirred.

"Joy," Paul said when we reached the door. "You seem like a nice young woman. Your whole life is ahead of you. Focus on what you've got rather than what you think you haven't, and you'll be all right."

"Yes," I said, turning to go. "Thank you for meeting with me."

"And—"

I looked back.

"Good luck," he said. "I wish you all the best."

He was holding with one hand on to the door frame, the dimple so prominent on his chin. And suddenly, in the lights of the hallway, his face looked so damaged to me. His expression seemed to be asking, Why did things happen the way they did? Engineers liked to have correct answers, but what was the answer to this?

WHEN I OPENED the car door, Lara said, "I'm sorry."

"Why?" I cried. "Why? I trusted you and you—"

"Coz you don't have a frontal lobe yet," she said calmly, as she strapped the seatbelt across Coby's chest.

I glared at her. "What?"

"You're a teenager. Teenagers don't have a frontal lobe. I mean, it's there, but it isn't fully developed yet. That's why we're so impulsive, prone to addictions, and have no judgement to speak of. That's also why we're incapable of making rational decisions. It sucks, I know. The frontal lobe develops fully only in our late twenties. I read all about it in a neurophysiology textbook. Only then do all the neurons connect together and we can take care of ourselves. Meanwhile, we feel confused and resentful. We hate our parents. Hey, quit with the thunder brows! I hate my parents too, okay? But I also care too much about you to see you do something that is certain to cause you pain. So there! I said it. Now, tell me I was wrong about that."

Her little speech failed to abate my anger. I felt so betrayed!

"What did you tell my parents?" I said through my teeth.

"Everything."

"Francine was on it?"

"Of course."

Oh, I could've slapped her right there and then!

"Go ahead," she said. "Do it! Slap me if that's what you want to do. It'll only go to prove my point. About the frontal lobe, I mean."

We drove home in silence. I watched the rain. Torrents of inky water stained the windshield.

We stopped at a gas station. She bought a box of doughnuts and two bottles of Diet Coke. I wasn't hungry. I couldn't imagine eating anything ever again. She, on the other hand, had no problem with digestion. I watched her stuff herself. I wanted to be sick. At one point, a glob of red jelly stuck to her upper lip. She'd look stupid with a moustache, I decided, if she were a boy, if due to some unknowable DNA process her dad had given her his Y chromosome instead of an X.

I winced every time a car overtook us. I shivered from cold. Then I cried.

As we got closer to home, I made a conscious effort to stop thinking about the talk I was bound to have with my parents. I knew it would be unbearably sad. I imagined my mother hovering by the front door, waiting to lecture me. Again. I needed the time to figure things out. To deconstruct everything on my own.

When I got home, though, there was no one at the front door. Which was strange. Instead, they were waiting for me at the dining room table, on which stood a half-full bottle of wine. I came in silently and sat down, bracing myself for the worst.

My mother said, "Hi."

"Hi," I said.

"How was it? Did you get what you were hoping for?"

"No," I said simply. "I didn't."

"What happened," my Dad asked.

I didn't reply to that. I couldn't. How could I possibly explain anything to them? How could I even begin to verbalize what I was feeling? What words could I use?

Only — that having met my biological father and seeing now my real dad, sitting across from me at the table, with the expression of complete misery on his face, I realized that I was forever indebted to him for being born. Because the thing was that my dad had made a conscious decision to have me with my mother and another man's sperm. He'd chosen to be my father. My parent. My forebear. He made me. Not Paul.

Only —

"I wish you'd told me sooner," I said, "about how I was conceived. It wasn't good that you didn't. It was —" I searched for the right word for a long moment. "Unkind."

My mother steepled her fingers.

"You're right," she said. "I'm sorry. I regret deeply that

we did not. It just goes to show that even adults who consider themselves smart and well educated sometimes make big mistakes. The irony is that I've read all these books on parenting, not to mention the novels of the classical canon. Great literature is supposed to teach us how to live a proper life. But it's hard to make out sometimes what 'proper' means, exactly, when you're in the middle of it."

She reached for my hand. "I'm not making excuses. Please don't think that I am. But sometimes I feel like parenthood is the game no one wins."

"Maybe it isn't about winning," Dad said. "Maybe it's about having played." He looked up at me. "People like to pretend that our genes define the truth for us. But I assure you, Joy, that's not the case."

I closed my eyes. I imagined the neurons firing away inside my frontal lobe. I was sure they were making important connections, but I didn't know what those connections were. Yet. Time was melting. Or maybe it was simply undulating, mutating as it coursed through chemical space. In my mind, I thought about the future. And what I saw was this: I was walking down a broad avenue, holding a woman's hand. There was a little girl skipping ahead of us. Our daughter. The three of us were smiling.

We were happy, I think.

Peptide *p*

or

The Association of Parapsychological Phenomena with
Resistance to Heart Break Disease in
Peptide *p*–Positive Children

ABSTRACT

Thirty-four kindergarten children who developed Heart
Break (HB) disease after consuming artificial meat and
two resistant children who ate the same meat but did
not develop HB disease underwent clinical trials at our
Bio Frontiers Research Institute (Division of Life). In this
paper, we present experimental evidence that resistance
to HB disease is not entirely biochemical, but may in fact
stem from specific paranormal abilities, at least in young
children. We identify a novel factor that may be responsible for these previously unexplained phenomena and
consider it highly significant, despite the small trial size
of this study. Our findings impact two great unknowns
of present-day cognitive science: the poorly understood
diversity of psychic phenomena, and their unexplained
abundance. As such, we pave the way for the rational design of new psycho-editing technologies.

INTRODUCTION

Mass production of meat in laboratories began a decade ago due to various environmental and ethical considerations. The original work involved the expansion of goldfish melanocytes in baths of cow blood. Within two years, researchers switched to stem cells from *Sus domesticus* (the common pig). The pig cells were placed on three-dimensional scaffolds shaped like steaks, ribs, leg bones, and the like, and coaxed to assemble by magnetic levitation. The cells grew slowly, however, until researchers in Denmark added human growth hormones to the culture medium. This prompted cells to expand rapidly into succulent muscle fibres.

The sales of artificial meat peaked thereafter and promised a bright future for the industry. But in March of 20___, reports of cases of a new human disease began to come out of Europe. This disease was limited to individuals who had consumed artificial meat. Tests revealed the presence of a previously unknown agent, peptide p, in their blood. Levels of peptide p in the blood increased steadily after consumption of artificial meat, and reached a lethal threshold of twelve parts per millilitre as early as six days post-consumption (see Fig. 1 below).

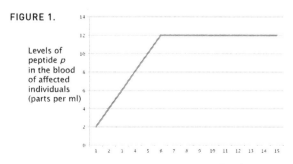

FIGURE 1.

Levels of peptide p in the blood of affected individuals (parts per ml)

Days post-consumption of artificial meat

Upon further investigation, researchers in Austria determined that peptide *p* was deposited in human heart cells, where it attached to normal proteins. This attachment resulted in the formation of large insoluble clusters, which expanded inside heart cells and broke them. The resulting disease, named Heart Break (HB), is progressively dementing, and is typically characterized by apathy, loss of motor function, and death within thirteen days. Whereas some infected adults remain asymptomatic, children exhibit the signs of HB quickly.

The production of artificial meat has been discontinued for the time being, but tainted meat products continue to surface. In May of this year, thirty-six kindergarten children in W—— were diagnosed with HB disease after consuming hot dogs in the school cafeteria. Curiously, two children (a boy and a girl) failed to progress to terminal stage, presenting us with a unique research opportunity. Initially, we were interested in investigating whether (as reported previously by J. Swift) levels of peptide *p* fluctuated during the day. As our experiments progressed, however, and we accumulated more data, it became apparent that more than blood biochemistry might be responsible for the observed effects, i.e., we became alerted to the possibility that so-called parapsychological abilities might account (at least partially) for the resistance to HB disease in these two extraordinary children. We investigated this possibility by conducting interviews with their caregivers.

MATERIALS AND METHODS

Children. Thirty-six children had an average age of 5.3 (range = 5–6) years and represented a variety of ethnicities (10% African, 25% Asian, 30% Caucasian, 5% Hispanic, 30% multiracial). During the trial, all subjects and their caregivers resided in the children's ward of our Institute under twenty-four-hour surveillance. Their diets and medication were uniformly controlled to exclude all outside agents.

Thirty-four children with the symptoms of HB were kept alive with blood transfusions for the duration of the trial and discharged at its conclusion to the care of their families, whereupon all progressed to terminal stage within two days. The two resistant children remained in the Institute until their transfer to the Centre of Cognitive Engineering in I———.

Peptide measurements. Previous work with human subjects (Zamyatin and co-workers) showed that peptide *p* diffused into saliva, matching its levels in the blood. Accordingly, we collected salivary samples from all children by instructing them to chew on a cotton ball for ten seconds. (Some children complained about fibrous threads being stuck in their teeth and some actually swallowed the balls. Thus, we recommend that in future experiments, cotton balls be soaked in warm water before giving them to children to chew on.) Each chewed-on cotton ball was sliced in two. One half was deposited in a glass test tube and assayed immediately. The other was stored in a cryofreeze vial at −80°C.

RESULTS

Thirty-four children who progressed to the terminal stage of HB showed a steady increase in salivary peptide *p* throughout the day (see Fig. 1). However, levels of peptide *p* in the saliva of the two resistant children fluctuated daily in a manner reminiscent of an electrocardiogram (Fig. 2).

FIGURE 2.

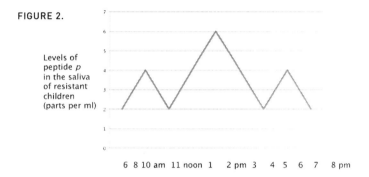

Levels of peptide *p* in the saliva of resistant children (parts per ml)

6 8 10 am 11 noon 1   2 pm 3   4   5   6   7   8 pm

As mentioned above, we controlled the diets of all children, thus excluding all outside agents that might have accounted for the observed fluctuations. After consulting a French bioethicist, Dr. Frederic P——, who hypothesized that children's psychological states might play a role in the decrease of peptide *p* levels at certain times during the day, we conducted interviews with their caregivers to explore this possibility.

*   *   *

Interview #1 conducted on _____ with the resistant boy's caregiver (Father).

Interviewer: Your son has unusual levels of a peptide agent in his blood.

Father: Unusual how?

I: The levels of this agent fluctuate dramatically during the day. Basically, they go up and down.

F: Why is that?

I: We don't know. That's why we're here: to try and figure this out. We'd like to ask you some questions.

F: I'm ready.

I: Could you please tell us about a typical day with your son? Specifically, what TV programs you watch, video games you play, books you read, and so on? What does your son get excited about?

F: He doesn't. I mean, my son is — a bit introverted. (Pauses.) Sometimes we watch the National Geographic or Discovery Channel. He likes animals. We read and just — hang out.

I: What kinds of animals does your son like?

F: All kinds. He's always been very caring. Once, I remember, we found a baby bird with a broken wing in the woods. He took it home and insisted we care for it. I convinced him to take it to the vet, of course. The vet said the bird was beyond help and put it out of its misery. My son cried for two days after that and decided to become a vegetarian.

I: Vegetarian?

F: Yes, he stopped eating meat. Just like that.

I: So, the hot dogs in the cafeteria that made everyone sick — why did he eat them?

F: Oh, he was forced to eat them by one of the teachers. I was very angry when I found out about it, but by then — well, it was too late.

I: We understand. Next question. According to the nurses' reports, the two of you go out often for walks in the Institute's garden. Is that true? How long do you usually walk there?

F: Half an hour, an hour at a time. Three, sometimes four times a day, depending on the weather. It's good exercise. We walk at home a lot too. There are woods around our house. We walk there with our dog and talk about things.

I: What kinds of things?

F: The usual things. School, space—he always asks me about planets and stars and satellites. Things like that. We also talk about his mother.

I: His mother?

F: Yes. He wants to know what she was like. We talk about her a lot. Karen died three years ago in an accident. I wrote it all out on the forms you gave me.

I: Sure, but could you please tell us more about your wife's accident anyway?

F: (Pauses.) Okay. Karen went for a run one Saturday morning and was hit by a car. I suppose you never wake up and think to yourself, Gee, today may be the last time I ever see my wife, right? (Shakes his head.) Anyway—it was three years ago.

I: Does your son have memories of her?

F: Oh yes. They were very close.

I: Could you tell us as much as you can recall about their relationship? Anything you can remember.

F: Well, they had this—affinity, I suppose I'd call it. It's almost as if they were one person. Karen was so in tune with him from the very beginning. That's what she called it, *in tune*. She knew she carried a boy. We were in our late thirties when we met—we didn't know if we'd have children. One day shortly after she got pregnant, she was standing in the kitchen washing the dishes, then she turned to me with the sort of expression that makes you pause and drop everything—you know the kind of expression I mean—it was like that. She turned to me and said, "We're going to have a boy."

I: What made her so sure?

F: She said she just knew.

I: Did Karen take any fertility drugs?

F: No, she conceived naturally.

I: How did her pregnancy go?

F: Great. She blossomed. Look, I know it's an awful cliché, but she really was glowing in this beautiful way. I remember the first time we saw our son's heart beating on an ultrasound, about ten weeks in, it must've been. He was so tiny, like this little shrimp, floating inside a bubble. Karen was thirty-nine at the time, so they did many tests on her. But she was her own ultrasound machine. I remember this because it was so weird. She'd say things like, "His heart is beating at a rate of a hundred and eighty beats per minute, twice the speed of my own. How can you *not* hear it?"

I: What happened after Karen gave birth?

F: It was a challenging time for her, I think. I couldn't take any time off work. I travelled on business a lot while she stayed at home and looked after our boy. I don't know if it was because of all the time they spent together, but they were inseparable. It wasn't easy for me, to be honest. I'd arrive home exhausted and try to spend time with my son. He'd be happy to see me and say "Dada" a few times, but that's about it. He just clung to her like a diaper. And she too, I mean, she wanted him to. She breastfed him until the day she was killed—the autopsy report said her breasts were filled with milk.

I: We are very sorry for your loss. Is there anything else you remember about their relationship?

F: Yes. When he was almost two, he began to understand what we were saying. And he expressed himself quite well. Better, I think, than most toddlers his age. So he would ask us perceptive questions, like, for example, why did the bunny laying eggs at Easter. Things like that.

I: Why did the bunny lay eggs at Easter?

F: Exactly. (Laughs.) You don't know, right? Most people know what Easter stands for, but they don't know why the Easter Bunny brings the eggs. It's a perfectly reasonable question to ask, isn't it, but most people never ask it. So let me tell you. Apparently, a long time ago, a goddess named Eoster—her name comes from German—was walking one winter day in a forest and saw a little bird. A terrible storm was coming. The bird was shivering from cold, and the goddess realized it had little chance of surviving. So she turned the little bird into a rabbit to save its life. The warm fur saw the bunny through the winter, and when spring came, it laid colourful eggs to thank the goddess for saving its life. That's how the tradition was born.

I: A wonderful tale. But what is your point?

F: My point is that my son wanted to understand why the Easter Bunny laid eggs. He's always trying to get to the bottom of things, to look for meaning behind them. At first I thought it was normal development, but Karen knew right away that he was a little bit — I don't want to sound spooky about it or anything — but she said he was extra-sensory. She read all these books about babies who could remember what happened to them in the womb, so one evening she asked him if he remembered being inside her stomach. He said, "Yes, Mama." She asked him to describe what it was like, and he went to the bathroom, filled the bathtub with water, climbed into it, and said, "Like zhat!" Stranger still, she asked him if he remembered anything about his birth and he went to the living room, rolled a carpet into a tube, and crawled through it! (Laughs.) I couldn't believe it.

I: What happened after Karen died?

F: He just — closed. Like a book. I couldn't read him. He waited for her. He'd wait for hours by the front door, asking me, "Where's Mama?" or stand by the stove on his little chair, like he'd done when she was alive. His soup chair, he called it, because they made soup together. Or he'd sit on the stairs and stare at me as though demanding an explanation. I tried not to cry in front of him. What was the point? What was I going to do? Unravel? No. I had to keep on living. (Clears throat.) In any event, I had to sell my business to take care of him. He understands now that she's gone. Every night he says, "Good night, Mama." She sings to him in his dreams, he says. I believe him.

I: You said you talked with your son about Karen during the day?

F: Yes. I tell him how proud she'd be of him for being a part of this trial, for helping to find the cure.

I: When do you talk to him about her?

F: When?

I: Yes. Try to be as specific as possible about the time of day when you mention Karen to the boy.

F: We talk about her at least twice a day. When we go for walks in the mornings, around ten in the morning, I guess, and in the evenings, after supper, around eight, when I read to him in bed.

I: Do you talk about her at any time in the afternoon?

F: Hmm, I guess she comes up in the afternoon too. When I put him down for a nap, he always asks me to tuck him in like a baby bird. Karen used to say that to him, "I'm tucking you in like a baby bird in a nest."

I: What time does your son usually nap in the afternoon?

F: Around two.

I: Does he dream?

F: All the time.

I: Does he tell you about his dreams?

F: All the time, as I told you. He used to sleepwalk. The doctors said he had something called sleep arousals. I'm told it's fairly common in young children, especially if they've had trauma. Shortly after Karen died, he started to get up in the middle of the night and walk around the house. His eyes were closed, but his arms moved around and he *looked* awake. I had to install gates on the top of the stairs to make sure he didn't fall down.

I: You said he *used to* sleepwalk. Has he stopped?

F: Yes. The last episode happened—let me see—at least six months ago.

I: You mentioned he tells you sometimes about his dreams. What does he say he dreams about?

F: About the same thing, every time. He says he can see the future.

I: What do you mean?

F: He says he sees things that are going to happen. The dreams often start with a room where he's sitting on a chair, waiting for someone. Sometimes he's waiting for me, sometimes for another person who is going to care for him in the future. But it's not going to be for a long time, in any case, he says. I mean he says that he isn't going to be around for a long time. There're usually two windows in this room but no doors. After a while he gets up off the chair, walks to the window, and looks out. He sees people, dressed in white robes, walking around. The thing is — (Hesitates.)

I: Please continue. It's very important that you tell us everything you know about his dreams.

F: The thing is, he says the people he sees in his dreams are not alive. They aren't dead, exactly. No. But they are bleeding through their clothes. Except there is no blood anywhere, because they have no blood left. I know it doesn't make very much sense, but that's what he says. He says their bodies have been eaten. Everything has been eaten away.

I: Eaten?

F: Yes.

I: Eaten by whom?

F: He doesn't say.

I: What else does your son see in his dreams?

F: Plants.

I: What kind of plants?

F: Plants that have become sentient beings — or rather, plants that were *made* into them. Plants that can feel emotions and respond to unspoken thoughts. He imagines them suffering, feeling stressed. He says the people in the white robes tried to make the plants different.

I: Different in what way?

F: They tried to make them behave differently. To make them more like animals by inserting things inside them. Except it didn't work. The people failed.

I: What colour are the plants in his dreams?

F: Red.

I: Not green?

F: (Shakes head.) No. Red.

I: You said your son saw the future in his dreams. So everything you just described, about the people in the white robes and the red plants with feelings, will happen in the future, according to him?

F: That's right.

I: Is there anything else — unusual, would you say, about your son?

F: I've always felt that he was unusual, especially after what happened to Karen. He knew something bad was going to happen to her. He didn't want her to go for a run that morning. I hate thinking about it, so I try not to. But that morning, that Saturday, when she wanted to go outside — it was a perfectly ordinary morning. She was getting dressed, putting her running shoes on. When he realized what she was going to do, he screamed. He threw himself on her. He wouldn't let go, no matter how hard I tried to pry him off her. He lost it, basically. He had a terrible fit, but she wouldn't listen. I wouldn't listen. She was feeling stressed that day. And when she felt stressed, she went for a run.

I: But you did pry him off her. Eventually.

F: Yes. Yes, I did that.

End of the first interview.

★   ★   ★

Interview #2 conducted on _____ with the resistant girl's caregiver (Mother).

Interviewer: Your daughter has unusual levels of a peptide agent in her blood.

Mother: Is that why she doesn't get sick?

I: We can't be certain at this point. That's why we're here: to try and figure this out. We'd like to ask you some questions.

M: Sure.

I: Can you please tell us about a typical day with your daughter? Specifically, what TV programs you watch, video games you play, books you read, and so on? What does your daughter get excited about?

M: She doesn't get excited easily. She's shy.

I: Introverted?

M: Yes, shy.

I: Has she always been shy?

M: More or less, yes.

I: Does she like animals?

M: Yes, but mostly she likes trees.

I: Trees?

M: Yes, she talks to the trees sometimes. She says they whisper secrets to her. Her favourite colour is green, and she likes patterns. She collects different kinds of leaves and arranges them in patterns. There's nothing wrong with her.

I: Of course not.

M: Good. She likes to eat leafy things, too. The greener, the better.

I: Like broccoli?

M: Yes. And spinach. And kale. And arugula. Even mustard greens. That kid—I swear, I've never met another kid like her. All other children, her friends, eat—I don't know—pasta?

I: Does she have a lot of friends? Does she play well with other children?

M: Sometimes. But mostly she plays on her own. She has an imaginary friend. Alex. I asked her if Alex was a boy or a girl. She said it depended. Sometimes Alex was a boy, sometimes a girl.

I: Can you give us an example of your daughter's typical imaginary play with Alex?

M: She likes to take care of him. Feed him. Give him warm baths. Cuddle. Put him to bed. She's a very caring little girl. Actually, sometimes she complains to him about being bored. I remember this one time, a friend of mine and I took her out to a fancy restaurant. We ordered some green food for her – cucumber sandwiches, peas. We were having a good time, sitting there talking. A man played guitar. It was, as I said, a fancy restaurant, so he was walking around with the guitar strung around his shoulders, playing a nice song. My little girl listened and drew things on napkins for a while. Then she turned to the empty seat next to her and spoke to Alex.

I: What did she say?

M: She said, "I know, Alex. That man killed her too."

I: "That man killed her"? What do you think she meant by it?

M: It was during the time when a man killed his wife in the area. They wrote all about it in the newspapers. Mind, I don't read newspapers or watch the news, but I knew about it because of my daughter. (Pauses.) She told me what happened. She said she saw it inside her mind. Her mind was stuck on it. That's the word she used—*stuck*. The man's daughter went missing, so the cops were looking for her. He denied everything, said she ran away, but my daughter knew different. One day we were walking past the house where the murders happened, and she pulled me into the garden and stood there without moving, statue-like, for a long time. It was a beautiful garden. My daughter said the plants told her what happened. I didn't believe her, of course. I thought she was making it all up, like with Alex, but she insisted and made me take her to the police. The cops didn't believe her either, but they had no other leads.

I: What did your daughter say the plants had told her?

M: The plants saw everything that happened in that house on the day of the murders. The man killed his wife, chopped her up, ate her fingers. His little girl saw everything then hid under the bed, but he found her and killed her too. He didn't mind that his wife's body parts were found. He was proud of what he'd done to her, he said during the trial. (Cringes.) They fought a lot, according to the neighbours, and the wife always shook her fingers at him. But his little girl was different. He said he really loved her. So he choked her to death and then entombed her body in a wall in the basement, mixing her into cement. He was a brick mason, so that's what he did. The plants saw everything through the basement window and told my daughter about it. As I said, no one believed her at first. But then the cops went down there, broke the wall, and found the little girl's body.

I: Did your daughter tell you how plants were able to see what they saw?

M: Through the shadows.

I: How is that?

M: She said plants could tell the difference between light and shadows.

I: Okay. What happened after the police found the little girl's body in the basement wall?

M: A psychologist came to talk to my daughter. She told him the story about the dinosaurs. He wrote a report.

I: The story about the dinosaurs?

M: Yes, I'd heard it many times by then. It was about a planet where dinosaurs lived. They ate only plants. Then something changed. One dinosaur became very hungry. He was no longer satisfied with plants and decided to start eating meat. But there was no meat around except other dinosaurs, so he started eating his friends. He ate and he ate until there was nothing left but himself. So at the end, he had no choice but to eat himself too.

I: What do you think your daughter meant by this story?

M: She says the story is actually about people. That this is what is going to happen to people.

I: Does your daughter eat meat?

M: No. She never liked it. She eats green, leafy things, as I told you.

I: So the tainted hot dogs she ate in the school cafeteria—

M: The teachers made her eat it. She trusted them. She trusts adults.

I: We understand and we'll keep this in mind. Now, can you please tell us about what you do during the day with your daughter.

M: There isn't much to do around here, is there? We read a bit and go for walks with the resistant boy. I chat with the father. He's nice. A widower. He always remembers to put cream in my coffee.

I: What time of the day do you usually go for walks with them?

M: Whenever they go. My daughter sees them out in the garden from our window and then she wants to go out too.

I: Do the children get along?

M: Real well.

I: Even though your daughter is shy?

M: Yes, that's just it. My daughter is usually shy with other children, especially with boys, but this boy is different. They talk.

I: Do you know what about?

M: About space. He tells her about shooting stars and other galaxies. They also talk about the boy's mother. I mean, he does. His mother died several years ago in a car accident. The boy showed me her picture. She was very pretty.

I: Does your daughter see the resistant boy at any other time during the day?

M: We eat lunch together sometimes, but other than walking? No, me and my daughter spend most of our time in our room.

I: What do you do there?

M: We listen to music, colour pictures, watch a bit of TV — cartoons, mostly. Other than that, there're all these tests she must do, so our time is divided into tests and no tests.

I: What about around two o'clock in the afternoon? What do you do then?

M: She usually naps between one and three, so around two she's sleeping.

I: Does she dream?

M: Yes.

I: Does she tell you of her dreams?

M: No, but she draws things.

I: Like what?

M: She draws her brother. (Sighs.) I lost him eleven days after he was born. He was three months premature. The doctor said that there was nothing anyone could do. I was a mess for a long time afterward. If it weren't for my daughter—I don't know how I would've survived it.

I: And your husband?

M: Never had one. Never wanted to. I've got Dave, but he's a free spirit. A wanderer.

I: Is Dave the girl's father?

M: Dave sure is. I wanted to have a brother or sister for my girl. I believe that there must be two things. Two people, two parents, two everything. Like, for balance, you know? Two things make peace. A tree falls when the wind blows without another tree to hold it up.

I: What tree?

M: I'm just saying. It's an expression.

I: Okay. You mentioned your daughter draws things in her dreams. Can you tell us more about her drawings?

M: Not much to tell. It's the same thing, over and over.

I: What is it?

M: Like this — let me show you. (Takes pen and paper.)

She says it's two beings wrapped up in one blanket. I ask her, "What beings, honey?" and she says it's her and her brother.

I: Do you mind if we keep this drawing?

M: Go ahead.

I: You implied earlier that your daughter helped you overcome your depression, is that right?

M: For sure. She was my rock when I hit the bottom. To stand on, to save me from drowning. I've got to tell you that when I was pregnant with her, I felt so good. It was like I could see the insides of stars. That children's song, "Twinkle, twinkle"? Well, I didn't wonder why the stars twinkled. I just knew. I knew everything. And everything was lovely. After she was born, I couldn't put her down. Not for a minute, I couldn't. I slept with her in my bed. Dave kept saying I shouldn't do it, I should keep her in her crib. But I said to him, "Show me one animal in the wild that puts their young in a crib." He didn't make a peep after that. And then — when I was in a dark place, after my son died, she said, "Mommy, don't be sad. How can my brother come back to live with us if our house is sad?"

I: What do you think she meant by it?

M: She says her brother comes to talk to her in her dreams. To tell her about where he is now.

I: Where is he now?

M: She doesn't know the name of the place. Only that it's somewhere not far from here. Not far from anywhere, because it's all around us. We can't see it because it's behind an invisible curtain. But not many people are paying attention, so they don't realize this curtain exists.

I: But your daughter is paying attention.

M: Oh, yes. She sure is.

I: Would you say your daughter has a strong connection with you?

M: (Frowns. Thinks it over in silence.) I'd say it's more like she knows something about me no one else knows.

I: Last question. We'd like to ask you now about eight o'clock in the evening. What do you usually do at that time?

M: Eight o'clock? That's not a good time for me. My son died in the evening at eight o'clock. My daughter sits on the bed beside me and holds my hand.

End of the second interview.

DISCUSSION

The striking similarities between the two resistant children did not escape our notice. Both of them were said to be introverted and sensitive. Both loved imaginary play. Both had dream visions. Both were vegetarian and forced to consume tainted meat by their teachers. Both showed sensitivity toward living things — birds and animals by the boy, and plants, especially, by the girl. Both lost a close member of their family in early life and had a strong attachment to their mother. In relation to this last point, we demonstrated empirically that the levels of peptide *p* in the saliva of these two children did not remain constant during the day, but fluctuated dramatically, and that these fluctuations corresponded exactly with the times of day when these children were *thinking* about their mothers

(Fig. 2).

A possible correlation between maternal relationship and resistance to Heart Break disease has been reported previously. It is also well documented that orphans spend a lot of time thinking about their mothers, which may in fact explain the high level of resistance to HB disease in these individuals. Moreover, experiments with the bodies of persons who perished in the recent earthquake in J—— showed significantly lower levels of peptide p in their blood. It is thus not unreasonable to assume that those persons were thinking about their mothers immediately before death.

Much more unexpected, however, was our discovery that both resistant children appeared to have extrasensory abilities: namely, precognition, clairvoyance, and (notably in the case of the girl) telepathy with plants. Thus, after much discussion among ourselves, we hypothesized that parapsychic perceptions, regarded by many of our peers as pseudoscience, might account, in some way, for the resistance to HB disease.

The most intriguing question then became *How?* How might extrasensory talents in these two children counteract the destructive effects of peptide p on their hearts?

To help us answer this question, we turned to a well-known psychic researcher and chair at the Department of Parapsychology at N—— University, Professor James D.

Professor D. has argued for years that although paranormal sensing in humans cannot be at present explained by known biochemistry, the chemical nature of a human body cannot be discounted. It is his long-held belief that each living being—from the simplest amoeba to man—is an elaborate circuit, designed to integrate chemical data to elicit a behavioural response. Professor D. maintains that, much in the same way that caffeine produced by certain plants functions as a psychoactive agent that makes bees remember these plants and return to them for pollination, subtle chemical clues present in the environment trigger cognitive responses in human beings. To investigate what these chemical clues might be, Professor D. has conducted experiments with bacteria, fungi, and worms, hoping to uncover—as he put it—their chemical "thoughts." He has also hooked up plants to polygraph machines and tested the effects of common variables, such as temperature, gravity, and nutrients on their biology, and found that in many cases plants generated "rational" chemical response. As a consequence of these and other experiments, Professor D. has come up with a model of an integrated Universal brain, through which all living things communicate with one another and with the outside world.

In one particularly stunning experiment, Professor D. discovered that certain plants excreted a volatile agent upon "hearing" the sound of a deer chewing another plant. He isolated this agent from their sap, named it peptide *d*, and predicted that a similar agent (or agents) existed in human cells, where it remained dormant until a perceived outside threat activated it. Once activated, this agent diffused through the body and became poly-functional, i.e., it acted at different sites in different manners. Professor D. has proposed that most people are insensitive to this agent and thus hardly notice its effects in everyday life. But a select few individuals are extrasensory, and these are the persons who make what we know as "paranormal"

FIGURE 3.

Levels of
peptides *p*
and *d*
in the saliva
of resistant
children
(parts per ml)

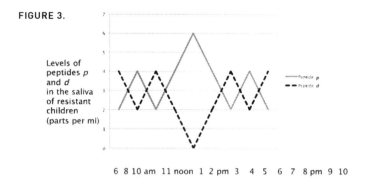

6 8 10 am 11 noon 1 2 pm 3 4 5 6 7 8 pm 9 10

claims. In this context, it is noteworthy that in his recent experiments with sixty-three French clairvoyants, Professor D. detected small quantities of peptide *d* in their blood.

Taking all of these factors into account, we reasoned that if Professor D.'s theory was correct and peptide *d* triggered in some way parapsychic abilities, then our two resistant children (both of whom appeared to be somewhat parapsychic) might have detectable levels of peptide *d* in their blood. And indeed, while we saw no traces of peptide *d* in the thirty-four subjects afflicted with HB disease, we found that peptide *d* was not only present in the saliva of the two resistant children but also that its levels rose and fell daily in direct opposition to the levels of peptide *p* (Fig. 3).

Strikingly, the union of peptides *p* and *d* resembles the dream vision the resistant girl described to her mother (see the drawing in the second interview). Peptide *d* may thus serve as peptide *p*'s partner, a molecular yin to its yang. Similar cases of molecular mimicry have been reported to occur in plants. As such, we postulate that resistance to HB disease in our two children might have been complemented by their vegetarian diets.

In a nutshell, it appears that a balance between these two peptides may exist in nature, which, when disturbed, leads to a shift. This shift then, not unlike an upset teeter-totter, may bring the affected organism down with disease. It is remarkable, certainly, that the mother of the resistant girl spoke of the "two things in nature making peace" and of the "curtain behind real things" of which most people remain unaware.

Many questions remain unanswered at present and may serve as guidelines for future research. How, for example, does peptide *d* in the blood of French clairvoyants account for their ability to gain information by unknown sensory means? Are these individuals, like the two resistant children we studied, also immune to HB disease? Since the answers to these questions are a matter of global security, we have applied to the French government for a special certificate that would enable us to hold all known clairvoyants in custody for an indefinite time.

Perhaps peptide *d*, as Professor D. predicted, is activated by a yet-to-be-discovered mechanism in response to external stimuli. Perhaps it then diffuses to the brain of susceptible individuals and finds suitable receptors to increase their sensory thresholds. Certain genetic factors may play a role in this process. The resistant boy's mother, let us remember, could hear her son's heartbeat before he was born.

The next step may be to restore the upset equilibrium between peptides *p* and *d* by artificial means. Plants from all over the world should be harvested and large quantities of peptide *d* should be isolated from them. Peptide *d* structure and its mode of action should be studied in detail.

Its effect on the human brain and embryonic tissue should be thoroughly investigated as well. Then, and only then, psycho-editing drugs may be designed and administered to select individuals to enhance their parapsychic skills.

One week ago, the two resistant children were transferred to the Centre of Cognitive Engineering (CCEI), where they will undergo further tests. In the first stage of the clinical trials there, they will be separated from their families to counter the effects of their attachment to them. In the second stage, they will be exposed to various "treatments" and the levels of peptides p and d in their blood will be quantified twenty-four hours a day, seven days a week, for several months. In the third and final stage, these children will be sacrificed via humane means (e.g., the variant of the Huxley technique). Their complete body chemistry will be then made public through the CCEI's Facebook page. In the meantime, we solicit public participation in this ongoing experiment through social media instruments of collective good and look hopefully to the future through the amber glass of our test tubes.

GONOS

LIFE IS REMARKABLY incorrect, Nikolai Larkov thought. Why is homology required for recombination? This process scrambles the parental genes, leading to new combinations in the offspring. If the offspring—

Someone sneezed, and he forced himself to stay focused. After all, he was in lecture and had to pay attention to what he was saying. His eyes scanned the two hundred under-graduate faces in his Biology 101 class.

"Let us examine now the key points of sexual differen-tiation," he said, and thought of his son. "How does a male become a male, for instance?"

"He has a penis?" someone suggested from the back of the room.

Everyone laughed.

"Testicles," offered a female with dark, shiny hair who sat in the front row. Her hips were sufficiently broad for childbirth, Larkov observed, and her genes were good, very good, judging by the symmetry of her smooth oval face.

He adjusted his bow tie.

"Certainly," he said. "Penis and testicles, ovaries and

vagina are the sexual parts appropriate to one's gender. Gender is the first thing we see in a person. It is also the first thing we ask of new parents. Is it a boy or a girl? But. Let me tell you that there is a molecular drama unfolding beneath."

"Why would you say *gender*?" another female to his left inquired. She had cropped red hair and large silver earrings.

Larkov looked up at her in amazement, his eyes large behind his high-index lenses.

"Pardon me?"

"One's gender has nothing to do with one's sex," the female said with conviction.

"No?" He straightened his shoulders. He could slide down a slippery slope here fast. It was imperative, *really important*, to nip this particular peach in its poisonous bud.

Meanwhile, the redhead continued, "In our Women's Studies course, we talk about gender as being about identity, about—"

"Bravo!" Larkov exclaimed. "You're probably right. I was only thinking of Greeks. The word *gender* comes to us from the Greek word *ghen*, which means 'root.' We know the Greek *ghen* as the gene, which has been the focus— and surely you can't argue with that—of this course."

It was ridiculous that in this country—No, he wasn't going to wade into another debate.

"Life makes more of itself," he went on quickly. "Fish, fern, and fowl—all procreate their kind. Sex is great. Sex is wonderful, really. We should attribute our very existence to the erotic habits of primitive cells in the primordial sludge."

At these words, his mind drifted off again. It was curious how he could be standing in front of the class, talking, and suddenly feel his body swell up as if filled with invisible gas. He'd rise up from the floor then and levitate above his students, all the while speaking and gesturing at the PowerPoint slides. In such moments, he thought deeply. About the bold propositions and intricate theories of his research. About his ex-wife, Nora, and how over the years he'd managed to mess their marriage up. About their only son, Eric, whose estrangement troubled him a great lot. And about the general flow of his life, which at present seemed somewhat tumultuous, tumbling, not unlike that of a treacherous river spilling over a tall dam.

On Monday, he'd been summoned to the dean's office and informed of yet another student's complaint. It was not the first time a charge of cultural insensitivity had been levelled against Professor Larkov. It would certainly not be the last.

"Nikolai," the dean said, chewing his moustache, "you must try and be more sensible, please. The consensus of faculty is that you are too preoccupied with your fruit flies. I will remind you that the principal role of this college is undergraduate teaching, not research. The curriculum committee has recommended that you teach an introductory course in biology this semester specifically with this role in mind."

The problem, Larkov had wanted to reply to the dean but had known better, was that he'd always felt misunderstood. He'd felt misunderstood as a child, as a lover, as a parent, and he'd most definitely felt misunderstood as a colleague. Actually, he'd felt misunderstood by the whole of Canada, ever since landing here at the age of nineteen. Sure he spoke both official languages, excelled academically, and won prestigious scholarships, but it was as though—he was—well, one might say a warm-blooded species transplanted onto an ice shelve of attitude. Students seemed entitled to do whatever they wanted. There was no respect.

He advanced to the next slide.

Where was he? Oh, yes. Gender.

No. He begged your pardon. Sex.

"Sex, however, is not required for good biological life," he said. "Single-cell organisms reproduce by division. Many plants propagate by offshoots. Earthworms are hermaphrodites and whiptail lizards are all female. But sexual reproduction provides a distinct advantage in an environment that is"—he waved his hand in the air, searching for the right word—"that might be, shall we say, unpredictably vague."

What that unpredictably vague environment might be, exactly, he'd learned a week ago, when Nora phoned to tell him about Eric's blog.

"I found out from Lisa," she said. "Eric doesn't know I know."

"Blog?" he said, rather surprised. His son wasn't known for his facility with composition. Rather—well, he hated to think about it, but Eric had never been academically inclined. "What's this blog about?"

"Read it," Nora said, exhaling loudly, and he visualized a black hair vibrating in a raisin-like mole above her lip. "There's something not quite right about it. I suspect he might be up to no good again."

"What makes you say that?"

"Read his blog, Nikolai. Then we'll talk."

He hung up and thought of a rainy evening, eight years ago and a month after Eric had moved out to his own place on Commercial Drive, when, upon arriving home late from his lab, Nora confronted him with, "I've met someone. I wish I could say that I'm sorry about it, but the truth is that I'm not. You can't be that surprised about it, can you? We've been strangers to each other for years, despite living under the same roof. I can't compete with your fruit flies now any more than I ever could. If it weren't for our son all these years, I would've been gone a long time ago."

He remembered exactly what she'd looked like when she uttered those awful words. She'd been perched on the top stair of their North Vancouver house, cradling a flute of pink champagne in her hands. As he listened to her, it occurred to him that he'd made a terrible mistake. That mistake had nothing to do with his family, strange as it was to have realized it then. No. It was about his experiments. Namely, with the traces of alcohol in the culture medium in petri plates. As he watched the tiny bubbles of carbon dioxide shimmer up through the pink liquid in Nora's glass, it came to him that the alcohol must've triggered the erratic behaviour in the *Drosophila* pupae, and before he could stop himself he cried out, "But of course, they were drunk!" Nora didn't remain on the stairs for long after that. She'd stood up slowly, gone to their bedroom, and slammed the door shut.

It might very well be, Larkov now acknowledged, that by drifting off at such an inopportune moment he'd proven the very point his wife was trying to make. But that was the crux of the matter, wasn't it? The distillation, one might say, of his life's research. Why — and this question bothered him greatly — why had his wife, his life partner, why had *she* never wondered about holometabolous larvae with reduced mouthparts? Why had she never questioned how it was possible to develop all cells in your body from one single fertilized egg? How was it at all conceivable that his own mother — whom he remembered as a strong, dignified matron in a floral babushka, always stirring borscht with a Khokhloma spoon — how was it at all conceivable that she too emerged from an eight-cell compacted morula, in the middle of heavy bombardment in Kiev during the Great Patriotic War?

No. Everyone had been designed for a reason: he was growing convinced of that with every breath he took. Everyone, even Nora, had been brought into being on purpose by a fantastic plan. It was this plan that Larkov studied, tirelessly trying to work out its patterns at night, when the dimmed lights in the Molecular Sciences Building cast ghoulish shadows on fly pupae crawling inside Erlenmeyer flasks.

Yet, as important as his work had been all these years, it all but ruined his relationship with his only son. When everything was said and done, at the end of his life, on his deathbed, would his research really be worth it? Would his theories atone in some measure for the fact he'd been practically absent from his son's life? He did not know. He hoped so, standing, as he was at present, in front of his students with his hands stuck behind his back.

But perhaps — it wasn't too late to restore their

relationship. His thoughts took an unexpected turn. After all, all organisms on the planet undergo DNA repair. Why not them? There was Kaya now, Eric's child, a once-removed particle of Larkov's original self. She had just turned a year old and was still perfectly innocent, unspoiled by the wicked ways of the world. Yes, yes. This baby could indeed become the new family nucleus around which they all might recrystallize. He could certainly facilitate this process by teaching her marvellous things about science, by explaining to her things about the birds and the bees. He'd already taken her to the Vancouver Aquarium to see the stunning exhibit of tropical fish. There would be other exhibits. There was also the whole Science World. He smiled, congratulated himself on his idea, and resolved to absolutely give it a go.

"Ah, Professor," he heard a male voice say, "can you explain what you meant by 'recrystallize'?"

Larkov squinted at the computer that stood on the podium in front of him.

"Hmm. Did I say that out loud?"

He took a moment to compose himself.

"Never mind that," he said. "We now turn to the most exciting part of our lecture. The egg."

Eric too had been an egg once, inside Nora's fallopian tubes. At the time, Larkov marvelled at how her skin stretched and perspired with the hormonal dew as the months of the pregnancy elapsed. He began to wonder what it was like being a female. What was it like to make eggs? Sperm production seemed easy. Sperm was motile, like men, speedy, efficient. The ejaculation of sperm was a relatively straightforward process. But to ovulate, one had to endure—physiologically speaking—cataclysmic events. The release of an egg into the uterine tube was bracketed by the follicular and luteal phases. A mature egg had a jelly coat. It had cortical granules. It had a magnificent ooplasm. Larkov was suddenly certain that had he ovulated, things would have turned out rather differently between him and his son. Because—

Last night he'd read Eric's blog again.

Thank you so much for your interest in my life. Many people ask me why I decided to become a female. But I haven't decided anything. My body made the decision for me. The truth is that I was living as someone else for so long I did not even know what it was like to be me. But despite the evidence between my legs, I have always known I was female. The strangest part is that I'm still attracted to women. I'm talking to my therapist about this all the time. He says that no person should have fewer rights simply because their genes did not activate in the correct direction. That the whole of life, and especially human life now, is unnatural in many ways. Drugs are unnatural. Politics is unnatural. The whole of human civilization is unnatural too. Nature is not organized. It never makes sense to anyone. It is one big accident. Gobbledygook of chemical soup. But here we all are, trying to overcome nature, each in our own way. And some of us are decent enough to help other human beings when they need help. So. If you wish to support my transition financially, which, as you can imagine, doesn't come cheap, please donate through the link to my PayPal account at the bottom of this page. It is only because of your generosity that I'm able to carry on.

Unlike Nora, Larkov wasn't shocked by the content of Eric's blog. Unlike her, he did not suspect that his son was up to no good. It was true that Eric had a history of duplicitous behaviour, but that behaviour could now be explained. All his life Eric must've felt deeply tormented by being trapped in the wrong body and so, understandably, he'd acted out because of this torment. Dropping out of high school, being always so desperate for money, finding ways to take advantage of people — Eric's transgender explained everything. Indeed, Larkov had always suspected that something was — well, *exceptional* about Eric's genes. What his son had written about them not activating in the "correct" direction struck Larkov as perfectly true. He'd guessed a long time ago that Eric's perceived amoral behaviour might be a consequence of some molecular process that happened *before* he was born. And how could a person be blamed for that?

No. Unlike Nora, Larkov was not scandalized by their son's impending sex change. Besides, he was a scientist and had come to appreciate the fluid nature of sex. How else would you explain the existence of sea lemons? Or, for that matter, a calcareous sponge? Unlike Nora, then, he'd welcome his son's transformation. He was convinced, furthermore, that once Eric became Erica, the damaged tissues between them would regenerate. He hadn't found the time to talk to Eric yet about any of it (understandably, as he was in the middle of a very busy semester), but he knew that he would, very soon.

Becalmed by these thoughts, Larkov looked up at his students and noticed that they'd spaced themselves evenly across the aisle, like the sister chromatids in the mitotic anaphase. This fact comforted him even further. He made up his mind to call Eric right after class.

"The egg begins everything," he said. "Once it is

fertilized, it increases in size and begins to divide. Two become four, four become eight, eight become sixteen, and so on."

"But —" someone interrupted him, "when does a person begin?"

"A person?"

"Yes. Like, each of us. When does each of us become *self*?"

"This is a very good question," Larkov said, and meant it. "There is a point in time when a cluster of cells becomes *you*. I would say that this point occurs at roughly fourteen days after fertilization, when the egg can no longer split into two. This is important to understand, you see, because how can *you* be *you* and *you* and *you*? There can only be one *you*. Unless you're Asian and your name is actually You."

No one laughed, so he cleared his throat and said quickly, "Excuse me. That was an unfortunate joke. As I was saying, once a cluster of cells may split no longer, it becomes an individual being, the *you*. It goes through all the developmental stages, from the infant to adulthood. *You* continues until *you* dies."

"And then?" The redhead on the left batted her eyelashes at him. "What happens to the *you* then?"

Larkov took off his spectacles and rubbed his eyes.

"I'm afraid I don't know," he said.

What he did know, however, was that he'd been happiest for about a year after Eric was born. He had kissed him terribly often, feeling incredible joy, and he knew back then already that he'd never feel the same joy toward anyone else ever again. He'd changed his diapers, fed him porridge with sugar and butter, and held his head in the crook of his arm. God almighty! If only he could go back for one moment to smell his son's baby skin again!

The next slide showed a hermaphroditic amphibian.

"The development into a male and a female in most animals," he said, "appears to be a matter of chance. The luck of molecular draw. In hermaphrodites, for example, we have individuals that possess both male and female gonads."

A hand shot in the air. "Gonads?"

"The term comes from the Greek word *gonos*. It means 'seed.' In the embryos, so-called all-purpose gonads develop into different types of sex cells. It is here that genes get activated, like the light switches in this lecture hall may be flipped on and off." He leaned toward the control panel on the podium and demonstrated what he'd meant. "The switching of genes is like a computer program, where commands are given by chemical signals, molecular zeros and ones. In a way, it is almost as if everything were —" He hesitated. "Almost as if everything were —"

"A game?" the girl with the dark, shiny hair said.

"Yes." He blinked. "A game."

BACK IN HIS office, Larkov sank into his chair. Outside, it began to rain. His hand travelled to the inside of his jacket. He brought out his smartphone and placed it on the top of his desk.

It rang.

He was startled.

"Yes," he answered, hoping to hear his son's voice.

"Hi," Nora said. "Where've you been?"

"I was teaching," he said, disappointed. "What do you want?"

"Eric's going to see a surgeon tomorrow. To do the—let me see here, where is it? Oh, yes. *Co-lo-va-gi-no-plasty.* What kind of word is that?"

"Google it," Larkov said evenly. "Seeing as you're already on the Internet."

There was a moment of silence followed by the violent tapping of computer keys on her end.

"Here we go. Wikipedia," Nora said. "'Colovaginoplasty is a surgical procedure where a vagina is created by cutting away a section of sigmoid colon and using it to form a vaginal lining—Dear God!"

"Well, if he wants to be a woman, Nora, he'll certainly need that."

"This is just the beginning." Her voice began to shake with emotion. "Don't you get it? Or care? What's going to happen to him?"

"Of course I care. This is why I'm going to support him all the way."

"But—what's going to happen—how are we—What's going to happen to us?"

"Us?" Larkov said. "What does it have to do with us, Nora? *We* are not changing sex."

"Fool," she said flatly. "I'm thinking about Kaya. Have you thought about how she might be affected by this?"

Of course he had thought about it. As a matter of fact, he was worried about Kaya too. And that was precisely why, he now decided, he'd start his conversation with Eric by mentioning her. It made perfect sense that of all people, Kaya, his granddaughter, should be an enzyme, one might say, a biological catalyst, to break the proverbial ice between them.

"I'll call you tomorrow," he said to Nora, hung up on her, and found Eric's name in his list of contacts.

"Eric?" he said when his son answered the phone. "Your father here."

"Dad?" Eric said, and fell silent for a long moment. "Is everything okay?"

"Yes, okay," Larkov said quickly. "I'm sorry to bother you like this, out of the blue — but we need to talk."

"What is it?"

Larkov took a deep breath.

"Your mother has brought up a question. An important question for all of us. She feels that perhaps it's important for me to ask you the same question." He was rambling on but couldn't help it. "To bring this question to your attention, because I'm worried about Kaya. We are all worried about her. She is such an angel, and your mother and I — we are a little bit concerned about the situation. The situation with which, by the way, now that I've mentioned it, I'm perfectly, completely, one hundred and twenty-five percent okay with. I want you to know that. I'm worried about your health, yes, there's that. These sorts of things have been done before, so I'm sure everything will be fine. I found records of five operations, all successful. But I have to tell you that I'm worried about Kaya and how difficult this transition might be for her."

At last he stopped talking and swallowed hard.

"What are you talking about?" Eric said.

Larkov placed a palm on his forehead to steady his mind.

"I'm talking about your transition to be a female. To become Erica. About everything you write on your blog.

I'm okay with all of it. Really. I'm so sorry I didn't know. All these years, I've tried to be a good father to you. I was not perfect. I know that. I'm sorry you had to go through it on your own. I would like to—make amends, I suppose—if I can. If you want me to, that is. I'm speaking to you from the heart."

The wind was picking up strength outside, throwing water against the window.

Eric said, "Wow, Dad. Listen—I'm—I've got to disappoint you again, I guess."

"No, no," Larkov said quickly. "I'm not disappointed. But here's what I think. I think you should tell Kaya everything as soon as she can understand what's what. Be honest with her. Be straightforward. Don't hide anything from her, because—"

"Stop," Eric said, and Larkov heard what sounded like cackling on the other end of the line. "You're killing me right now. You really are."

"I just wish you'd told me sooner," Larkov said.

At this, Eric laughed. Unmistakably now, it was all-out, hearty laughter.

"Jesus, Dad! Let me tell you something. I've written the blog out of boredom. Did you know that I'm so fucking, mind-numbingly bored these days with this baby, with this constant crying and feeding, night after bloody night? It's like she's sucking the life out of me, I'm telling you. I think I'll go mad soon. Lisa is back at work now and I'm stuck here in this place, which by the way smells like shit all day, every day."

Larkov said, very quietly, "Eric, do you mean to say that you are *not* transitioning to be a female?"

Eric roared with laughter again.

"Lisa, come here!" he called out. "Come here!"

To Larkov, he said, "Wait, Dad. This is too much. Honestly, it's too much."

There was the shuffling of feet and muted whispers. Larkov overheard Lisa say, "I didn't know she'd tell him. Besides, I thought she knew!"

Eric said, "Here's the thing, Dad. It started off as a game. This guy I know — we used to play hockey together. His name is Grace now, but it used to be Jim. Jim Cornwall. Anyway, *Jim* is transitioning, and Lisa — it was, by the way, her idea — suggested that I pretend to be transitioning too and see what happens. So I started this blog. There wasn't much interest in the beginning, but then people began to write to me and actually offer me money, to support my quote-unquote transition financially, with no strings attached. I couldn't believe how easy it was. I linked my blog to the PayPal account and the money just poured in. Let me ask you something: would you turn the tap off in your kitchen if gold started to pour out of it?"

Slowly, Larkov placed his phone face down on the table. He stood up and looked out of the window.

"Dad? Are you still there?" he heard Eric's muted voice.

Nausea flooded him. He felt dizzy. The spectacles fell from his hand to the floor.

He was tired.

He stepped out into the hallway, closed the door carefully behind him, and walked down the hall to his lab.

On one of the benches, the fruit flies were crawling on beds of molasses in five-inch glass tubes, plugged with cotton balls. He dragged a lab stool over, sat down, and brought his face closer to them. It never ceased to amaze him how much biological power was hidden inside their brown bodies, each one no longer than a grain of rice.

"You know," he said out loud, although there was no one else in the room, "we've discussed this many times already, but up until now I think I've failed to see. Every bit is in its proper place in your body, organized from the front to the back. There is the head and the mouth, the opening for the food intake. There is a hole at the back for the waste to come out. All animals are organized in this way. But there are always exceptions. Do you know why? I don't. Look here. I give you nutritious broth. I watch over you. I observe you. I record your size, body temperature, and the shape of your wings. But you remain a mystery to me. It will always be so. Because I make not the tiniest difference in the grand scheme of things. You are programmed to be who you are before I put you in test tubes. Humans are the same way. None of us are free."

The flies made no answer, just kept moving around and swallowing food.

He stayed in the lab for a while, then went back to his office and put on his rain boots and coat. Outside the building, he saw a small boy wearing sneakers and standing in a deep puddle of rain. His mother was urging him to come out, to hurry home, she had to make dinner before Daddy got back from work. The boy was ignoring her and kept grinning at Larkov, as though daring him to do something about it.

At last, the mother waded into the puddle, grabbed her son by the collar, and pulled him out onto dry land.

Larkov looked up at the sky. The universe was an egg,

it came to him suddenly. It would go on dividing forever. Two, four, eight, sixteen. Life was remarkably correct, after all, to make a boy like that.

The wind moved the clouds overheard. There were stars seeded up there, their light moving away from the Earth.

THE BIG ONE

IT'S THE MORNING of an ordinary day in early March. I've been up since four, reading yesterday's newspaper.

It's raining.

"The sun," M says, "is taking a shower."

She's sitting on a pink chair and scooping puddles of milk with a spoon. My grandmother left me her silver spoons. She used to say, "Spoons are maps to men's hearts." She was right, I think.

There's a smoky ornament of oxidation on the spoon M is holding. I should clean it. Some other time. Speaking of time, we're late.

"Finish up and let's go," I say. "Brush your teeth and get dressed. Look at the time!"

M swirls the spoon pensively in her bowl.

"Mama, what is time?" she asks.

"Excellent question. What do you think time is?"

She looks out of the window. Eighteen storeys below, people are driving cars on broad streets.

"There are four times," she says. "We're late time. We're on time time. And we're early time."

"Very good."

She's defined past, present, and future.

"And the fourth?"

"The fourth time is a vegetable," she says.

"Time is not a vegetable." I laugh. "You're funny."

I go to the kitchen to prepare her lunch. I slice cucumber. Wait a second—

I put down the knife and walk back to her table.

"What vegetable?"

"Cauliflower."

"Why?"

"Because," she says, and begins to colour in a dinosaur.

"*Because* is not an answer."

She puts down the marker. "It's like a cauliflower. We grew it last year. First, we had a seed. We put it in a pot. It became a small plant, then a big one. There was a tiny cauliflower in it. We waited. It grew. We cut it and cooked it and ate it."

She picks up her marker and resumes colouring.

Okay, I think, time is a vegetable.

"WHY DIDN'T YOU MAKE YOURSELF PRETTY?" M asks me as we step into the elevator, ten minutes later than usual.

"I'll make myself pretty after I drop you off at daycare, don't worry."

"Okay," she says, and smiles at herself in the mirror. The digits above the door descend predictably: 16–15–14.

I wipe her nose with a tissue.

13–12–11.

The elevator stops. The door opens. An old lady and a poodle in a leather coat come in. The same two were in the gym yesterday. The old lady was on the bike. The poodle was on the treadmill.

"Hi," M says. "How are you?"

"Very well, little girl. Going to school?"

"Daycare." M points to the dog. "Nice coat."

9–8–7.

"How old are you?" the old lady asks. "You seem bright."

"Four and three-quarters." M hops on one leg.

3–2–L.

The elevator stops again. The door opens. The old lady says, "Have a good day," and goes out. The poodle follows.

P1–P2–P3.

We walk toward our car. Our building has three underground levels. The ceiling is low. Black pipes slither below it. Yellow lines demarcate parking slots. Numbers are stencilled in grey blocks on white walls. Our parking spot is 339. I hate having to go through two security gates and then circle and circle and circle to get in or out of the building. M usually rolls down her window, looks at herself in the giant mirrors at each corner, and waves.

What if, I think, the Big One happens today? The One everyone keeps talking about. Not late time or early time but on time time. As in right now. Why are we late this morning? Why weren't we late yesterday? Why does the old lady come in on the tenth floor and delay us? If the Big One happened today, how would I deal with it?

Then it begins.

M is two metres ahead of me. The air convulses and drinks dust. A crack zigzags through the ceiling. Pillars kneel. Cars crinkle. Walls melt. A glass door explodes like a Popsicle dropped on the asphalt.

I stumble forward and sink my fingers in M's collar. I pull her toward me. I crouch, move her body beneath me, assume the fetal position, and cradle her head with my hands. I whisper, "Don't be afraid."

The ceiling collapses, folds on a wrecked pillar, and canopies us with pasted stone.

M screams.

The shaking stops after several minutes. I spit grit out of my mouth and cough. I feel M's body with my hands and understand for the first time in my life what it's like to be blind.

I bring my BlackBerry out of my pocket and use it as a flashlight to explore our surroundings. We are immured in a stone sleeping bag.

How to stay calm? How? How to die gracefully?

I try to raise my head but bump it on hard rock.

"Where are we, Mama?"

"In a fort. Like the one in your room — It's going to be all right, you'll see. Someone will come and help us."

M throws her arms around my neck.

The fort in her room is a bedsheet tied with strings at two corners and my lover's scarf on the third. Will my lover miss me?

I check my BlackBerry's messenger.

X Service denied.

"Mom," M whimpers. "You're always on your BlackBerry. You're not paying attention!"

My daughter is here. I will die gracefully because of her.

I put the BlackBerry down and touch her cheek.

"Of course I'm paying attention!"

Who is going to pay attention to me?

"No, you're not," she cries. "I asked you this morning to help me turn the water down in my bathroom one hundred times. And you didn't."

"Really? Did you leave the water running in the bathroom?"

What was it in Poe? Why am I thinking of Poe? I must think of nothing but M. Nothing. Oh, yes, "The Cask of Amontillado." A murderer entombs his victim alive in a brick wall. Who read it to me? My mother. She told me, "The reader is walled up too."

"Yes, I did!"

"I'm sorry."

We find each other's hands and interlace our fingers. The ruins of the twenty-two-storey tower groan above us. The air draws closer. It smells of burned rubber. Both of us breathe heavily. We need more air.

"I want to get out of here, Mama," M cries. "I want to get out right now!"

"Me too. But we have to wait for the men to clear the roads. They'll clear the roads, get people out of the building, get all this stuff on top cleaned up, and off we'll go. Today you won't have to go to daycare, I promise you. What would you like to do today?"

"I want to go skating," she says, "and have hot chocolate."

"Me too."

M sneezes. I help her take the backpack off her shoulders and put it under her head.

"Let's play a word game while we're waiting."

M stops crying. "Okay."

"The word I'm thinking about starts with the letter" —I touch her hair— "G."

"Giraffe," M says.

"No."

"Giant."

Please do not let anything be crushed unevenly. All must be crushed at once.

Men. Men with tools will come and rescue us. "I'm grateful that not everyone is like you and me," my lover said the other day. "Nothing would ever get done otherwise. The artists bullshit while people do real work."

What will it be like to die?

I wonder if I should tell M about God now. Would it even matter?

"Nope."

"Gorilla."

"Try again."

"I give up."

"Already?"

"Give me a hand."

"A hint, you mean."

"Yes."

"Ask me a question."

"Is it big?"

"Very."

"Gino."

"Who's Gino?"

"A boy in my daycare."

"Is he big?"

"He's five. He takes stuff from other kids."

"Like God."

"What?"

"Nothing. What kind of stuff?"

"Important things. Like, he—uh—one time he took my juice when I was thirsty."

"What did you drink?"

"Nothing. My teacher told me to drink water, but I didn't want to."

"Why not?"

"Because Mama doesn't

drink water. She drinks wine."

I kiss her forehead.

"Maybe Gino didn't know it was your juice when he took it."

"He didn't."

"Then he took it by mistake."

"He still took it."

"Yes. Anyway, the word I was thinking about is not Gino."

"What is it?"

"Guess."

"That's a funny word."

"No, guess what the word I'm thinking about is."

"I don't want to play anymore. It's too hard." She sniffles. "Right now, I'm exhausted about you."

We lie silently for a little while and stare at the screen of my BlackBerry.

"Gravity," I say.

"What is that?"

"Gravity is a force of nature. It's the reason why space is filled with things. It's the reason why two

Can a sweater be tender? I think M's sweater is tender to the touch.

God is Gino and Gino can take your juice any time. Maybe he already has. And you have to deal with that too.

What's the word you're thinking about right now?

I wonder if M will resent me one day for all the things I thought she should do.

bodies, like us, always fall together."

"I don't like it."

"You may not like it, but it's everywhere. When two people come together in a small place like this— wonderful things can happen. Wonderful."

Maybe the big bang was a big crunch.

"Like what?"

"Well, for one thing, we get to play the word game and make stuff up. For another, we get to be together. Togetherness is very important."

"Why?"

"Because. Our parents had to be together to make us."

Because is the perfect answer.

She's silent for a few moments.

I ask her if she wants to look at the photos saved on my BlackBerry.

We look happy in the photographs.

"Do you remember you told me you wanted to write stories?" I ask.

"No."

I don't want to die unpretty. God, I wish I'd taken two minutes this morning to make myself pretty for you.

"Yes, you did. I asked you once what you wanted to do when you grew up and you told me that you wanted to write stories so that parents all over the world read them to little boys and girls before they fell asleep."

"I remember now."

"What would your stories be about?"

She crinkles her nose. "About a little person in a green hat."

"What is this person doing?"

"He's walking around and finds people who are unhappy."

"And then?"

"He makes them happier."

"Is he a doctor?"

"No."

"Who is he?"

"Just a person in a green hat."

"Why is he little?"

"You don't have to be big to make someone happy."

It's amazing how easily people abandon you. The only person who's never abandoned me is my mother. Not everyone is so lucky. I wish I could Skype with her right now. I'd tell her, "I love you. I've always loved you. I'll love you until the day I die."

"That's true. You don't
have to wear a green hat."

"But he does wear it,
Mama."

"Why green?"

"Green is a happy col-
our. It's good for you. Like
vegetables."

"Like life."

"What is life, Mama?"

"Life?"

"Yes."

"My life, your life, or life
in general?"

"Life in general."

"Okay, well, it's like
this. It starts with a small
space, like where we are
right now. It's important to
separate yourself from the
rest—"

"The rest?"

"The rest of the stuff out
there." I knock on cement
with my knuckles. "You
and I are two living things,
enclosed in this pocket.
Now, if we find a way to
get in and out of it, every
once in a while—"

"To do what?"

We live in vegetable time.

"Well, to eat, for one thing. Living things must eat."

"And kaka."

"Definitely. So eat and kaka." I hold my finger up, and she makes a fist around it. "If we make a baby and another and another and so on, we—"

"Continue."

"Yes. We continue."

The BlackBerry screen goes black. I don't press any buttons. We lie in darkness for a while and listen to our breathing.

"I want to tell you something," I say.

"Yes."

"I'm stupid."

She laughs. "*Stupid* is a funny word."

"It is. I fall in love with all the wrong people."

"I don't want to hear it."

"No?"

"Not right now."

"When, then?"

"When I'm bigger. Maybe when I'm five."

I wish I were a Buddhist. I'd close my eyes and hum myself into nothingness. No, I don't wish that at all! I want to scratch my way out with my nails right now! Until I have no fingers left. I will never give up!

I should've frozen my eggs. Someone would've inseminated them, and I would've continued.

"Okay."

I kiss the top of her head.

"Mama, I want to go home."

"I know, baby, I want to go home too, but we have to be a little bit more patient. Listen, when I was a little girl, my grandmother and I got locked in a closet — I don't remember now how it happened — and we couldn't get out of it for a long time.""

"Really?"

"Yes! Just like we're trapped except that we didn't even have a Black-Berry to see anything, It was pitch-black and we sat there for hours and couldn't get out. You know what we did?"

"What?"

"She sang songs. We ate baked apples. She made these amazing apples when I was small and brought them to the skating rink. She took me to the skat-

My grandmother used to kiss the top of my head like that. She always put chicken wings on my plate because she said children who ate chicken wings were able to fly away to a better life.

Before I gave birth to M, I sat on the edge of the bed and cried with happiness. All of my ancestors were folded in the small of my back. They were all there, crying of happiness with me.

ing rink in winter, almost every morning we went. It was dark and cold, the snow crinkling.

"Did someone save you?"

"We saved ourselves. My grandmother was a strong woman, although she was small. During the war, she was a cartographer—"

"What's that?"

"A cartographer is someone who makes maps. Maps are important because people don't want to get lost. That little man in the green hat you want to write about? Maybe he makes people happier because he helps them find their way. Anyway—my grandmother made maps, and she figured out that there must be a mechanism on the door to unlock it. She felt with her hands everywhere—the sides, top, bottom, everywhere. It was an old door made of wood with metal hinges and nails, and she found the lock and picked it."

I know exactly what I'd do at my grandmother's grave. She's buried in White Russia. I'd fall on my knees and ask for forgiveness for flying away.

Love is the most intense preoccupation of our imagination.

"Picked it?"

"Oh, yes."

"How?"

"She used her imagination."

The rubble on top of us gives a terrific sigh and shifts weight. I draw M to my chest. I see blinding lights.

Without imagination, life makes no sense.

THE BLOOD KEEPER

1

My father, Viktor A. Mishkin, was the keeper of Lenin's mummy. Yes, the very same Franken-fish of the Great Communist Chief they still keep on display in the Red Square Mausoleum. Every week there, in a secret chamber, he conducted what he called *adjustments*, wiping the mummy with hydrogen peroxide, treating its wrinkles with acetic acid, and painting its waxy face with bifonazole. Every six months, his assistants moved the thing to a sterilized room, disassembled its body parts, and immersed all of them in a glass bathtub filled with glycerin. Yet, despite all attempts to curb life, fungi crept along the mummy's neck, the skin of its ears turned blue, and brown spots became visible on the pads of its fingers.

Life went on as life always does.

I remember my father as clever. He was also inventive and good with practical things. He fixed refrigerators and cupboards, toilet bowls and mechanical clocks. He was fond of Romantic poets, especially Pushkin, and fine cognac, which he called *balsam* for the soul. Balsam was the embalming fluid the Russians came up with in 1924. Its exact chemical composition was a state secret my father would take with him to his grave.

Of course, I'd always thought of my father as trust-worthy, the sort of man with whom one would not hesitate to go behind enemy lines. But his singular skill, his *gift*, as my grandmother put it, was people. He'd look at someone, ask them a question, and know their truth. Perhaps that ability came out of his work. Perhaps it was necessary to dissect human beings, to slice into their flesh, before one could begin to understand them.

My conjuror, my mother had called him, Doctor Faustus.

They met in 1964. There was a student production of *Doctor Faustus*, in which my mother acted the parts of all seven deadly sins. My father was in the audience, smitten, like so many others, with her. During that production, a bull raged on the stage. It was one of those mythological creatures, half beast and half man. After the performance, my father made his way backstage, presented my mother with orchids, which were extremely rare in Russia, and said, "For you, I'll kill a bull." After they got married, it became a sort of joke between them. Every year on the anniversary of their meeting, they'd go out to have steaks. I wondered sometimes if thirteen years of tenderloins amounted to a whole bull, in the end.

Although my father had never taken me to the Mauso-leum, he'd brought me with him once to his other work. In addition to taking care of Lenin's mummy, he also chaired the Department of Pathology at the Moscow Medical

Institute. I remember the white-tiled room that smelled of disinfectant and the bile-green peristaltic pump. Pink, poisonous-looking liquids scowled through Erlenmeyer flasks. On the table in front of me that morning lay the body of a young girl. She was six, maybe seven, with a blue headband holding her hair back. I was told she'd been hit by a car that morning and died on impact.

One of my father's assistants had extracted her liver and was weighting it in a tin balance pan. The expression on his face, I will never forget it, shone with absolute awe. He spoke some medical terms into the microphone wire that hung suspended from a ceiling beam. Then he turned to me and, holding out a chunk of liver, pointed to the dark channels inside it, filled with brown liquid. The child's tissues were too delicate, he said, too fragile to preserve her hepatocytes.

Nausea flooded me. I lunged toward the window, looking for air, unable to breathe. But my mind was too fast for my body, and my foot slipped on the floor. I swooned, looking for balance, trying to hold on to something, anything, beating my arms through the air like a child who couldn't swim. But it was too late. I was falling already. I hit my head on the table on my way down and passed out cold.

"I'd be worried about you if you didn't feel sick, Verka," my father said to me that evening at dinner, pausing to sip his borscht from a silver spoon. "But you cannot deny that death is fascinating. No one can wrap their head around it."

My grandmother, who sat at the table with us, knitting and watching my father with narrowed eyes, leaned forward to get a cube of sugar, lifted it out of the bowl with her fingers, and stuck it under her tongue.

"So speaks the one who was trained to heal the living, and ended up pickling the dead," she said.

My grandmother was eighty. Three years earlier, she'd moved to the country to sulk. There, alongside a female companion, she cared for sick chickens, crossbred peonies, and entertained semi-mystical thoughts. She spoke of the secret teachings in Asian religions and expressed her emotions through sacred chants. "Life is so ugly," she'd said to me once in between singing. "One must surround herself with beautiful things." Every once in a while, unannounced, she'd come up to our apartment in Moscow to cook and dish out judgement to us.

Anyway, whether it was the revulsion I'd felt in my father's laboratory or something else, conceivably guilt at what he did in his lab, I took my grandmother's advice. By July of 1994, when my father was called to Pyongyang, I'd finished my third year at Moscow University, where I studied botany. I was twenty-one years old, serious and bookish. Boys didn't interest me, or rather, boys weren't interested in me because I was rather plain-looking. I wore khaki pants and black leather jackets, and pulled my hair into a tight ponytail. In the mornings, I was busy with classes; in the afternoons, I swam laps in a public pool; and in the evenings, I did my homework or read obscure volumes on herbology to learn about the active ingredients in medicinal plants. In those days I was also interested in pollination observed in certain species of orchids, especially in the *Coryanthes* that Darwin had described.

In the middle of August, my father wrote to me. His team, his letter said, had encountered many skin complications on the corpse of Kim Il Sung and, as such, he'd have to stay in Pyongyang a while yet, possibly until May. It was a long time for us to be away from each other, so he suggested I come to Pyongyang on a student exchange. He had visited the Botanical Gardens there and was impressed with what he saw. He was certain a field project in North Korea would be a nice addition to my dissertation on tropical plants.

I reread my father's letter several times because it struck me as rather odd. First of all, he addressed me as Vera, instead of Verka, which was his usual pet name for me. Second, I thought, North Korea? Wasn't there some kind of crisis, post–Cold War and all that? I recalled having read something about famine, about the Russians shutting off the natural gas. What was the political situation over there? Last time I heard, it was a Stalinist state. I could not understand why my father imagined I'd be okay with going over there on a student exchange.

Moreover, the nine months he'd proposed for my exchange was a long time to be away from school. In nine months, provided I stayed in Moscow, I could already be in graduate school.

I also wondered why he'd write me a letter. Why didn't he just call me on the phone? But after speaking with his secretary at the Medical Institute, I realized that he was, in fact, cut off. Apparently, due to the state of deep mourning in the Democratic Republic of Korean People, no international calls were allowed to go in or out of its capital.

Then I thought, okay, I'd always wanted to travel, and had never been anywhere farther than Brest. Besides, a chance to work with rare orchids in a foreign country, even if that country was North Korea, might be the chance of a lifetime. Nevertheless, something must've felt wrong to me, because I wavered, thinking things over, and delayed dispatching my reply letter with the diplomatic post.

I went to the university library and did research on the Botanical Gardens in Pyongyang. I learned that the Gardens were established at the foot of Mountain Taesŏng in 1959. Spread over twenty hectares and divided into fourteen sections, the collection included at least fourteen thousand species of ornamental plants. There was an orchard, a tree nursery, a herbarium, a meteorological station, and a botanical museum of some renown. In the state-of-the-art orchid greenhouses, the article I'd found said, scientists cultivated Kimilsungia (*Dendrobium*) and Kimjongilia (*Begonia tuberhybrida*) flowers, to great international acclaim.

Still my heart was filled with foreboding. I kept dreaming about snakes. I decided to see my grandmother, and took a Sunday train to the countryside. She read my father's letter three times out loud and then once to herself. Then she moved to the veranda, collapsed in a rocking chair, and frowned into the sunset. Finally, she brought out a flask of cognac from under her apron, took a large swig from it, and held it out to me.

She said, "Something's the matter. But he wouldn't have asked you to come if he didn't mean it. That much we know. You should go."

2

My thesis adviser was delighted with my decision and asked me to take careful notes on the orchid compost. How many parts of coniferous bark did North Koreans use? How much perlite? Did they add pumice, loam, or sand as supplements to the soil? He asked me to pay particular attention to the ratio of nitrogen to potassium in fertilizers, the mineral composition of the water, and the air movement in the orchid greenhouses achieved by electric fans. Finally, he procured a Zenit camera and four rolls of Kodak 35-millimetre film, each with twenty-four exposures, and requested that I photograph the most unusual specimen I came across.

On the morning of September 8, at ten minutes after 9 p.m. Moscow time, I boarded an Aeroflot plane to Vladivostok, and ten hours later connected to an Air Koryo flight to Pyongyang. The second plane was an ancient Soviet-made Ilyushin with a cabin that reeked of kimchee. Far worse, though, were the strong winds blowing off the Sea of Japan that kept tossing the plane as if it were an empty tin. A middle-aged North Korean stewardess, wearing a Kim Il Sung badge on the lapel of her brown suit, braved the turbulence to bring me a bottle of Coca-Cola, a "bag for my refuses," and a Russian-language guidebook.

Time passed slowly. It seemed to have actually stopped. I saw myself from a great distance, tossing inside that stinking plane like a pitiful ant, and asking myself all sorts of rhetorical questions, the chief among them being, "Why am I doing this?" Normally, I was not prone to brooding, but if negative thoughts came, they tended to suck me right in. In an effort to lighten my mood, I began to flip through the guidebook.

The Korean name *Pyongyang* translated to "Flat Land," but it was once called Ryugyong, which meant "willow city," and apparently there were lots of them in the capital, thanks to the tireless tree-planting efforts of Kim Il Sung. Following his amazing victories in the Korean War, the Great Leader rebuilt the city out of the ashes, applying his motto, "The people are my God." These days all visitors to Pyongyang were overwhelmed by the city's great beauty, especially by its many parks, countless monuments, and magnificent gardens, inhabited by beautiful birds.

Honestly, I thought. What a load of baloney. Magnificent gardens. Beautiful birds. That was not what my father's acquaintance and a former diplomat in Seoul, Pavel, had told me about Pyongyang. Two days before I left Moscow, he took me out to a new Japanese restaurant on Tverskoi Boulevard, taught me how to use chopsticks, and went over the key travel essentials to DRKP. Rule number one, he told me: do not disrespect the Kims. Never. Not ever. Doing so would be a sure ticket home. Worse, if they thought you were subversive, you could be sent to a labour camp. When I laughed at that, he said, "Trust me, even your father, with all his connections, wouldn't be able to do anything about it." Rule number two: do not disobey orders and always do what you're told. Three: refrain from passing negative comments when you see something that rubs you the wrong way. Not that the new Russia, Pavel acknowledged, was exactly a paradigm of democracy yet. Still, it would be unwise to react negatively to the propaganda; asking questions, seeking out explanations, even pointing out the obvious wasn't going to change anyone's mind. Everyone was so completely brainwashed over there, they might actually think you're deranged if you tried. And deranged people belonged in mental institutions, if I was catching his drift. So. Good behaviour was expected of me at all times. Assume all rooms were bugged. Don't take photographs of anything without permission, and be careful which newspaper you sit on. A translator Pavel knew once foolishly sat on the front page of a newspaper that bore Kim Il Sung's holy face. It was noticed, and he was criticized for his inattention, and then no one heard from him ever again.

Pavel's face darkened and he leaned closer to me. "And don't underestimate the skills of the North Korean intelligence agents. Over the years, the so-called Division 19 has outsmarted many powerful adversaries. Not only have they obtained nuclear weapons, they also earned a lot of money for the regime."

"How?" I asked him.

"Counterfeit money, embezzlement of foreign aid funds. Drug trafficking, also. North Koreans are experts at that."

My ears popped. I opened my eyes. The plane began to descend. On the ground below me, I saw flat brown land. Some distance off to the south lay what looked like a strangely symmetrical city, under a carpet of dingy fog.

The plane landed, coasted on the tarmac for maybe a minute, and came to a stop. An ancient disembarking ladder was rolled up to the front door. I gathered my things, stuck the guidebook into my backpack, and walked down the aisle on wobbly legs.

The first thing I saw outside was a huge portrait of

Kim Il Sung. It hung on the terminal building, covering its entire facade. The building itself was three-storied and shabby. It squatted much more than stood on the cracking asphalt. It looked deserted. I saw no lights inside. Eerily, there were no other planes on the tarmac, no workers busying themselves with luggage carts. No other passengers. No other people. No one. None of the bustle one usually sees in the big airports of capital cities was apparent in Pyongyang.

It was like the city was dead.

In the late afternoon, the light was already fading. It looked as if a storm might be coming too. Under the gathering clouds, I followed the other passengers through a metal barrier into a vast empty hall, at the end of which stood a granite counter with a man sitting behind it. As I began walking toward him, unsure what to do, a stout male official in a suit made of polyester and a young woman wearing a blue uniform approached me. She introduced herself to me in Russian as Comrade Song; she would be my translator. Her companion's name was Comrade Lee. She was pretty, my age, perhaps slightly older, and wore white face powder and bright red lipstick, the combined effect of which made her look as though she'd just finished drinking blood.

After measuring me with her dark eyes, she inquired about my health, and then proceeded to greet me enthusiastically in the name of Kim Il Sung. In her speech, she referred to him in the present tense as if he were still living, and at one point her eyes welled up with tears and she actually cried. Once she'd fished a handkerchief out of her pocket and dabbed her eyes with it, she composed herself.

Her voice became softer. She said she hoped I'd had a pleasant journey and inquired about my health again. I thanked her and said I was well and excited to land in Pyongyang at last. I was, however, quite tired, I admitted, unsurprisingly after two flights. She bowed slightly to me at those words but said nothing, and beckoned me to follow her.

In the customs office, I had to sign several papers confirming that I hadn't brought any firearms with me. No, I did not have any drugs or telecommunications equipment either. My luggage, which had materialized by my side, was then unpacked and inspected by two malnourished-looking soldiers in oversized uniforms. I was allowed to keep my flashlight and Walkman, but not the camera and none of the tapes I'd brought from Moscow with me.

"Madonna is not allowed in our country," one of the soldiers said, lifting the *Erotica* cassette out of my bag on the tip of a pencil and holding it some distance away from himself.

"Don't worry," Song assured me, "everything will be returned to you when you leave."

At long last, I was given a slip of paper with my visa stamped on it in red ink. No stamp in my passport — I'd understand later — meant that there would be no evidence of my arrival in Pyongyang.

Outside, a black Mercedes waited for us by the curb. It hadn't started to rain yet, but I smelled ozone in the air and knew it was only a matter of time. Comrade Lee held the back door open for us, then slammed it shut after Song and I got in. He squeezed into the passenger seat, said something quickly to the driver, and we drove off in a cloud of dust.

The road was in good condition, but the scenery outside was depressingly barren, with no people or other cars in sight. We drove for about thirty minutes in silence and entered the city with broad, willow-lined streets. Just ahead, I could see blocks of apartment buildings. A rusting Soviet-made pickup truck lumbered past. Closer to the city's centre, groups of people, dressed in identical plain-cut clothes, were shuffling along the sidewalks. At one intersection, a dozen old women were sweeping the road with brooms.

Across the river, a gigantic candle cast spooky red shadows on the darkening sky. I recognized it from the guidebook. The Tower of Juche Idea, the tallest obelisk in the world. Unveiled in 1982 for Kim Il Sung's seventieth birthday and made out of 25,500 granite slabs — one for each of his days on Earth.

We drove farther into the city.

"Look!" Song pointed out the window. "The Grand Monument on Mansu Hill."

Kim Il Sung's bronze statue was colossal and submerged in flowers up to its knees. It did not just stand on the hill overlooking the city but dominated it, stretching its arm toward it like some benevolent god.

A large crowd of people had gathered in front of the statue, at least a thousand strong.

"What are they doing?" I asked Song.

"Paying their respects. Our great nation has suffered an incomprehensible loss."

"But it's been almost two months since Kim Il Sung died," I pointed out.

"It will never stop. Never. A foreigner cannot possibly understand the depth of our love."

She folded her arms, looking awkward, then pointed to the right side of the road, where a troupe of children in red scarves were marching in perfect step. They stopped as we drove past them and saluted us in unison.

"They recognize that inside this Mercedes ride important persons," Song said. "From an early age, children in our country are taught respect. Of course, Kim Il Sung was the source of everything good in their lives, so they honoured him first of all."

She sounded like a robot, like one of those text-reading machines. Somehow I was sure she'd said all of that not for my benefit but for the benefit of Comrade Lee.

Ten minutes later, the car climbed a small hill. As we drove through the stone gates, Song said, "Welcome to Kim Il Sung's University campus, founded on October 1, 1946. It's the first people's university of the Democratic Republic of North Korea and an undisputed leader in higher education all over the world. Its many buildings and libraries form a harmonious picture of learning to the envy of all other universities. It has thirteen faculties, three colleges, nine research institutes, and two hundred departments, with state-of-the-art laboratories. Kim Il Sung himself provided on-the-spot guidance on more than five hundred occasions here, giving important instruction to scientists."

I wanted to burst out laughing but, recalling Pavel's advice, refrained.

"I feel incredibly honoured to be here," I managed to say with a straight face. "But just now I feel somewhat tired from the long journey, and would like to get some rest."

Shortly we came to a stop near a concrete ten-storey

building and got out of the car. Comrade Lee remained in the passenger seat, and drove off the moment I took my suitcase out of the trunk.

Song led me into the ground-floor security office, where a tall officer waited for us. He took his time inspecting my visa and wrote down the details of my passport in a logbook. Then he looked up, met my gaze, and smiled broadly, revealing a large gap in his front teeth. Through Song, he told me that I'd been assigned a room on the fifth floor and that I'd share that room with Song.

The Party provided each student with meals and textbooks, he said next. Everyone wore blue uniforms. Seeing that I was going to be a student here, I was expected to wear one too. There was a bathroom facility on every floor and an elevator, although it was switched off at present to save electricity.

We went over the rules again. I wasn't allowed to use cellphones, binoculars, or telephoto lenses. No disrespectful posing in front of Kim Il Sung's portraits or statues. The same rules applied for Kim Jong Il's. I was prohibited from giving food to anyone, including children, who might ask for it on the street. Finally, I was forbidden to approach or speak to North Korean citizens, unless those citizens had been approved for contact with me.

After I signed another paper, affirming my understanding of the above rules, I was given a blue suit—skirt and jacket—and a white collared shirt to be worn under it. I was also issued a booklet of twenty-one ration tickets for my meals in the university canteen. The ration tickets would be renewed every week, the officer told me, sounding as if he rather regretted having to give the meal tickets to me. Then he carried my suitcase up five flights of stairs and down a dimly lit corridor.

We stopped at a plywood door.

The room was small and claustrophobic. It stank of mildew. A pane of dusty glass under the ceiling allowed some light to seep through. The furniture was bolted to the floor and included two punishing-looking beds. There was also a dresser with pulled-out drawers, an oblong writing table, and two chairs with metal frames. A radio dish was mounted on the wall, next to the portrait of Kim Il Sung. The portrait was to be kept in good order at all times, Song informed me as soon as we stepped inside. For that purpose, she'd clean it twice a day, with a brush made of camel hair, kept in a special box.

I looked up at the window again and noticed that it couldn't be opened. I wouldn't be able to jump out, I thought with a shudder, even if I wanted to.

"What about the key?" I asked the security officer.

"The room can't be locked, so there's no need for it."

"When can I see my father?"

"Soon," he said. "Maybe next week."

"Next week? Why not tomorrow?"

Song sighed. "There's much for us to do, Comrade Vera, while we wait for the permit to come through. If everything goes well, the permit will be given to you. In the meantime, don't rush things. That's not revolutionary. We must work patiently during these hard times. Our great nation has suffered a great loss. Each of us must follow the Juche principles of self-reliance and find solace in our work."

"What permit?" I asked her.

"The permit for your work in the Botanical Gardens."

It took me a moment to process that information.

"But—" I started. "Surely my father has arranged everything."

"Your father has arranged your student visa, but to work in the Botanical Gardens you'll have to get the special permit. Everything in North Korea requires a permit," she said matter-of-factly, as though relating a basic truth. "As I said, we don't like to rush things."

I was too tired to think straight. Fatigue washed over me. I wanted to fall asleep and then wake up in Moscow, as if from a weird dream. But no, I wasn't dreaming. I'd come here of my own accord. I tried to comfort myself by thinking that maybe the reason everything seemed so weird was that Song's Russian wasn't so good. Maybe she was lost in translation, as I seemed to be lost in Pyongyang. Yet in my heart I felt a terrible foreboding. A frightening thought lodged in my mind. Dear God, I thought, maybe, just maybe, I'd come here on the wrong kind of exchange.

3

The moment the security officer left our room, Song became different. It was as if her entire body had undergone a transformation. Her back straightened. Her face brightened up. The grimness, so pronounced in her face just moments ago, had given way to something resembling cheer. Which was a strange thing to see in someone apparently so aggrieved.

She sat on one of the beds and bounced up and down.

"I've passed my first assignment," she said, and grinned from ear to ear.

"What's that?"

"You."

I accepted her words at face value. Pavel had warned me that I'd have a minder in North Korea, and Song didn't seem too bad. I could've got a far creepier person, I imagined, and silently thanked my lucky stars. At the same time, I was intrigued by her metamorphosis and waited to see what would happen next. She was silent, however, so I set my suitcase on the bed and began to unpack. As I was taking my clothes out, I sensed an oncoming headache.

A jug of water stood on the table. I poured myself a glass. Then I fished an aspirin out of my backpack, popped it into my mouth, and ground down on the bitter pill.

Song was watching me from the bed, still bouncing on it.

"Dinner's in an hour," she said.

I turned to face her. "I won't go. I'm tired. I have no appetite anyway. I just feel like sleeping. I think I'll just wash up and go to bed."

She stopped bouncing and for a few moments sat perfectly still, like a statue, her hands folded neatly on her knees.

"Okay," she said finally. "I'll accompany you to the bathroom when you're ready."

"There's no need." I laughed. "The bathroom is just down the hall, right? I'm sure I'll find it. "

"No." She shook her head vigorously. "You don't

understand. I must go with you everywhere you go. Those are my orders."

Okay, I thought, this will be interesting, and turned back to my suitcase.

Song, meanwhile, reached for her own satchel and brought out a small notebook. Gazing sideways at me, she wrote something down in it in pencil, tore the page out, and passed it to me.

It read: WAIT TILL NIGHT FALLS TOMORROW.

I started and began to open my mouth to say something, although I had no idea what that something would be, when she silently pointed to the ceiling with a finger and then brought it to her lips. Suddenly she lunged toward me and snatched the note out of my hands. In another instant she crumpled it, stuffed it into her mouth, and swallowed it whole.

I was so shocked by her actions I had to sit down on the bed.

We stared at each other in silence, trying to read each other's thoughts.

"I'm ready to go to the bathroom now, Comrade," I said at last, louder than I meant to. "Please, show me the way."

At the other end of the dim hallway was a tiled room with a long, trough-like sink. The toilet stalls had no doors, and it took me a moment to realize what that meant for doing what my grandmother called "poopeeri." I'd have to go to the toilet in plain sight of anyone who happened to be nearby. And, as I'd find out later, I'd have to do it into toilets that didn't always flush. I also noticed that there were no showers, or in fact any large basins that could double as baths.

"So, how do we wash our bodies?" I asked Song.

"In the public bathhouse on Tuesdays," she said, and opened a tap. The water that ran out was shockingly cold. "They have a sauna and a swimming pool there, which I am sure you will appreciate."

We returned to our room.

I took off my clothes, changed into my flannel pyjamas, and crawled under the thin grey sheets.

"Such unheard luxuries," Song said, tucking my feet in. The gesture was unexpected but also, I thought, rather sweet.

"Pardon me?"

"Your pyjamas. I've never seen anything like it in my life. Well, good night, Comrade Vera," she said, and turned off the lights.

AND SO IT began—my life in the Democratic Republic of Korean People, while I waited for the official permit to work in the Botanical Gardens to come through.

Song was my main, no, my only contact in those early days, and in many ways I was grateful to her, for the time I'd spend with her during that period prepared me for what would happen with Shin. Then again, as I'd come to understand later, everything I did in Pyongyang back then, everyone I encountered, and everywhere I went was designed to prepare me for him.

For the first couple of days, she spoke to me in a mechanical manner, as though articulating some programmed ritual. She inserted "Kim," "Kim Il Sung," "Comrade Kim," or "Our Great Leader" into practically every sentence, and ended many of them with "as Kim Il Sung said." But gradually, as we spent more time together, I began to discover a different Song, a profound, albeit somewhat lost, young woman, who was nothing like a robot at all. For one thing, she cared deeply about her family, especially her mother. For another, she played violin, and, as I was led to understand, played it rather well. She wasn't allowed to keep the violin in the dorm for some reason, but she often pretend-played it for me. Then the fingers of her left hand curled around the invisible strings and ran up and down them, while her right hand sawed across with the invisible bow.

Alas, the note she'd swallowed on the first evening with such drama turned out to be anticlimactic in the end. I was quite disappointed because after that performance I'd expected some big secret or terrible intrigue to unfold the next day. But it turned out that she simply wanted to talk to me about herself, to tell me about her childhood and her family.

She was, on balance, a roommate of contrasts — cold and unfeeling with me one moment, genuine and caring the next. One day she'd reprimand me in a harsh, unforgiving manner for something as minor as forgetting to wash my hands, but then she'd show incredible patience with me when I tried to say something in Korean. She also burst into tears. A lot. Especially when tender melodies played on the radio, or children recited poetry written by Kim Il Sung.

The first Song, cold and unfeeling, was her Party Persona, I realized. Indeed, at night she shed it like a snake might slough off its skin.

"The violin was my life when I was a child," she told me

one evening. "I performed in many concerts and competitions as a soloist in a large group. My instructors praised me for my technique. They said I had talented fingers. I hoped one day to perform for Kim Il Sung."

"Why didn't you continue? If you were so good at it, I mean."

She seemed unsure how to respond to my question.

"Because of my family's financial difficulties, I had to give music up. With the wise counsel and helpful assistance of a Party leader, I decided to dedicate my life to medicine instead. Medicine is more useful to people than music. Don't you think so? But, you know, music helped me with languages. By the time I graduated from high school, I could speak Russian, English, and French. That is why, when the Party was looking for someone to be your translator, they selected me for the job. Tell me, is my Russian adequate for your needs?"

I assured her that it was. It was true that her Russian was pretty good. But it was also highly formal, especially when she tried to elongate syllables in complicated words. At the same time, though, what she said to me about being my translator wasn't as simple as that. I knew, for example, that every evening she went downstairs to the security office to deliver her daily report on me. She watched me constantly, at all hours. Sometimes I felt as though she watched me when I was asleep. I also knew for a fact that she went through my clothing when I swam in the bathhouse on Tuesdays. How did I know that? Because one day when we went there I conducted a test: I pencilled "Long Live Comrade Song!" on a piece of paper, folded it into a square, and tied one of my hairs around it with a knot. I then placed the note in the pocket of my jacket before I went swimming. Afterward, I checked it. The note was there, but the hair was gone.

TO IMAGINE MY days, picture waking up at dawn to the sound of a siren. It turned off about thirty seconds later, but its screech haunted me for hours afterward. The radio, which was always fixed to the central government station, switched on automatically. A brass band usually played a vigorous march. To its accompaniment, every morning, Song performed what she called her "gymnastics" routine. She'd balance her body in various poses, lunge forward and sideways, or twist her arms at impossible angles behind her back. When her gymnastics was over, we washed in the bathroom with icy water, and then came down to the parade ground for the general assembly. A Party secretary gave a brief address and read the front page of the Party's newspaper. Important announcements were made. Thereafter, the students dispersed to their classes, while Song and I made excursions around the city or spent time in the library. There were only a few botanical books in Russian, but I also found a volume of Korean folk tales. In that book, the Russian translations were accompanied by the original Korean text, and Song was very patient with me as I tackled the Hangeul alphabet.

During the first week, we visited the Revolutionary Museum. The war wasn't over, a stern-looking guide there told me. Military manoeuvres were more important than ever before. With Kim Il Sung's untimely passing, the filthy Americans would love nothing better than to take over his beloved fatherland. Did I know that American spies were everywhere? Just the other day, one of their agents, posing as a tourist, derailed a freight train in Wŏnsan.

Pyongyang's centre was clean and manicured, full of fountains, stadiums, and green parks with leafy trees, but farther away, toward the suburbs, apartment buildings bore the telltale signs of neglect — peeling paint, crumbling plaster, and black stains of mould.

On a few occasions we took the subway, which resembled the Moscow metro, except that the escalators in Pyongyang were longer, the tunnels deeper, and the socialist murals in its stations more elaborate. Many murals depicted scenes of happy peasants reaping wheat on collective farms. There were also muscular workers casting steel rails in factories. But most often the murals featured a broadly smiling Kim Il Sung. He was frequently surrounded by laughing children and behind him rose rays of luminous sun to convey the idea that he was the omniscient deity who had descended to Earth.

Aboveground, the streets of Pyongyang were virtually empty of traffic. Small children bounced limp soccer balls on the road. Men rode occasional bikes, but most people walked along the sidewalks carrying plastic bags. I was struck by the absence of pets. Song told me people didn't keep pets in Pyongyang. "Children may have fish. Maybe pigeons. In the country, dogs cohabit sometimes with the livestock. But in the capital, space is limited for human beings. There is no room for stupid pets."

In the canteen, Song and I ate our meals at a separate table; in the library, we had a study room to ourselves; and during political sessions, we always sat in the back row of a lecture hall. The students I did see on campus were taciturn and unfriendly toward me. Most of them wore serious, determined expressions and walked past me briskly, with bowed heads. If our paths did cross on campus or in the hallways of buildings, they made a point of steering clear of me, as if I'd been infected with some deadly contagion or an incurable viral disease. I hated the feeling of being excluded. It unsettled me. Besides, I wanted to practise my Korean as Song had begun to teach it to me. I thought it was ironic that human beings had come up with language to share with one another their experiences of the world, but there I was, trying to learn Korean and living in virtual isolation, deprived of all meaningful human contact except with Song.

Every day, I asked Song about my father. When could I see him? What was keeping him away? Her response was always the same: he's busy. He's busy with his important work. "But," she'd add quickly, "he expresses his never-ending respect for you, of course." One day I'd had enough of it, went downstairs to the security office, and demanded to be taken to see him immediately. A security officer I hadn't seen before, a bold man with a bad rash on his hands, gestured to me with them to indicate that he didn't speak Russian at all. But if I wrote my request down on paper, he'd be sure to pass it on to his boss.

I did write my request on a piece of paper, and the following day Song and I were called into the security office as we were heading out to the assembly.

"Why do you want to complain to your father?" another officer asked me. "Are you treated badly by your translator? Is that what it is? We're happy to replace her if she isn't good for you."

"Of course not," I said, wanting to scream at him and beat him as hard as I could with my fists. "That is not what it's about. I want to see my father. That's all."

Pleading to see my father, however, was of no use at all. Every day in Pyongyang was like that American movie where the character had to relive the same day over and over again.

I thought of my mother more often. In fact, the thoughts of her pursued me throughout my days. Like a sick child who runs to her mother when she needs comfort the most, I ran to the memories of her for strength. Especially when I despaired, when I didn't feel like being strong anymore. In my mind, I replayed the happy images of my childhood in Moscow, which seemed so far away. I remembered swimming in an outdoor pool with her, ice-skating on frozen ponds, or eating jam, right out of the jar, in the kitchen of our apartment, after she came home tired and hungry from her theatre rehearsals, very late at night.

I missed Russian food. Actually, I missed eating. Korean cuisine disagreed with my stomach. Indeed, I had a terrible time with it in the first couple of weeks in Pyongyang. On most days our meals in the canteen consisted of corn gruel. Sometimes we were given a soup of dried vegetables, or a cucumber salad with slimy seaweed. Once a week, a piece of fried fish appeared, its stench permeating my skin, it seemed. The side dishes — provided there were any — featured kimchee, which I detested, or mashed yellow turnips with red pepper paste.

One day, I remember, at breakfast, a public announcement came on. I didn't understand what was being said, of course, but caught the word *boshintang*, repeated several times. Everyone got very excited, especially Song. She began to jump up and down, her cheeks turning pink with joy. Wanting to share her enthusiasm, I asked her what *boshintang* was.

"It's a meat stew," she beamed at me. "Simply delicious. It has green onions, dandelion, and mint leaves. The main ingredient, though, is dog meat."

Needless to say, I couldn't do it. I couldn't eat dog. I kept thinking of all the dogs my grandmother rescued over the years and I couldn't bring myself even to look at it. I'd started having stomach cramps by then from the lack of food. Things weren't helped by the fact that the following day I was extremely hungry and ate a lot. My digestive tract went into overdrive. The pain was unbearable. I thought I might die. For two days I lay in bed, moaning and swearing never to eat anything ever again in my life. Song sat by my bed and commiserated with me by holding cold compresses to my forehead.

A nurse was called to our room. Half blind with pain, I watched her roll up her sleeves and give me two shots. When I woke up the next morning, I felt much better but wondered if it had all been a dream. Song insisted the nurse had been real and had given me special medicine to relieve my pain. "What medicine?" I asked her. She wasn't sure, only that it had contained ginseng. "Traditional medicine is good for you," she said. "It cures cancer, you know."

WHILE SONG TAUGHT me Korean, I taught her botanical terms. She liked to hear me talk of angiosperms and monocotyledons, but especially about orchids, the most common but least understood flowers of all. The first orchid I ever saw, I told her, was at my mother's funeral. A man she'd known from her student days but whom I'd never met before brought orchids to her memorial service in a large translucent pot. The roots were visible through the plastic, like thin whitish fingers with green, glowing tips. It was the most exquisite plant I'd ever seen, not only because of its dramatic flowers but also because of its scent. It smelled so delicate, sweet, yet also bitter, with hints of almond, nutmeg, and rose. The man was Asian — Chinese or Mongolian; I couldn't place him better than that. He spoke quietly to my father for a minute and then left the orchid at my mother's feet. It stood there, quivering in the currents of air, spun by the overhead fan, and it seemed to me as though its pale, smoky flowers were sprouting right from her toes. I'd identify that orchid six years later and grow it from seed in my lab. *Trichopilia fragrans*, subfamily Vandoideae, native to Trinidad. If you looked it up in a manual of cultivated orchids, you'd find it among the medium-sized epiphytes, which means that it grows in the wild on trees, attaching its roots to bark.

Song usually yawned when I used scientific jargon. She preferred to hear stories instead. I obliged and recounted legends about orchids, some of which were as exciting as the flowers themselves. I told her, for instance, that the word *orchis* comes from the Greek. It means "testicles" because many orchids have tuberous roots. After a Greek physician named Dioscorides proposed in his *Materia medica* that orchids were aphrodisiacs, they became synonymous with reproduction, or, more specifically, with sex. In the Middle Ages, for example, people ate orchids to arouse themselves. Meanwhile, German Jesuits thought that orchids sprang from the seminal fluid of mating animals. In Japan, legend said, the emperor's sterile wife inhaled the perfume of *Bletia hyacinthine* and went on to have thirteen kids. Turks ground roots of *Orchis mascula* to make a thickening agent to add into ice cream. And dried leaves of *Maxillaria cucullata* were said to cause such pronounced paralysis that people who had swallowed them were often mistaken for dead.

SONG TOLD ME she was born in Pyongyang twenty-five years ago to a family of schoolteachers. She had no brothers or sisters, and her father had died of lung cancer when she was three. After that, it was just her and her mother, brought together and made very close by unfortunate circumstance. They lived in a one-bedroom apartment with central heating, which was a rare and special thing. The words *lucky, fortunate, special* were common in Song's vocabulary, which I found so odd, so peculiar really, considering where she lived.

Song's mother was a chemistry teacher who prepared students for medical school. When Song was growing up, they'd always found the time to have dinners together and to talk about books. It was hard to find time for family in North Korea because most people worked very hard. Even on weekends, everyone was required to volunteer their labour on construction sites. As such, most families saw very little of each other, except in the mornings and before they went to bed. But her mother made a point of finding time to spend with her daughter and to read good books together. Most people in North Korea didn't read fiction because they didn't have time. They were too exhausted to read after workdays, and if they weren't, they read Kim Il Sung's works.

Her mother loved Maxim Gorky, the true proletarian writer. Song, meanwhile, liked Dostoyevsky and Gogol, because, as she put it, "of their tormented souls." In fact, one of the reasons she learned Russian in high school was in order to read *Crime and Punishment* in the original text. Reading the Russians was like entering regions of darkness, she said, and she liked darkness a lot. Things could be done in the night, she once told me, her eyes sparkling with a mischievous glow, that could never be done during the day.

I'd been brought up to read widely in Moscow, all kinds of authors and all kinds of books, and I couldn't help but wonder if the fact that North Korea was a nation of apparent non-readers contributed to the success of Kim Il Sung's regime. Or the fact that they didn't keep pets in their homes. That they ate dogs in stews.

Another strange thing was that I'd never, not once on campus, seen a couple hold hands.

"What about romance?" I asked Song one evening, about two weeks after I arrived. "Where do students go on dates, for example? Is there such a thing?"

"Dates?"

"Yes. Where do students meet to spend time together? To whisper sweet nothings, to talk of love?"

"Sweet nothings?" She blinked. "I don't understand you, Comrade Vera. Please explain what you mean."

"You know," I said, growing annoyed with her. She wasn't twelve, was she? She was twenty-five. "A man, a woman" — I demonstrated what I meant with my fingers — "a baby."

She blushed terribly and turned her face away from me.

"I'm sorry," I said. "My culture is different from yours. I thought —"

"Please, say no more." She held a hand in front of her face as if defending herself from a blow. "There is no such thing as sweet nothings in our country. North Korea is very traditional. Understand that. If a couple is caught — making love, they may be punished and asked to criticize themselves. Romance before marriage is forbidden. Confucian principles teach us so. Besides, what does love have to do with our way of life? How does love benefit us?"

I wanted to say, "The future," but, registering her discomfort, bit my tongue. Instead, I asked her to tell me more about Confucian principles, admitting that I didn't know much about them.

"A friendship between members of the opposite sex isn't considered normal," she said. "When a man speaks to a woman his own age, he addresses her informally, but the woman is obliged to use formal language when she speaks to a man. As with all relations, courtship follows a strict hierarchy, and the institution of marriage is stratified. Marrying a foreigner is a big taboo, of course, because of the purity of our blood."

I thought I misheard her and asked for clarification.

"Korean blood is the purest. The Party believes it is so. The Party believes in eugenics, that people with undesirable characteristics should be — no more. In this way, our race remains pure. It was always meant to be so. Like the clearest spring from the sacred mountain, our blood must be kept free of silt."

That was the final drop in my tolerance bucket. I could stand it no more. I didn't need to be strong any longer. I was weak and I wanted to go home.

"Listen, Song," I said. "Can you please tell your chief comrade that I want to go back to Moscow? Tomorrow would be ideal, but I suppose I can wait another day."

4

The next morning, it began to rain heavily as if a plug had been pulled out of the sky. A small, intense-looking man came to our room and introduced himself to me in Russian as Comrade Park. He wore a dull brown suit and battered white sneakers that made squeaking noises as he paced the floorboards. His long, scrawny neck, bulging eyes, and long nose hooked on the bottom brought to mind a villain in science fiction movies of old.

"Esteemed Professor Viktor has made unparalleled progress with his work," he said in a sugary tone of voice. "He'd be delighted to dine with you this evening in the world-famous restaurant called the Red Lantern. I'll pick you up at the front gates at six o'clock this evening. It'll rain, so bring your coats and don't be late."

In the library that day, Song showed me the Red Lantern on the map of Pyongyang. It was located on the bank of the Taedong River, between Moran Hull and the Okryu Bridge. She described it to me as a public noodle house, and became very excited about the house specialty. The cold buckwheat noodles would make my mouth water, she promised, smacking her red lava lips. Meanwhile, I suspected that I'd be too excited at seeing my father to eat anything at all.

As promised, at six o'clock that evening a black Mercedes drove up to the main gates. Comrade Park had been right about the weather: the rain poured out of the sky unabated all day. He got out of the car, opened a black umbrella, and stood looking skyward as we got in.

The Red Lantern turned out to be an impressive two-storey building designed in traditional Korean style. It had curved gable eaves covered in green tiles that glistened like the scales of some mythical dragon under incandescent street lights. As we climbed up the granite stairs to the heavy oak door, Comrade Park informed me that more than three thousand people could have a meal there at any given time. The restaurant had hundred-seat banquet halls as well as private dining rooms. At least twenty expert chefs and "an army" of sous-chefs worked there to preserve the country's authentic cuisine.

We were expected. A petite woman in a traditional dress greeted us as we entered, making deep bows to each of us in turn. She led us inside, taking us to the right of the marble staircase and along a brightly lit passage, stopping at the last door. She opened it and invited us to enter with another bow.

The room was octagonal and large, about thirty metres square. The walls were covered in garish pink paper, and in the centre of the ornamented ceiling hung a large crystal ball. Dozens of people sat in groups around the tables, moving chopsticks to and from their lips. The chairs were covered with white cotton shrouds, and resembled, I thought for some reason, marshmallows with legs. Two pairs of French doors on the other side of the room over-looked the river and afforded a view of the glowing amusement park on the opposite bank.

My father stood at the far end of the room, in the corner, leaning against the wall. He wore crumpled grey trousers and a blue shirt, unbuttoned at the collar and missing his usual bow tie. Days, possibly weeks, of sleep deprivation pooled in dark circles under his eyes. He'd lost weight, and his hair, which had been always so neat and tidy, looked as though it hadn't been brushed for days.

The change in his appearance was so striking that I had to stifle a cry of disbelief. Sickened with worry, I crossed the dining hall, weaving my way between tables through to him. But before I could greet him or say anything out loud, he reached out quickly to embrace me.

If he was surprised by the change in my own appearance — for I too must've seemed changed to him — he didn't show it. After we separated, he smiled weakly at me and brushed his hair down self-consciously with both hands.

"I'm sorry it's taken so long for me to see you, Verka," he said. "I hope you've been well."

"You're here now," I said, kissing him on the cheek. "That's all that matters to me."

Someone guffawed at the next table. My father flinched and, as if remembering suddenly where we were, motioned for us to sit. Other patrons glared at us as we settled around the table.

My father and I exchanged glances as if to say, "Well, here we are. Now what?"

Comrade Park said, "It's truly wonderful to see the

father-and-daughter reunion in our great country. Our new leader works constantly toward victory that will surely bring an end to all separations in the world."

"Everyone eats plentifully well here," Song offered.

"Speaking of eating," Comrade Park went on, "foreigners who come here are usually shown into private rooms. But you two are such special guests of our country that the Party decided you should eat with everyone else."

A waitress materialized at our table, carrying four small brass bowls on a plastic tray. She placed the bowls carefully on the table in front of Comrade Park, and then launched into a speech in Korean, making eye contact only with him.

"Ah," he said after she finished speaking. "Today's special is *raengmyeon*. I've gone ahead and ordered it for all of us. It's a wonderful dish. And let's also have ginger beer!" He clapped his hands.

After the waitress departed, he leaned back in his chair, looking exceedingly pleased with himself.

"Comrade Vera. Comrade Viktor. Tonight we celebrate. Both of you must be so pleased to meet again. We must love our families. Every day. Because who knows what might happen to any of us at any given moment? Life is unpredictable that way. Take the original architect of this restaurant, for example. His name was Ahn Young-gi. He built this beautiful place, but unluckily for him did not get a chance to see it bloom. Very sad, no? His wife and the mother of his seven children waited for him to come home, but, unhappily for them, he did not return." He leaned toward me as if confiding a big secret. "Because Ahn Young-gi was not just an architect. He was also a

special agent. Yes! It is hard to believe. But North Koreans
love their country more than anything else in the world.
So, there's no greater honour than to serve the fatherland.
In the West, children are brought up to believe that the
most precious thing in the world is their life. But how
foolish it is! No! Kim Il Sung was very wise. He said man
was a social being. Man develops only through social life.
A man's mind is a social attribute that must work inside
the collective for the benefit of everyone." He turned to
my father. "You agree, Professor Viktor?"

My father and I glanced at each other.

"I do," my father said.

"Ahn Young-gi was sent to the South on an important
assignment," Comrade Park went on, "but was betrayed
by his friends. Some say he's still alive down there, impris-
oned and longing to return home."

"Why was he sent to the South?" I asked, unable to
help myself.

Comrade Park blinked. "He was sent there by the Party.
That is all one needs to know."

The waitress brought in four beers and decanted dark
copper liquid into each glass. Comrade Park raised his
glass to my father and gestured toward me. "What a
daughter you have, Professor Viktor! I congratulate you
with all my heart!"

My father's eyes remained on me while he was drinking his beer, willing me to remain calm. I was trying to
figure out what Comrade Park's bizarre story was all
about. What had he actually meant? Was it some kind of
warning? A threat? Perhaps both. I also wasn't sure what
to make of my father's agreement with him. I knew for a

fact that my father prized individual freedom above all else, despite being brought up in the Soviet Union, or perhaps because of it. So, clearly, he was trying to tell me something by agreeing with Comrade Park. The whole thing, this dinner, was weird. It frustrated me no end. I wished we could talk in the open, shovelling all the doublespeak out of the way.

I was also disturbed by my father's demeanour, which seemed very submissive. He sat across from me at the table with hunched shoulders and lowered head, casting futile glances about him as though he thought he was trapped. At one point it struck me that he looked like a little boy who had broken a school rule and was now waiting, in the principal's office, to find out what his punishment would be.

I could tell as soon as I walked through the door of the dining hall that something was the matter with him. My father and I had always been quite close. Perhaps it was my mother's death that had brought us together, making our relationship stronger than a typical parent–child bond. But whatever the cause of our closeness might have been, it allowed us to communicate without words. Sometimes a gesture or a tilt of the head from one of us could tell the other everything they needed to know. I'd seen such closeness between my parents. That evening, as my father sat across from me at the table in the Red Lantern, he communicated to me that he wasn't okay.

Our food was brought in: four stainless bowls of soup, each with coils of noodles submerged in yellow broth. A pair of scissors was placed discreetly on the table next to me.

"Ah." Comrade Park rubbed his hands together and grinned broadly, revealing a set of small teeth. "Frankly speaking, this is the best bowl of noodles I've ever seen. Now I'll show you how to eat them. You've got to bring art into it." He motioned to the scissors. "Forget about those. The noodles are meant to be eaten without cutting them up. Not, in any case, with scissors. You've got your teeth for that."

He reached for the mustard sauce and scooped a spoonful of it into his bowl. Then, using his chopsticks he mixed the sauce into the noodles, took a deep breath, and said, "Begin!"

He ate quickly. It was amazing to watch the noodles disappear into his mouth with such dexterous speed. Song, who had sprinkled vinegar into her bowl of soup instead of mustard, was wasting no time eating her noodles too.

My father, meanwhile, was probing around his bowl with the chopsticks as though uncertain how to begin.

Other patrons at their tables were laughing and having a good time. Now and then the glum-looking waiters emerged from behind the swivelling door of the kitchen, carrying loaded trays. The door kept banging open. I smelled burned cooking oil. My stomach lurched. Despite having eaten a meagre lunch, I didn't feel hungry at all. I looked into my bowl. The noodles looked grey. Green onion, red chilies, and a thin oval of sliced boiled egg floated on the top. The bowl of soup was unappetizing, not the sort of food I'd ever enjoy.

Comrade Park must've registered my expression and misunderstood it, because he said, "Comrade Vera, do not fear to eat noodles. They won't bite your tongue."

Song guffawed and brought her hand to her mouth.

I started to say, "No, it isn't that. I just don't—"

"Now," Comrade Park cut me off, "there is, as I said, a whole art to it. Watch me, okay? First, coil a bundle around your chopsticks. Next, bring them up to your mouth, like that. If some noodles end up hanging out of your mouth, simply bite through them with your teeth. Suck the rest up, but do it gently. One must be careful not to suck too hard."

He winked at my father, and for a moment I was certain I would be sick. I gulped for air. My head began to spin. I knew that if I looked at my father, I would start to cry. And so, to compose myself, I pretended to look around the room.

"Comrade Vera," Comrade Park called to me as though from a great distance. "You must eat!"

"She will," my father said, "just give her a moment. She's not used to using chopsticks."

They were all watching me now in silence, and reluctantly I picked up the chopsticks and sank them into my bowl. I tried to grasp the egg or the green onions, anything, all to no avail. The noodles kept sliding down the chopsticks, splashing back into the broth.

Comrade Park said, "My grandmother told me long ago that eating noodles was a bit like acting. Your mother, Comrade Vera, she's an actress too?"

"She was," I said, trying to keep my voice even. "She died of leukemia when I was thirteen."

He stared at me for a moment, without saying anything. Then he stretched his lips into a thin smile and mumbled, "Forgive me, I didn't know. Please accept my sincerest condolences."

My father said, "Vera's mother was a terrific actress. She acted in many revolutionary films. It may please Comrade Park to know that in her third film, for example, she played a war heroine. This heroine was very young, only twenty, but in the movie she found herself behind enemy lines. She was quite alone, but very brave and very clever. She kept her wits about her and survived."

That wasn't true, of course. Both of my mother's movies had been romantic comedies.

Comrade Park nodded with appreciation. "Very good. I must watch that movie soon."

"Movies are entertaining," my father continued, looking pointedly at me now, "but I think our young people should spend their valuable time learning more useful things. Like science, for instance, which reminds me — Vera, how has your work in the Botanical Gardens been going? Has the research there been useful to you?"

Song's chopsticks froze in mid-air.

Comrade Park cleared his throat.

I began to open my mouth to tell my father that I hadn't as yet been allowed to go, that I was waiting for the official permit for my work in the Botanical Gardens and was surprised that he didn't know that, when out of the corner of my eye I saw Comrade Park lift his bowl off the table, hold it up in both his hands, and tilt it toward himself. In another moment, unbelievably, he began to slurp the broth.

My father and I turned to watch him in silent fascination.

"I know what you might be thinking," Comrade Park said, pausing to wipe his lips. "Slurping in Russia is rude, am I right? But in our culture it isn't. In our culture slurping lets the cook know that you've enjoyed their food. Slurping is therefore not only encouraged, it is in fact recommended. So." He motioned to our own bowls encouragingly, "Go ahead and enjoy yourselves."

I tasted bile climbing out of my stomach. Desperately, I gazed around the table for something to help me push it back. I settled for beer, but when I brought it up to my lips, it smelled acrid, like burned rubber, and made me feel worse.

Meanwhile, Comrade Park's face began to glisten. He burped loudly, laughed, and patted his stomach.

"A most excellent meal," he said.

"Vera." My father drummed his fingers impatiently on the table. "You were going to tell me about your work."

Comrade Park sighed. "Dear Professor, the thing is, we are still waiting for Vera's permit. As you know, everything in our country requires official authorization. That's how it works. Things are moving ahead, I assure you, but the Party, in its infinite wisdom, must consider all facts."

"What facts?" my father asked, thrusting his chin forward, the way he always did when he was upset.

"The facts the Party always considers in assigning work," Comrade Park said. "Comrade Vera is an honoured guest of our country, but she must be treated like everyone else. There is no preferential treatment for anyone here. This is the essence of our success."

My father looked at me. It was hard to say what he was thinking. His eyes seemed to be searching for some kind of sign from me. And in that moment I understood that I wouldn't be able to go home after all, because they weren't going to let me leave.

"I see," my father said slowly. "But what does the final decision depend on?"

"It depends on good behaviour." Comrade Park turned to Song. "I understand that Comrade Vera has been behaving herself very well. Should she continue to do so, I anticipate no problems down the line. But of course, it's up to our glorious leaders to decide such matters, not humble workers like me."

"Did you hear him, Vera?" my father said, avoiding my eyes. "Comrade Park doesn't anticipate any problems provided that you behave yourself. Please be patient and be strong, my darling. All of us must do our best."

THAT NIGHT, THE rain finally stopped. At least that was something, I thought, as I lay in my bed, turning my father's words over in my head. More than anything else in the world, that evening I'd wanted my father to tell me that he'd take care of me and that everything would be okay. Instead, he'd made it clear that he was in no position to help me, that I was, in effect, like the young heroine of my mother's fictional movie, "behind enemy lines" entirely on my own.

Song kept tossing in her own bed also, until at last she gave up and called softly to me, "Comrade Vera, are you asleep?"

"Yes," I said.

She giggled.

"It was great to meet Professor Viktor. Your father is a truly exceptional man."

I didn't feel the need to respond to that assessment, just shrugged into the dark.

She cleared her throat, straining to get the conversation going, I thought.

"We had so much to eat," she said. "My stomach is hurting."

"I feel upset," I blurted out, and regretted having done so right away.

"I'm awfully sorry about your mother," Song said, misunderstanding what I'd meant. "Please accept my deepest regrets."

"Thank you. But I'd rather not talk about it. Let's sleep."

"Okay." She shifted her body in bed and fell silent.

"Good night, Song," I said.

"Actually" — she sat up — "I want to ask you something about your father's work. I wanted to ask him so many questions this evening, but of course it was not my place." She took a deep breath. "Did he preserve your mother?"

"What?" I bolted out of bed and began to pace around. "Of course not! No! Never! He never touched her. He didn't let anyone touch her, okay?" I stopped in front of her, trying to compose myself. "Her body was cremated. We scattered her ashes at sea. That's it!"

"I'm sorry," Song said, and stretched a pale hand toward me. It glowed like some ghoulish limb in the moonlight, terrifying me. I took a step back.

"There's a popular saying in our country," she said next. "From ashes, mystical mountains rise. There is another: When tigers die, they leave leather behind, but when people die, they leave their blood behind. I wonder if perhaps you know —" She hesitated, moving her face closer to mine. "I wonder if perhaps you know what happens to all the blood?"

"The blood?"

"The blood of corpses your father works with. To preserve bodies, he removes their blood, yes?"

"Oh," I said, shivering and rubbing my arms for warmth. "They replace it with balsam."

"Balsam?"

"Yes, it's a chemical solution that preserves the flesh."

"I see. Do they use a pump?"

"A pump?"

"To get the balsam in?"

"Yes! No! I don't know!" I cried. "Honestly, must we pursue this? I'm tired. I want to sleep." I walked back to my bunk and collapsed onto it, lacing my hands behind my head.

"But where does the blood go?" she insisted.

"Down the drain," I said.

Would you just shut up! I thought, exasperated. *Shut up and leave me alone!*

"They don't keep it for anything?"

"No. Once you're dead, your blood—it sort of spoils."

"Okay," she said, and turned to the wall.

Soon, she was snoring.

Amazing, I thought. Nothing short of a nuclear war, I imagined, could disturb her. I envied her that.

5

The following Tuesday, I woke up to find the official permit for my work in the Botanical Gardens slipped under the door of our room, and after breakfast Song and I donned plastic ponchos and headed eastward in the city, riding our bikes in the rain. Neither the miserable weather nor the fact that the hem of my poncho kept catching up in my bike's chain (every so often I had to dismount and tear strips of it off) could dampen my spirits. I was so excited to finally start working with orchids, I could hardly contain myself.

We rode past the Kumsusan Palace, crossed a rusting bridge, and entered a vast wood-like area dominated by ash trees. Turning north onto a dirt road, we dismounted and walked our bikes through a grove of crabapple trees, at the end of which stood iron gates. A chain-link fence topped by barbed wire encircled the grounds as far as the eye could see.

"Now what?" I asked Song.

She left her bike on the ground, walked to a low wooden hut that stood to the left of the gates, and peeked inside a small, grimy window. As she raised her fist to knock on it, a soldier ran out and pointed a Kalashnikov at her.

A bit much, I thought, but put my hands up just in case. The Botanical Gardens seemed a rather odd place to be guarded by military. What was it exactly they were trying to protect?

Song spoke with the soldier for several minutes, pointing at me and then at herself. He examined our papers for a long time, snorted, and waved his hand in disgust. Then he rummaged in his trouser pocket and extracted a key. Next he approached the gates, unlocked them, and motioned for us to go through. As I led my bike past him into the Gardens, he glared at me in silence, and then spat at my feet through his teeth.

I found the encounter highly unpleasant, but resolved not to let it affect my mood. By then I'd grown quite used to people treating me with disdain, and the best way to deal with it, as far as I could see, was to ignore it.

We'd come upon what seemed to be a service road. On the right stood a cluster of buildings with painted blue roofs.

Within minutes, a beautiful trail opened in front of us, planted with hundreds of trees and shrubs. There were Japanese maples and gingko trees, persimmons and chestnuts. I recognized also jujubes and hazels, cherries and plums. The opposite side of the grassy meadow was lined with Dutch elms. And just ahead, past a copse of silver birches, lilac bushes sloped toward a pond walled by white stones.

"We were expected in the orchids greenhouse," Song said. "If I remember correctly, it must be just past the Flowery Brook."

"How many greenhouses are here?" I asked her as we approached a glass structure that abutted a brick wall.

"Let's see," she said, leading me down the gravel path that skirted to the right. "There is one for the ferns and one for the tropicals, one for the begonias and one for the herbs. Then there is the Exhibition Centre and the Hall of the Arids. That one is my favourite of all. There is also a Chinese garden, a rose garden, and a big plot of land for the shades. A tree nursery is over there, next to the meteorological station." She motioned toward a whitewashed building with a dome on the top. "An insectarium recently opened just off the alpine trail. Finally, there is a toxic plants station. But we aren't allowed to go in there, so never do."

"How come you know so much about this place?" I asked her. "I thought you studied medicine before you agreed to translate for me?"

"I was assigned to translate for you, Comrade Vera. Of course, I agreed. But if you must know, in preparation for your visit, I spent two weeks here, familiarizing myself with everything. I had to learn the names of all the plants in Russian, among other things."

She sighed in a way that made me feel guilty, but also left me with the feeling that there was more to it than simply that.

The gravel path widened, merged with another, and began to climb a small hill. A man in dark overalls walked past us wheeling a barrel of compost. Here and there I saw people in knee-high gumboots digging in flower beds.

"In case you're wondering why there aren't any visitors in the Gardens, our people are still in a state of deep mourning," Song said. "All entertainments, including trips here, are strictly forbidden, for now."

The rain began to come down harder, and we quickened our pace, coming shortly to a large, three-tiered building covered with a vaulted glass roof.

"This is the Exhibition Centre." Song pointed to its narrow wing. "The Room of Living Sculptures and the Hall of the Arids are in there. Let's leave our bikes here and peek in."

"Aren't we expected at the orchids greenhouse?" I asked her, surprised by her proposition. I'd never seen her disobey the smallest instruction before.

"Don't worry," she said, sprinting forward eagerly. "They'll wait for us there. Meanwhile, it might stop raining.

There's no reason for us to get soaked."

I ran after her then, and soon we let ourselves inside a vast empty hall. The sound of the rain faded behind us as we pulled off our ponchos. It was so quiet. No one was around. In the middle of the hall stood a fountain basin, floored with blue tiles. Coated with a layer of dust and without water, it looked exceedingly sad.

"Hello?" something compelled me to call out in Russian. My voice bounced off the walls. "Anyone here?"

"Be quiet!" Song hissed at me, and beckoned for me to follow her down the passage on the right.

Beyond the moon-shaped doors was a room filled with miniature trees. Bonsai, I realized, although not a kind I'd ever seen. On granite pedestal-like tables stood entire bonsai landscapes. There were pine forests and fruit orchards, trees in bloom and trees growing on rocky outcrops. Many displays included model houses and animal figurines.

"What are these?" I asked Song.

"Penjings. Chinese bonsai. Each has a traditional meaning, you know. This one, for example" — she pointed to a group of small flowering trees — "is the apricot orchard. It symbolizes purity in intention, inherent in everyone."

The first room led into the second through a red wooden door. It was a dry, arid place, like a desert, unbearably hot. All the moisture seemed to have been sucked out of my mouth the moment I stepped inside.

Cacti of various lengths grew in beds of sandy soil, each bordered by slabs of red granite. The flagstone floor was covered with an orangey substance that crunched under my feet. In the far corner I spotted a flowering cactus, a peyote plant famous for its hallucinogenic effects.

To our left, two women in hairnets were bent over a glass table, slicing plant stems with curved metal blades.

"I love how warm it is here," Song said. "When I was growing up, I was always cold. Since I discovered this room, I come here whenever I can to keep warm."

One woman looked up at us, and Song waved to her.

"They know me here. They don't mind that I visit, every once in a while. The scientists here study the breeding systems of cacti. They pay special interest to their medicinal effects." Her voice shifted to a whisper. "I'm sure I'm not supposed to tell you, but ten years ago Kim Il Sung in his infinite wisdom established a seed bank. In this way, in North Korea we can grow any plant whenever we like. Isn't that clever?" She paused. "The women you see over there are working on extracting the seeds."

Interesting, I thought. They paid special attention to their medicinal effects. Alkaloids, I was willing to bet anything on it, the compounds known for their neurological effects. Anaesthetics, stimulants, painkillers, perhaps even entheogens. The latter induced an altered state of consciousness, their name meaning "generating the divine within." Except that in North Korea there was already a powerful deity, a benevolent, omniscient Kim Il God, so what was the actual purpose, I wondered, of that little room? To isolate alkaloids from biological sources, sparing no expense. And suddenly the soldier with the Kalashnikov, the gates with iron bars, the chain-link fence, and the special permit for me to work here made perfect sense.

The question, though, was why Song was showing that room to me. What was I supposed to take note of in here?

There remained no doubt in my mind any longer that Song had led me there on purpose, and certainly not because she was "cold." Then I remembered how I'd told her once about my interest in the alkaloid content in some species of orchids — *Dendrobium*, *Phalaenopsis*, and *Catasetum*. About how in the lab in Moscow I'd found additional positive alkaloid reactions in *Paphiopedilum* and *Liparis*. About how, after screening for alkaloids in different species and purifying many of them myself, I'd begun to work out the common steps in their biochemical pathways in order to synthesize them on an industrial scale.

I grew frightened. Was that the real reason I'd been brought to Pyongyang? Could it be — no, I hated to ask the very question — could it be that my father was involved in the making of drugs? I felt sweat spreading under my shirt and was beginning to panic when I saw a funny-looking man heading our way. He was wearing a yellow raincoat with a hood at the back, and his pointed ears and fidgety manner made him look remarkably like a garden elf.

"Good day, Comrade," he said to Song in Korean, and then spoke to me.

"He says he saw our bicycles outside," Song translated. "He sincerely apologizes for missing us at the gates. The begonias kept him very busy. His name is Comrade Ting."

Even his name sounded elfish, I thought as I shook his tiny hand.

Ting seemed unable to stay still, even for a moment, swivelling to and fro on the balls of his feet. His hands were soft and delicate, though, I noticed, and his fingernails clean. Despite what he'd told us about being busy with the begonias, I doubted that he worked with any plants.

We went outside through the Exhibition Hall to collect our bikes and ponchos, and ten minutes later arrived at the wooden fence that formed a screen around a greenhouse. Inside, orchids of hundreds of species grew in translucent pots. Benches and high tables were covered with rows upon rows of magnificent specimens. Some plants dangled upside down from the ceiling, their green roots like thin fingers grabbing on to chunks of soggy bark. The humid air was heavy and pungent, crowded with the orchid scents. At one point I caught the rotten-flesh reek of *Bulbophyllum*, and hurried along down the aisle.

But how lovely everything was there! How lovely and humid and green! Everywhere, it seemed, orchid stems burst with blooms of fantastic shapes — some concave, some convex, some oblong. Their colours made me dizzy. Their scents made my head spin. The deprivations of the past several weeks seemed so trivial now, so unimportant, such a small price to pay for all this! As I followed Ting along the narrow passage that ran between the rows of plants, the orchid flowers seemed to nod their greetings to me. *Welcome, Vera,* they seemed to be saying. *We're so glad you could come.*

A work table, strewn with sheets of paper, stood at the far end. To the right was a small office-like room with a separate entrance that opened into a courtyard. On a shelf above the table stood a portable light microscope. Next to it perched a glass bottle of alkaline stain on a leather-bound book. I tilted my head to read the silver letters engraved on its spine, and was happy to see that it was the Russian translation of Darwin's *On the Fertilization of Orchids*, the book I'd read so often in Moscow that I knew parts of it by heart.

A man sat on the ledge of the window, with a book opened on his lap. He'd removed his glasses, and was tapping their handles against his knee, apparently lost in thought. His face was cast in shadow, profiled against the light, but in its silhouette I could see the sharp contour of his jaw.

"This is our esteemed orchidologist," Song translated Ting's words. "Comrade Shin, meet Comrade Vera. Comrade Vera, say hello to Comrade Shin."

The man looked up, closed his book quickly, and stood up. Then he put his glasses back on, walked over to us, and offered me his hand.

He was older than me, perhaps twenty-seven, with well-defined cheekbones and a high-bridged, narrow nose. I thought right away that he didn't look North Korean because he was not undernourished, like most others I'd met in Pyongyang. Also, there wasn't anything grim about his expression, nothing uneasy, nothing to suggest an unhappy life. When he spoke to me, his dark eyes sparkled with excitement, as though he'd just solved an intricate puzzle that had preoccupied him for a long time. Life was so interesting, his open face seemed to be saying, if you just looked around you.

"Hello," I said, feeling slightly confused.

"Welcome." He spoke in Russian. "I look forward to our association. I've heard a lot of good things about you."

I must've frowned, wondering from whom he might've heard the good things about me, because in the next moment he added, "From your father. Professor Viktor visited here one month ago. He was impressed by our collection of orchids and told me about your interest in their biochemistry. I suggested then you come here as an exchange student and work with me. I believe our collaboration might benefit both of us. Perhaps not unlike a symbiotic relationship between two organisms that complement each other's strengths."

His Russian was correct, albeit awkward.

I nodded self-consciously and said that I appreciated the sentiments he'd expressed.

He moved over to a small orchid with white flowers covered in purple spots.

"Do you know this one?" he asked me.

I approached closer to examine it.

Dorsal sepal ovate, about three centimetres long, *Synsepalum* much smaller. Leaves elliptic, dark green, with grey markings on upper surface and purple-spotted beneath. The telltale sign was the pellets of calcium carbonate in the soil.

Yes, I certainly knew it.

"*Paphiopedium niveum*, also known as a dwarf herb," I said. "A terrestrial orchid, found in Southeast Asia and restricted to limestone outcrops. Rather exacting in its nutritional requirements and notoriously hard to breed."

"And this one?" He took hold of the stem of another orchid with dramatically shaped scarlet blooms.

"A *Masdevallia* species. Perhaps *militaris*. The lip is an insignificant feature in this genera. Lithophytic. Grows in South America, at high altitudes. I read a paper recently that suggested that the increased amount of ultraviolet radiation led to a higher mutation rate in these plants."

"Yes, I suppose it's possible," Shin said. "UV radiation mutates DNA. Your father has led me to understand that you were interested in orchids that thrive in environmental extremes. What else interests you? Tell me."

"Sex. Specifically, chemical scents given out by the orchid flowers and their visual stimuli of colour and shape. So far I've concentrated on studying *Stanhopea* alliance with Euglossine bees. In my lab in Moscow we've analyzed the fragrances that attract only one kind of bees. In one experiment, we deposited them on artificial gels, and as expected, bees of only one species landed on them."

"So you tricked them," Song said, exchanging glances with Ting.

"You can put it that way," I admitted. "But our goal was to confirm their identity. Orchid flowers are extremely selective about which pollinator they allow to get inside. Over thousands of years, they've evolved the most elaborate mechanisms of molecular mimicry to attract just the right kind."

"Then you must know a little about this very special orchid." Shin motioned toward a plant with complex, innervated leaves. I recognized its grotesque flowers immediately. There was no mistaking it.

"*Coryathes Hooker*," I said. How many times had I seen it in Darwin's books? "They attract their pollinators by their strong odour and then drop them in a water pool." I beckoned to Song to come closer and look inside the bloom. "These flowers have glands that distill water to fill a vase on the bottom of their lip. The pollinators who fall into this vase can stay where they are and drown or crawl out to safety through the narrow gap over here, do you see? The botanists call it the tunnel of love because it is coated with pollen. As the insects squeeze through, they become covered with it, which allows them to pollinate other flowers with high efficiency."

I lifted my eyes at Shin. "Do I pass the test?"

He laughed, without taking his eyes off me. "It isn't a test. I only wondered if you were as serious about the orchids as I was, and now I see that you are."

After Ting left, Shin led us into his office and motioned for us to sit.

"Now," he said, looking at us over the top of his glasses. "There are four other people who work here besides me. One of them is a menial labourer, who washes the floors. He also humidifies the air and takes care of electrical fans. There are also two students who work with me on breeding orchids resistant to red spider mites. A few years ago we had a bad infestation and lost many valuable plants. The other person is the Academy scientist, who extracts lipids and studies them on chromatography plates. I supervise all of them in their duties and make up work schedules every day. Every person has their workstation and is expected to help with housekeeping things."

He turned to me.

"Since you've indicated your interest in the investigation of the climatic factors, I suggest that you start looking at the effects of the temperature shifts first. It may be difficult to mimic in the greenhouse the condition of high irradiation, but I might be able to procure some UV lamps. In the meantime, the temperature control chambers are functional and are at your disposal whenever you like. By the way, we heat this greenhouse with hot-water pipes. There is a coal-powered furnace out in the courtyard."

He spoke clearly and calmly, and once again I was struck by his self-assured poise. Nothing seemed rushed or strained with him. Nothing extraneous. Everything seemed to fit perfectly in its right place. He also treated me like an equal, and the prospect of working with him made my unease about my father and my feelings of alienation evaporate into the humid air.

"Comrade Song's responsibility will be to assist you with language and anything else you might need. I expect both of you to become familiar with the workings of this greenhouse and follow its rules at all times. Plants, as you know, don't have regular hours. They don't take time off on weekends. Your work hours may thus be irregular also, but I'm sure will bring their rewards at the end. As with most things in life, you get out what you put into it. Isn't that right, Comrade Song? Comrade Vera, if something troubles you or you aren't sure about something, come and talk to me about it. Orchids, as you well know, tend to have strong feelings. Special care must be taken with them at all times. Otherwise, they get angry, and their idea of angry is to die."

Song guffawed loudly and covered her mouth with a hand. It was painfully obvious to me that she was as smitten with Shin as I was.

"Now, let me show you to your station. We have a whole day of work still ahead of us."

My work with the orchids gave me purpose and made me forget about the world beyond the garden walls. I didn't think about going back to campus, or about having to sleep another night in our dorm room. I forgot all about having to eat food I detested and about seeing other students who looked right through me as if I didn't exist. All of that fell away when I worked in the greenhouse. When I was near Shin. I felt a sense of promise: the promise of something completely unknown and yet utterly thrilling underneath.

6

In my dreams now, I often see myself in the greenhouse, mixing the compost—six parts pine bark, one part pumice, one part sieved peat, one part charcoal. I'm chopping green sphagnum moss, melting agar, or setting up UV lamps to irradiate meristems. Shin is laying cut orchid canes on damp sand to let plantlets develop from their dormant eyes. His movements are uncomplicated and tender. His body is divine, like a curve of a flower.

I began to desire him from the moment I met him, although my feelings toward him back then, in those early days, were naive and childlike, not unlike that of a young student falling in love with her first-year professor. I spent my days thinking of little else but him. I could be riding my bike with Song, listening to her proverbs, lining up for morning assembly, or swimming in the bathhouse. I could be doing all of those things, and at the same time I would be thinking of him. On occasion I went further and created elaborate fantasies that involved him touching me intimately in the places I'd never let anyone touch me before. Never before had I thought of another person in such a racy, scandalous way. I'd have visions of thrusting hips, eager mouths, wet, penetrating flesh. Those strange, unfamiliar feelings confused me. It was like the slow burn of a dynamite fuse. The spark kept on running toward the detonator, with nothing to prevent the blow.

Through it all, I tried to reason with myself, cognizant of my naïveté. I tried, for example, to ascribe my sudden desire for Shin to boredom. He was, I told myself, the most exciting person I'd met in a month. It was perfectly natural that I'd be drawn to him. He knew so much about the plants. He was always friendly toward me. He treated me like an equal, unlike the other North Koreans I'd met in Pyongyang. The others had treated me as if I were an invasive species, threatening their natural habitat. But not Shin. Never Shin. He never, not once, made me feel wrong. Nor was he impatient with my questions. He was calm, kind to me, sometimes almost indulgent. He was also incredibly good-looking. Yes, there was that.

I watched him care for the most capricious orchids, responding to their every whim. In my mind, he embodied their complexity. He understood their souls. I'd heard him speak once to a pair of *Cypripedium* species, one yellow, one strikingly blue. In many ways he reminded me of my father, and perhaps that was the main reason I was drawn to him.

In the canteen every morning, Song and I got two lunch packages in paper bags. On most days, our lunches consisted of corn porridge packed into paper cups. We'd wash those down with green tea around noon in the courtyard, if it wasn't raining, or walk down to the pond to sit under the willow tree. Sometimes Shin joined us, and Song would take over the conversation completely, asking him trivial questions about plant structure and growth. How does the vascular tissue system develop? What are meristems? If humans could capture the energy of light, would humans look like plants? He'd indulge her by not answering her questions directly but rather inviting her to explore the questions herself. He was incredibly gracious about it, I thought, patient and warm.

In the greenhouse, Song watched closely over everything I did. I'd had time by then to grow used to her ever-present company, and even begun to welcome it. She was, after all, the only person I could talk to about my feelings, although it had taken me a while to come around to actually doing it. I couldn't talk to my father. Not in the open, in any case. Even though I saw him every second Wednesday for dinner at the Red Lantern, we were never left alone. Comrade Park was always with us, watching us closely and listening to our every word. He'd made it abundantly clear that I'd be allowed to work in the Botanical Gardens as long as I behaved myself. And so I did. At those dinners I tried to show myself at my best. Sometimes going overboard even, pretending to be a diligent worker, a good student, an expert noodle eater—the whole lot.

It might sound strange, but despite my initial impression, I'd come to be quite fond of Comrade Park, as one might become fond of a piece of ugly furniture that got more benign-looking with time. Indeed, there was something almost endearing in his squeaky white sneakers and overblown Party talk. He could sit through an entire meal in silence, gazing moodily into his soup, but then he'd raise his finger suddenly to interrupt me and ask me a question about orchids, which was often well thought out.

What did we talk about at those dinners? My work, of course. The Botanical Gardens. Shin's name came up a few times. My father never spoke of his work, except to say that it was progressing as well as it should. But for the most part, our talk revolved around the Party, as Comrade Park updated us on its historic achievements and Kim Jong Il's on-the-spot guidance in the farmers' fields.

One Wednesday, three weeks after I met Shin, Comrade Park announced that there was to be a labour mobilization. In October of each year, he told me, dedicated workers from the Botanical Gardens went to the country to collect medicinal plants. The work usually lasted two to three weeks, sometimes longer, and brought in a bounty of herbal remedies. The most prized crop, however, were the roots of ginseng. Did I wish to join the work brigade? As a guest of his great country, I wasn't obliged to do so, but perhaps in the shared spirit of Communist labour it would be advisable that I went. Comrade Shin would be leading our party, as he had the most experience with the fieldwork.

I pretended to think it over for a few moments, and then said, "Okay."

Comrade Park laughed. "That's the spirit! It's settled, then. Make sure you pack warm clothes. You'll be provided with standard-issue padded jackets, but the weather is unpredictable up in the mountains, farther up north. Last year, middle school students from Wŏnsan were snowed in near Ulim waterfalls. They would've frozen to death if it weren't for the infinite kindness of the Great Leader who saved them."

SONG DID NOT seem too excited about the prospect of our trip to the country, as she'd gone on many trips like it in the past. In North Korea, she told me later, all students from elementary school onward were expected to help out with the harvest in the countryside. For my part, I was looking forward to our trip for several reasons, not the least of which was Shin. Of course, I welcomed the chance to see the native plants in the field: that was perfectly true. But if I had to be honest, I hoped most of all that while we were there we'd be able to spend time together, just the two of us, without Song.

Why did I think he'd be interested in me? After all, he hadn't given me any indication to that effect. His demeanour toward me had been always courteous, but strictly professional too. Only — one day in the greenhouse, I forgot myself. As he was working near me, I stared unguardedly at him until he looked up and met my gaze. He smiled then, shook his head slightly, and moved his chin toward my work. Was it my imagination or was he conscious of me too? I was afraid to even contemplate that question, unprepared for what it might mean.

The first week in the country, the weather was splendid. It was warm and bright. The sky was high and the air was honeyed with the scent of wild thyme. The light wind kissed the leaves off the tree branches, and then spiralled them through the air like strange crimson birds.

There were twenty-two of us in our work unit: eight females and fourteen males. The canvas-covered truck drove us from Pyongyang for three hours, on a paved highway first and then up a steep dirt road. We entered the mountainous region. It was bumpy. The crates, packed with food provisions, tents, and sleeping bags, kept sliding up and down the bed of the truck.

In the valley that separated Frog's Knee Mountain from the hill on which we set up camp was a village of twelve thatched huts, two silos, and a mill. On the other side of the hill the ground fell away into long slopes of rice fields and beyond them was a lake.

We came down to it on the first evening of our trip.

"The water is seasonal here," Shin told us. "Salt concentration varies with the fall of the rain. Spotted brown frogs used to breed here, but the locals caught them all for food. One especially dry year, the villagers tried to use the lake for shrimp farming, but they didn't know what they were doing, so nothing came of it." He laughed. "Some say the lake is enchanted. But I think it's just old wives' tales. It's an ancient lake, though, because trilobite fossils have been found on the bottom here, under the layer of silt."

I thought about his words the next morning, looking up at the sky. Clumps of mist sailed down from the mountains into the valley, making the land seem bewitched. Song and I crawled out of our tent into the milky air at daybreak to gather wood, boil water, and make corn gruel for everyone. It was through the cooking and dishing out of food that I'd got the most acknowledgement of my existence in North Korea. As I scooped spoonfuls of porridge into people's bowls, they smiled at me and nodded their heads, gesturing for me to give them more. Song, meanwhile, dispersed small cubes of sugar. Men installed those between their front teeth to drink tea through. Women ate their sugar differently, taking discreet little bites. Many of them didn't eat the sugar at all, but wrapped it carefully in their handkerchiefs.

After breakfast, we made our way up the mountain and deep into the woods, men carrying large canvas sacks and short, sharp-nosed spades. The woods, smelling of pine needles and sprinkled with yellow anemones, were lovely. Here and there, lily-of-the-valley nodded their bell-shaped heads. Brown-capped mushrooms peeked out of carpets of green moss.

The ginseng plants were highly sought after by locals, who bartered them for food, clothing, or cigarettes, but a man named Jung who had grown up in the area knew its secret locations and made a big difference to our quest.

"Look under the poplars for the companion plants," Song translated his instructions for me. "Jack-in-the-pulpit and bloodroot. These plants favour the same growth conditions — moist hardwoods and lots of shade. You want mature plants with three leaves and red berries, but examine the neck of the plants first. The neck must have five or more scars on it, from the previous years' growth."

When it came to digging the roots out, Jung showed me how to use a screwdriver to avoid damaging the adjacent plants. After carefully extracting the root from the soil, I'd call Shin over to show it to him. He'd approach slowly and crouch next to me to inspect the plant in my hand. If he found it satisfactory, he'd pluck the red berries off, squeeze them tightly in the palm of his hand to get the seeds out, and plant each one in the soil around the extracted root. In those moments I'd feel a swell of desire rising up from somewhere deep inside me, and I'd wish more than anything in the world that I were a red ginseng berry he was crushing in his hands.

But the work was exhausting. After returning to the

camp in the evening, men collapsed into sleep in their clothes. Women, meanwhile, laid out the gathered ginseng roots to dry on sheets of newspaper, and then came down to the lake to bathe.

The weather turned foul on Sunday. A fierce easterly wind blew in. Bruised clouds gathered above us, caking the sky with ashy paste. The pine trunks creaked in feeble protest, as gusts of wind tore at their tops. The lake, meanwhile, crusted over with a thin layer of ice. It threatened to snow.

As night fell, Song and I huddled together in one sleeping bag for warmth, and the following morning we swaddled our upper bodies in additional layers of clothing and donned padded peasant pants.

On Monday evening, upon returning to camp from the mountains, we found two local men roasting what looked like a piglet on a spit. Upon closer inspection, the piglet turned out to be a skinned dog with short, wiry legs. A terrier of some kind, I thought. A gift to our work brigade from the village, Song said. The men from the village had also brought home-brewed rice wine, in exchange for our help with the rice harvest, which due to the abrupt change in weather had to be completed quickly, before the snow came.

The rice wine turned out to be very tasty. It was brewed with a blend of traditional spices, Song said. Lychee wolfberry, and yarrow, among other things. Consumed on an empty stomach, it spread its magnificent cheer through my bloodstream in no time at all, and unable to stand the smell of roasted meat any longer, I caved in and wolfed down a piece of dog meat. It tasted like chicken. It was pretty good.

The following morning, blowing warm air into our mittens and stamping our feet, we came down the hill into the village and were given steel blades. The mechanical thresher was under repair and no one knew how long it might take to fix it. We'd have to cut the rice plants off the ground and use the ox-driven cart to bring them up to the mill.

The sun made a reluctant appearance as we spread out over the field. I bent over the rice plants, gathered the stalks in my hand, and tried to cut through them with my blade. The blade, though, was as blunt as a wood plank, and after three hours of trying to work with it, my back felt like a stiff board that had been stuffed with nails.

I sat on the ground to rest when there came the noise of a sputtering engine and shortly a mechanical thresher appeared on the top of the hill. It moved its bulk down the road, spewing black plumes of burned diesel and tooting its horn. We cheered, ran to it, and began to throw the cut plants into it to separate the grain from the stalks.

We worked fast as we had been promised a decent meal at the end of the day. The farmers would give us eight cups of freshly threshed rice in payment for our help. Song was beside herself with excitement and practically skipped her way up the hill back to camp. The men made a quick fire and sat around it, watching the women cook rice. After eating, more sated than any of us remembered being in a very long time, we gathered around the bonfire in silence, watching a slice of moon climb into the dark sky.

At some point, a group of young people, apparently energized by the rice, began to jump over the fire, calling out to the others to try. Soon they began to compete with each other, and Song joined in the fun.

Shin came to sit next to me and handed me a cup of green tea.

"It's going to snow tonight," he said. "We can't risk the ginseng turning mouldy. I sent a message via the radio. They're coming to pick us up."

"We go back to Pyongyang tomorrow?"

"I doubt it will be tomorrow. It'll take them longer to get here, over the mountains, in this weather, but soon in any case."

A shout to our right made us turn in that direction. A man with his pants on fire was rolling on the ground, hollering wildly for help. The others ran to him, yanked off their jackets, and began to beat down the flames.

Song came over to us.

"What are you doing?" she asked.

Shin raised his eyes to her.

"The lake is freezing over," he said. "We should go for a skate."

"Skate?" Song cried. "The ice is too thin. You'll fall through and drown. Or get hypothermia. No way. I'm responsible for her." She pointed to me and then batted her lashes flirtatiously at him. "Comrade Shin, please, no."

"The lake is shallow." Shin got up to his feet. "The locals skate all winter long on it, and nobody has drowned yet. I'll go down to the village to see what I can find." He looked at me. "What's your size?"

"Seven," I said cheerfully. "I love skating. I used to skate with my mother in Moscow when I was a little girl."

"It's settled, then." He smiled at me and turned to Song. "And you?"

"I'll watch," she said.

He shrugged his shoulders, glanced at me, and walked off.

That night, I couldn't sleep from excitement. Song snored next to me. She lay on her side with her mouth open and her hand stuck under her cheek. Provided that Shin found skates for us in the village and the ice on the lake held, he'd be impressed with my skating ability, I was sure of it. That would be great. But what a fool I'd been for boasting that I loved skating, that I had skated when I was a little girl. Because, if I hadn't, he wouldn't have known it, in which case he might have to hold my hand. He'd have to guide me when we stepped on the ice together, perhaps even catch me in his arms. God! What was I thinking? I was mad at myself for being hasty, for lacking the foresight to moderate myself.

The next morning, as word reached us that a truck was coming from Pyongyang to get us, Shin presented me with a pair of black, battered skates. Size eight.

"Another pair of socks should solve the size problem," he grinned.

"When you do fall through the ice," Song said, yawning, "I might get you out. Then again, I might not. But in any case, I'm looking forward to the satisfaction of saying 'I told you so.'"

After dinner, in the gathering darkness, the three of us came down to the lake. Shin walked down to a cluster of cattails and cut off three long stalks. Then he brought out a small jar from his pocket, scooped some wax out, and smeared it over each sausage-shaped spike. He lit a match, set one spike on fire, and handed it to Song.

"We can use them as torches. Hold it up high so we can see."

In no time, I laced up my skates.

"How do they fit?" Shin asked me.

"Great," I lied.

"Go ahead, then." Shin passed a torch to me. "I'll follow you."

I stepped onto the ice. Slowly, stretching my free arm out for balance, I began to glide. Tentatively at first, but soon surer and faster. The ice crackled here and there under my blades. My muscles remembered the strides, despite the fact that the skates were too big. I wasn't afraid. It was shallow here. I could see through the ice all the way to the bottom by the light of the flame in my hand. The blades were blunt and rusty, but I managed to carve curlicue scars in the ice. In the stillness of night I thought I heard my mother's voice calling to me. "Bend your knees, Verochka. Push sideways. Find your rhythm. One and two. One and two. One and two and three."

After making three wide circles around the lake, I felt brave enough to launch into a spinning spiral. Shin wasn't good at skating, but he could stand on his feet. He hobbled over to me.

"Can you do that again?" he said. "That spiral. I want to see you do it again."

"Yes," I said, and repeated it again. And again. And again.

Song marched along the shoreline, watching us and waving her torch.

"Can you come closer?" she yelled. "I can't see you! Skate closer to the shore!"

"Listen," Shin said as I came to a stop next to him. "When we get back to Pyongyang, we will be separated again. What I mean is, we won't be able to talk. With

Song always present, we won't be able to talk like this." He refocused his eyes on me through his glasses for a moment and let his torch down, away from his face. "But the thing is — there are so many things I want to say to you. I wonder if you know what I mean."

"I don't like it that you're so far away!" Song yelled from the shore. "I don't like it one little bit!"

I hesitated. I didn't know what to say. My heart pounded in my chest. I waited to see if he'd continue talking, if he'd say something else, when in the light of his lowered torch I noticed a dark clump under the ice. Bending down over it and bringing my own torch closer to it, I saw that it was a frog, frozen under the ice. Its legs were contracted, as if it had just landed after a jump. The creature was brown in colour, with large, bulging eyes.

"Look!" I cried in surprise, pointing toward the frog and dropping my torch on the ice.

He bent over too quickly to pick it up. For a moment he wobbled on his skates, looking for balance, and, finding none, he collapsed on the ice. Turning awkwardly on his side, he managed to slide toward the torch and lift it off the ice. His glasses, I was happy to see, were still perched on his nose. He came up to his knees, brushed the snow off his chest, and leaned over the ice to look at the frog.

"Frogs are cold-blooded animals," he said. "They can't control their body heat. The weather changes, they change with it. I've seen experiments like these."

"Experiments? Where?"

"In the Botanical Gardens. Scientists from the Academy come sometimes to freeze frogs in our pond. They say they are interested in organ preservation because human organs do not last very long. If you freeze human organs, they lose water rapidly, get damaged quickly, and die. But without the freezing there's decomposition, so the organs can't be used for transplants. Frogs don't die, however, when they freeze. They enter a state of suspended animation."

"How do they manage it? Doesn't ice break their cells?"

"Most cells, yes. Human cells. But frogs have special proteins. These proteins cause the water in their blood to freeze first. Meanwhile, the frog's liver begins to make large amounts of sugar. The frog's cells become crystals of honey. If you were to eat this one right now, it would be very sweet."

I was astonished.

"Human beings don't make sugar after they die," I said. "Which is why their cells break."

He nodded. "Which is also why humans get frostbite." He reached for my fingers. "See what I mean? We'd better get you some tea."

"I don't appreciate it," Song shouted from the shore, "when you ignore me! What's the matter with Comrade Shin? Why is he sitting? My torch will go out soon. If we can't see where we're going, how are we supposed to find our way back?"

"Comrade Shin is all right, Song!" I shouted back to her. "Just a few more turns!"

Shin said, "Anyway, forget what I said. It doesn't matter. In Pyongyang, we'll still see each other in the greenhouse, yes? But we won't be able to skate there, so let's do it right now." He stood up and took my hand.

What a feeling it was to skate there, together, above the sweet brown frog encased in the ice. In the sky above us

I could see smudges of light. Were those meteor showers? Shooting stars? Spy satellites? I didn't know and I didn't care. We were together and he was holding my hand.

The next morning, in the back of an army truck, as we were bumping down the frozen road, I parted the canvas curtains to take a last look at the countryside. In my heart I knew that I'd never return here, and for some reason it made me terribly sad. There were some things in life you never forgot, and skating above frozen frogs by the light of cattail torches was one of them. I tried to imagine what would happen to the frozen frog in the spring when the weather changed. The warm air will come up from the south. The ice will melt. The water will rush back into the frog's cells and heat up its blood. The frog will reanimate and resume living as if nothing has happened to it at all. Amazing! If only things were that simple with humans. If only people could reanimate like that.

7

In the days following our return from the countryside, my work in the orchid greenhouse continued as before. Shin seemed indifferent to me, preoccupied with his chores, a strictly professional comrade again. My conversations with him were all work-related and limited to the necessities of the day. It was as though we'd never skated together, gazed at each other over the bonfire, or held trembling hands. He seemed so distant with me, so unfeeling, and less inclined to respond to my questions, I thought. Perhaps he'd been warned against becoming too friendly with me. Perhaps our attraction, or rather what I had so foolishly made out of it, was a figment of my juvenile imagination. I simply didn't know.

As one day leaked into another, and a month passed since we'd come back from the countryside, I'd accepted the fact that nothing would ever happen between us and sunk back into my work. It was for the best, I decided, and even began to feel slightly ashamed of myself. Romancing a North Korean? What was I thinking? How could that ever work?

By the end of November, Song and I had settled into a routine. October's orange foliage gave way to browns and greys. The ground turned liver-coloured, the grass frosted away. The rose bushes had been covered up with canvas sacks, and the Hall of the Arids had been locked. The daylight seemed tired, washed out, like an ancient linen sheet. On most days we worked until dusk, sometimes later, and then rode back to campus with flashlights clipped to the bars of our bikes. By then we'd found another way into the Gardens, and the guards there were friendly toward us. Song had buttered them up with cubes of sugar and cigarettes, procured from where, I didn't know. She smoked cigarettes herself sometimes, and on a few occasions I smoked with her. Her face changed when she smoked, I noticed, becoming much less of the Party Song's face. Perhaps in the nicotine she tasted freedom: she seemed a lot more capable of independent thought.

One time, we were having lunch by the pond. She brought a pack of Russian cigarettes out of her pocket and held it out to me.

"I got these especially for you," she said. "Please have one."

I'd experimented with smoking as a teenager, but it had never caught on. Besides, it was an awful brand of tobacco. Nonetheless, not wanting to appear ungrateful, I extracted one reluctantly from the pack.

"I was just thinking about my mother," I said, watching her strike a match. "There's a park in Moscow. It has a pond, just like this one. My mother used to take me for walks there when I was small. We'd have lemonade or ice cream, and just sit on the bench and watch people go by." I leaned over to her to light my cigarette. "She invented this game where we had to decide which famous person someone resembled, or in what historical era they might fit best. There was one woman who fed the swans. Her name was Fiona, but she looked exactly like Catherine the Great. Another man looked like Einstein, yet another like Stalin himself. My mother said that everything, even people, repeated over time. That everything and everyone returned in some way."

Song tapped the ash from her cigarette. The smoke drifted into the space between us and then dissolved into the air like a ghost.

"You wish to return to your mother," she said.

"I suppose so, or, rather, I wished for her to be returned to me. It's funny that when I was a kid I was keenly aware of her holding my hand. Kids never think about that. About holding hands with their parents, I mean. It's the most natural thing in the world. But I did think about it. Even then. I must've known that something was going to happen to her, and that I wouldn't get to hold hands with her for very long. You know?"

She didn't reply for a while, but leaned back on her

elbows and took her time exhaling smoke through her nose.

"Today is my birthday," she said. "But it isn't a big deal. Birthdays are not celebrated here. The Party discourages it. But one year, when I turned ten years old, my mother did give me a special gift. It was a tortoiseshell that had been in her family for generations, and that her own mother had given to her when she turned ten. The shell was meant to remind me how fortunate I was to have been born. Because most people, you see, do not get to live at all."

"What do you mean?"

"Just what I said. Most people never get born. Genetically speaking. To have us, our parents combine their genes in just one way. But all other millions of possible gene combinations never make it. And yet those that are born don't appreciate their own specialness. They waste their time doing stupid things. Worrying about trivialities. But I wonder—if what you were talking about was true and everything and everyone did return in some way, where would I fit in? Who would I have been in history? Whom would I repeat?"

ONE FRIDAY, AT the end of November, I was sitting at my work table and mixing compost. Shin walked toward me carrying a dropper of acid. It was unusual for him to approach me. Customarily, if I had a question or wanted to consult him about something, I'd go to him. At eight o'clock that morning we'd had our usual meeting in his office and gone over the plan for that day. It was two in the afternoon now. Song, perched on her stool within earshot, was cleaning her nails with a paper clip.

"Comrade Vera, it's advisable to have the water ana-lyzed," Shin whispered to me. "If the local supply is too alkaline, some method of shifting it to the acidic side must be arranged." And before I knew what was happening, he'd clasped my hand under the table, brought it to his lips, and kissed the inside of my wrist.

I gasped, but had the presence of mind not to cry out.

Song appeared at our side.

"What's happening?"

"I was just telling Comrade Vera that I've found the book she was looking for," Shin said, holding my gaze. "I'll leave it on the desk in my office. Please come to get it there at the end of the day."

He nodded at Song slightly and walked away.

I resumed mixing the compost, willing myself to remain calm. My thoughts raced. My heart thundered inside my chest. I had no idea what to make of what had just happened. What to make of his kiss. I looked down. My knees were shaking, my hands were trembling, and sweat beaded on my forehead.

Song was watching me.

"What book were you looking for?"

I had to think quickly. "The one on clonal multiplication. It describes the new technique of tissue culture that—"

But she'd grown bored already. She yawned.

"Okay." She went back to her nails.

It was excruciating to wait until the end of the day to go to his office.

"Wait here," I instructed Song when the radio chimed five o'clock. I was hoping beyond all hope that for once she'd leave me alone.

"Wait." She jumped off the stool. "I'll go with you. I must go with you wherever you go."

Shin's office was empty. The door stood ajar. The desk was strewn with handwritten notes and orchid drawings, coloured crayons and metal spatulas. A book lay in the middle, bookmarked with a pen.

The Collected Works of Charles Darwin.

I flipped it open.

A passage was underlined in blue ink:

It is certain that with most of our common Orchids insects are absolutely necessary for their fertilization; for without their agency, the pollen-masses are never removed and wither within their pouches.

The text came from the *Fertilization of Orchids*, which Shin knew that I knew well. There was no doubt in my mind what he'd meant by it, after what had happened that afternoon.

"What is it?" Song asked me, peeking over my shoulder. I had to think on my feet.

I turned to her.

"Now I remember." I slapped my forehead. "It's Darwin. Comrade Shin and I had a debate about him." I lifted the book from the desk to show her the cover. "We argued about his description of certain — molecular mimicry. I see Comrade Shin was right about it. He proved me wrong, yet again. He underlined the right passage, you see here, like that." I hesitated, looking around the office, unsure what to do next. "If you give me a moment" — I turned back to the desk and picked up the red crayon — "I have to make a note for him to let him know that I understood what he meant."

Quickly, I flipped a page forward to find what I was looking for. How brilliant it was of him, I thought, how perfectly brilliant to use the text I knew so well to communicate with me.

I took a deep breath to steady my hand and underlined the following passage:

> We now come to the Bee Orchid (Ophrys apifera), which presents a very different case. We must admit that the natural falling out of the pollen-masses of this Orchid demands a special contrivance.

There! That was my response. If I were right about his meaning, and there was no doubt in my mind that I was, then my reply should encourage him, but also convey my understanding of the dangers involved. After all, I didn't want to appear too eager. Or too stupid. I knew better than that.

The bike ride back to campus was like a blur. In my mind's eye, I kept seeing Shin kissing my wrist. Song, meanwhile, whistled a cheerful tune and pedalled ahead of me. She'd scored a Marlboro cigarette from a guard at the main gates and was looking forward to smoking it in our room. How could she be so carefree? I thought, looking at her. How could she not see that the world had changed for me?

THE FOLLOWING AFTERNOON, Shin came down the aisle with a touch of concern on his face.

"Comrade Song" — he spoke to Song in Russian, clearly for my benefit — "I need your help with something very important. It's about the sphagnum moss. I don't quite know how it happened, but we're getting low on it right now. As you might know, our work with *Calanthe sylvatica* is very important, perhaps the most important work we do. If it were any other plants, I could do without the moss for maybe a week, but with the *Calanthes* I simply cannot. I'm in the middle of an important experiment at the moment, and" — he looked at what I was doing— "Comrade Vera seems to have just started hers. It's therefore you whom I must ask to go to the warehouse and fetch me a bag of moss. I understand there was a shipment this morning—"

Song didn't let him finish.

"I can't leave her." She shook her head. "You know this, Comrade Shin. My instructions are very clear. I'm never to leave Comrade Vera on her own."

Shin swallowed. "I realize that. But this is an emergency. I'm sure the Party will understand. Do you have any idea how long it took us to cultivate the *Calanthes*? Five years! And, as you might know, these particular flowers were beloved of Kim Il Sung. If they die because you refused to help me, how do you think the Party might react?"

It was a load of baloney. The *Calanthes* could wait for the moss for a week, even for two. But Song didn't know that. She hesitated. I could see the torment she was going through as she decided what to do. If she were to leave me, she could get in trouble. But if the flowers died, it might be far, far worse for her.

At last she made a decision. The only decision she could've made.

"Fine," she said, her face flushed with resentment. "I'll go. But I want you to know that in my report this evening I'll express my full concern."

"As you should," Shin said calmly. "Indeed, I encourage you to do so. Now. When you get to the warehouse, give Comrade Ting this note from me." He handed her a slip of paper. "And while you're there, if you don't mind, please collect some dung. A bag or two will suffice for the moment. Take the wheelbarrow out front."

We looked at each other the moment she disappeared down the aisle. The warehouse was a ten-minute walk away. With a wheelbarrow, it might take her longer to get there, to say nothing of getting back.

Stepping toward me, Shin whispered, "I sent everyone else away."

I got off my chair.

In the silence that followed Song's footsteps, we stood facing each other, afraid to breathe. Outside, we heard her lifting up the wheelbarrow and then pushing it down the hill.

"Come here," I said, stretching my hand toward him. "Be with me."

He started but paused, as if thinking it over, then moved quickly toward me and took my face in his hands. He kissed me. It was a chaste kiss at first, tentative even, but then I felt the tip of his tongue.

How long did we kiss? I didn't know. I didn't care. I never wanted it to stop.

But it did stop.

There was a sound, a bang, like a clap, outside. We heard voices. Footsteps approached and walked past, disappearing somewhere beyond the courtyard.

I turned from him then, blushed deeply, and ran my hand through my ponytail in dismay.

We stood apart for a moment, an ocean between us. I thought my heart would explode.

The heat and humidity clung to us. When everything became quiet again, he reached for my ponytail, took a hold of my hair, and slowly released it from its elastic band.

I shook out my hair. It fell to my shoulders. He ran his fingers through my hair, then suddenly let me go.

No! I screamed in silence. Not now! Not ever! Do not let me go!

He turned to the right, toward his office, but instead of walking away, he began to clear a space on the bench, moving the orchid pots around and lowering them to the floor. When a space large enough to hold both of us had opened up, he pulled me forward and kissed me again, deeper, rougher this time, and with new urgency. Sliding his hands down, he touched me now through the fabric of my skirt, tugging it up and sliding his fingers under it.

I closed my eyes. How does it feel to be loved like that?

Afterward, he clung to me for a long time in silence, as if he too was afraid to let me go.

"I love you," I whispered. "I've loved you since the day we met."

He turned me, kissed my eyes, and wiped the sweat off my forehead.

I leaned into his shoulder as one leans into the light.

"What are we going to do now?" I asked.

"We carry on."

"I want to do it again."

"We must be careful."

He kissed me again.

"Tell me," he said, "how did you know what the messages I left for you in the Darwin book meant?"

"I didn't know for sure," I admitted. "Only hoped."

We heard voices outside.

Quickly, we separated.

"We'd better arrange ourselves," he said. "What would Comrade Song think?"

He tucked his shirt back into his pants, smoothed his hair, and began to move the orchid pots back up on the shelf. I straightened my clothes, retied my hair, then walked to the sink in the corner and wiped myself off. Outside, the light seemed to have tilted, become denser, as if weighted down with lead. My body felt strange, unfamiliar, as though it were a stick of butter, dropped into a saucepan to melt.

"We communicate through books from now on," Shin said when I walked back to him. "You can circle letters in red pencil to spell out words for me. I'll do the same in blue. I use erasable crayons for floral drawings, so you can erase my messages after you read them. Song may become suspicious if we use the same book all of the time, so let's alternate them. I'll arrange the books up on the shelf in my office in the order we should use them, okay? We'll start with the book to the left of Darwin and move on to the next in line after that."

The door to the greenhouse rattled. Song was coming back.

"Vera." Shin squeezed my fingers. "Listen to me. I've been thinking. I have narcoleptic drugs, plant extracts.

They're quite harmless but have powerful temporary effects. If you want to — if you'd be able to, you could give some to Song."

"Do you mean to make her sleep? How?"

"She drinks tea, doesn't she? She boils water for it on the electric stove. You'll have to mix the drugs in."

"When?"

"Tomorrow if you want to. Or the day after tomorrow. Whenever you think you'd be able to. Look under the pot next to your desk. I'll mark it with something. A piece of tape."

"What about the others?"

"The others?"

"The other people who work here? What about them? We can't make all of them sleep, can we?"

"I'll give them other tasks. I'll send them away —"

Song shouted, "Hello there!"

We leapt apart.

In an instant she was beside us, holding her hands on her hips.

"There wasn't any moss in the warehouse," she said pointedly to Shin. "A shipment is coming next week. Comrade Ting was rather surprised you didn't know that. He said he'd gone over the schedule with you last week."

"I see." Shin adjusted his glasses. "I must've written the wrong date by mistake."

She was watching us suspiciously, taking in our crumpled clothes.

"Comrade Vera was just helping me to repot some plants," Shin said. "We had to move heavy things around."

Song's face darkened. "I bet."

There was a silence. It was important to change the subject quickly. But for the life of me I couldn't think of anything to say.

Shin cleared his throat. "Did you get the dung, Comrade? We really need the dung."

"Yes, I did," Song said, somewhat testily. "Practically broke my ankle doing it, too. Slipping and sliding with that awful barrow, loaded with a pile of shit."

I burst out laughing. Song gave me a murderous look.

"Very well, then. Thank you, Comrade Song," Shin said. "You've done us all a great service. I'll commend your dedication to the Party, you can be sure of that." He turned to me. "And I thank you, Comrade Vera, also. Your assistance was much appreciated this afternoon."

And with that, he withdrew to his office, leaving a hole in my heart.

8

That night, I wasn't able to sleep a wink. I lay flat on my back wide awake, listening to the blood pounding through my veins. When I closed my eyes, I smelled vanilla on his fingers or felt his lips on the back of my neck. All night long I fretted, pining for Shin. I was also afraid. Afraid of what our love meant. For me, for my father, but most of all for Shin. It was exhausting, and by the morning I was drained of all feeling because of a migraine. I willed myself to get up and carry on with my day, just as Shin had said: *We carry on.* Everything would be okay, I told myself, because on Monday I would see him again.

When Song and I arrived at the greenhouse on Monday, however, Shin wasn't there. He'd been sent away. For how long? I asked one of the workers. He didn't know. The coal-fired engine needed repair. Comrade Shin had gone out to take care of it.

I sat at my work table that Monday, dipping my fingers mindlessly in methanol. It was strange to think that a small gulp of that water-like liquid could blind me or, worse, strike me dead. There it swished in the flask, so innocent-looking. I lifted the flask off the table and held it up to the light. Suddenly, I was tempted to try it, to drink it, to see what would happen to me if I did. What would it actually feel like to start dying? Would I be in terrible pain? I knew how things would work biochemically, which enzymes would be shut down and so on. But what would it actually feel like to have poison work on my body? What would the last moment of living be like?

Dear God, I caught myself thinking. I was going insane.

To my right, Song was perched on her stool, flipping through a magazine. She must've sensed me looking at her, because she raised her eyes to me.

"Something's the matter?" she asked me.

I shook my head, turned back to my work table, and began scheming at once. Shin had proposed that I mix drugs in Song's tea to make her sleep. For how long? It depended on the dose, I supposed. We'd work out the details later, he told me, but for now, in his absence, I decided to try an experiment to investigate just how easy it might be to drop something into her cup.

While we were having lunch in the greenhouse, I pointed to a small red-chested bird in the courtyard. It was hopping around, chirp-chirping, and leaving tracks in the snow.

"What kind of bird is it?" I asked her.

She spun around to look. I stretched my hand over her teacup and imitated dropping something into it.

"A robin," she said, growing thoughtful. "No, maybe a finch of some kind. Are there any red-chested finches? I don't know, but it looks very fine."

Suddenly, the bird fell silent and tilted its head to one side. A shadow moved across the snow, and the bird gave out a shrill cry.

"A squirrel must have frightened it," Song said, disappointed. "What a pretty little bird it was."

She brought the teacup to her lips and emptied it.

I smiled to myself.

I had to wait a whole week yet to drug her for real, because that's how long it took for Shin to return. The worst day of all was that Wednesday, when I had another dinner with my father and had to pretend that all was well. The sight of the cold noodles stirred up such potent nausea inside me that I had to excuse myself. Song came with me to the bathroom and stood waiting for me on the other side of the stall. At least they had doors in the bathroom stalls in that restaurant. What a relief that was! When the nausea subsided, and we returned to the dining hall, all I wished for was to go back to our dorm.

When Shin was away, I despaired. My thoughts began to travel down unhappy paths. I replayed the scene of my lovemaking with Shin over and over in my mind, until our love turned. It became something disgraceful, dirty, something to be ashamed of. What would my father and grandmother say about it? What would my mother say?

But when Shin came back, I felt better. We talked via books. In his first message he told me he was very sorry he'd been called away. He also reminded me of his promise to leave the narcoleptic drugs in the designated place. He wasn't sure how Song would respond to them, so we had to be careful and wait. The first time, tomorrow, I should give her a very small dose. We'd watch her to see what happened and then adjust the dose.

Shortly after lunch the next day, Song began to sway sleepily on her stool. I said to her, "You look tired. Maybe you need a nap. Why don't you use my table. I won't tell anyone, okay? I'm tired too, actually. I can use a nap myself." I yawned to emphasize it.

"Thank you," she said eagerly, "but please don't tell anyone about this. I don't know what's wrong with me, honestly." She squeezed onto the bench beside me and laid her head on her hands. "I'll just lie down here for a bit. Just for a short little while."

In less than a minute, she fell into what looked like a deep sleep. She even began to snore. I looked at my watch, then let my hair out and ran to Shin's office.

He was at his desk.

"It worked," I said.

We embraced.

"We can't stay here," he said after a moment. "We need to time her today."

We walked back to my work table, holding hands.

We watched her for a minute, then turned to each other and began to kiss. Song gave a small cry and shifted. Her head rolled off her arm. Her cheek, squished and pushed up by the table, gave her a comical look. She smacked her lips a few times and went back to sleep.

"What happened last Friday—" Shin whispered, gazing into my eyes. "I can't offer you anything, I'm afraid."

"Other than sex, you mean?"

He looked hurt at that.

"No. That's not—You must understand. You're a foreigner here. You don't know how things work. I can't offer you anything because I am—" He clenched his jaw. "Because I'm poor. You must understand that."

I reached for him, held him closer, kissed him again.

"My love," I said. "That doesn't matter to me. That doesn't matter to me at all."

SONG SLEPT FOR fifteen minutes the first time, and after that Shin upped her dose. Thereafter, she'd sleep for a half or full hour, but never more than once a week. Shin was concerned that if we did it more often, she might become groggy, or have other side effects, which would inevitably make her suspicious and put a stop to our tête-à-têtes. On the days she wasn't sleeping, Shin and I communicated via books, and in that manner we told each other many things about our lives. I'd been so busy loving him during that month that I hadn't the time to pause and think about what I was doing, or how it all might end. I was naive. Perhaps foolhardy. But the truth also was that I didn't want to think about any of it. I wanted to live and love him in the moment because I knew that it wouldn't, or couldn't, last for long. I'd be leaving Pyongyang in five months. I must confess also that occasional doubts about Shin did cross my mind. Why had he chosen me? I wondered. What had he found attractive in me? But when those doubts arose, I forced them away. Everything was too alive, too vibrant, for any doubts to take root in my mind just then. An entirely new life seemed to have opened up before me, and I was determined to let it bloom.

Meanwhile, incredibly, my work went on. Somehow I managed to do important research. I'd discovered, for instance, that the infection with *Agrobacterim* could induce orchids' roots to grow. And I'd identified three phenolic compounds in the *Dendrobium* leaves that transformed their shoots. Every day there were seedlings to plant, plates of agar to pour, and lipids to analyze. By all appearances, then, my routine hadn't changed all that much, except now there was the centre to it, around which everything else revolved. Like a meristem of a plant from which all of its organs develop, this centre, my love for Shin, controlled everything. I felt it inside every cell of my body, in every molecule and every protein.

I wondered sometimes if Song could see the change in me. Surely anyone could. When I looked at myself in the mirror, I could see a distinct glow. Or perhaps it was all in my imagination, a reflection of how I felt on the inside. But no, there were real, physical changes that seemed to grow more pronounced with each passing day. I'd become stouter, solider somehow, although my diet hadn't changed. I felt hungrier than I'd ever felt in my life and ate more in the canteen. It must be hormonal, I figured; with all the sex I'd been having, my metabolism had understandably changed. Song, amazingly, didn't seem to think much of my new appetite. She was preoccupied with her own thoughts in those days, anyway. Worried, she told me, about some aunt's illness back home.

One day at breakfast, I must've daydreamed for too long, because, startled by the sudden quiet around me, I looked up to see Song staring at me over her bowl.

"What's up?" I asked her moodily.

She was silent for a moment, and then asked me, "What do you think of Comrade Shin?"

The question came as a shock to me.

I swallowed.

"He's great. Very helpful in my work."

"Do you find him attractive?"

"What?" I pretended to laugh. "Of course not. He's my supervisor." I drummed my fingers on the table. "He's taught me a lot."

"Well, I think he's very handsome. I have fantasies about him."

She was looking straight at me, without blinking. It was unnerving.

I said, "Really? What kind of fantasies? Do tell."

She smiled. "Like he's my husband. We live together. I make food for him. We take care of each other. We have five kids."

For some reason that made me very angry, but it was important not to let her see that she'd upset me.

"I see," I said breezily. "Maybe he secretly loves you. Maybe your little fantasy will come true. You'll get married to him and have lots of children together. I truly wish that for you."

I hated myself for saying it, especially the "truly" bit.

She lowered her eyes into her bowl for a moment, and then looked up at me again.

"Duck egg in a wide river," she said.

"What?"

"It's an ancient saying. The egg is so small, so alone, so stupid to jump in a wide river like that. Does the egg not realize in what terrible danger it puts itself?"

Panic gripped me. Did she know something, or—

"And you think I'm the egg, then?" I managed to say after a long moment.

She smiled again.

"Maybe you. Maybe me. Maybe no one. I don't know why I suddenly thought of that. As my grandmother used to say, Comrade Vera, it is darkest underneath the lamp."

EVERY SECOND WEDNESDAY, my dinners with my father continued at the Red Lantern. We talked about safe subjects, of course: my work in the greenhouse, the orchids, the biking in the snow, and the botanical museum. Shin's name came up once when Comrade Park asked me if I was happy with my supervisor. I said yes, very much. Comrade Shin was an excellent scientist. I was so lucky to work with him.

How I wished I could talk to my father! Really talk to him. Tell him everything. It wasn't easy to sit there and pretend everything was okay. I felt that by being silent I was betraying my father in some small but important way. It was not a nice feeling. But what could I do? Nothing. I could not tell him anything. Because I knew that the moment I did, my work in the Gardens would be finished. It would be all over for me and Shin. So I sat there, ate noodles, laughed at Comrade Park's jokes, embraced my father when the time came for us to part, and said goodbye, waving my hand.

Meanwhile, my father looked increasingly worn out. I watched him with a heavy heart. I decided that even if I were able to tell him about my love for Shin, I had no right to add more stress to his life. When we got back to Moscow, I'd tell him everything.

One Tuesday when December was almost over, and Shin and I had been lovers for a month, we were lying on the floor in his office and he told me his brother was dead.

"What happened to him?"

"He served in the navy. One night there was a terrible storm. They were in the open ocean. In the middle of it, he tried to secure something to the deck. He fell overboard and drowned. They didn't even try to rescue him."

He rolled over on his stomach, and I saw welts on his back. He told me he'd got them in the army. They'd whipped him with leather straps. He'd questioned the circumstances of his brother's death, and they'd whipped him for it.

Then, as though catching himself for having said something he hadn't meant to say, he tried to change the subject.

"Do women serve in the army in Russia?"

"No, women don't, although my grandmother did, during the war. She was a cartographer. You know, the person who draws maps. She was very good at it, actually. She earned many medals. One time a big general, I forget his name now, wanted her to draw maps for his situation room. When another cartographer showed up, he threw him out, and then screamed at everyone to find my grandmother at once and bring her to him."

"Did he love her?"

"What?" I laughed. "No. He was just a moody old man

who liked things just a certain way. He did win the war, though, so we must forgive him."

Shin took my hand.

"I want to map you," he said. "Find all your lines. Lines that can be rivers, or borders, or crossings to the other side." He kissed my palm. "I meant to ask you something. You don't have to answer if you don't want to."

"What is it?"

"Is there someone waiting for you in Moscow? A special friend?"

"No. There's never been anyone like you." I reached for him. "Not like this."

I kissed him.

"Do you like horses?" he asked me.

"I haven't been much around them," I said, startled at the change of subject. "Why do you ask me that?"

"When I was growing up, we kept horses, on our farm near Humhung. I loved how they made me feel, but then — things changed, my father was called away, they took our farm. My brother left for the navy, and my mother and I moved to Pyongyang. I often think that if I had another life somewhere, or if I could change this one, I'd want to spend it looking after horses, riding them in the wild. When I make love to you — I hear them neighing some- times. It's as though they are calling my name. Look here." He traced the lines on my palm again. "We could make a map of a horse ranch right here, spell out its geographic co-ordinates. If you're anything like your grandmother, you'd know how to read it, yes?"

His words touched something deep inside me. Tears welled up in my eyes. But I didn't want to cry in front of him, I dared not to, and so I turned my face away from him. He put his arms around me and held me tight for a little while, and when I looked back at him, he said, "There are rumours of underground networks smuggling illicit goods to China."

"What illicit goods?"

"Drugs. Ginseng. Snakes."

"Snakes?"

"Snakes are highly prized for their supposed aphrodisiac properties. And drugs—well, have you ever wondered what those buildings with blue-painted roofs were?"

"Of course I wondered, but I'm forbidden to come near them."

"Exactly. The buildings are run by the military. Inside are millions of dollars' worth of narcotics for distribution to the West."

"How do you know?"

"Everyone here knows it, and everyone is threatened with death not to know."

I raised myself on my elbows.

"The drugs are plant-based?"

"Some are, others are synthesized here. Trucks of chemical powders drive in and out at night. Someone is making a lot of money doing it."

"Why are you telling me this?"

"Because I thought your father might want to know about it. Tell him and see what he thinks."

Something occurred to me then. Something I hadn't realized before.

"Listen." I sat up. "You told me once that you couldn't offer me anything. But perhaps"—I tapped a finger against my lips — "perhaps I can offer you something."

"What do you mean?"

"What if I asked my father to get you out?"

"What?"

"Yes!" I tried to gather my thoughts. "It may sound far-fetched, but it could work. In exchange for the information about the drugs. I don't know much about my father's connection, only that he knows people who do this — sort of work. One of his friends told me, before I left Moscow. I know this is true. They are not all diplomats up there in the Russian embassy, you know. They all snoop on each other. The North Koreans spy on the Russians, the Russians spy on the Chinese. If what you said about the illicit goods being smuggled across the border with China is true, then people must be smuggled too. In Russia we hear stories about the refugees from the North sometimes. They surface in South Korea and give interviews to the press. How do they get there? They must escape!" Oh, I could've kicked myself for not thinking of this sooner. "My father would never risk something like that for a stranger, but if his daughter was involved — well then."

He looked unconvinced.

"Don't you see?" I cried. "That's our only chance!"

"But you'll have to tell him about us. Are you ready for that?" He lifted my chin, kissed it, and then shook his head. "In any case, it won't work, Vera. I want to believe that it would, but it won't. If they catch me, if they even as much as suspect me, you have no idea what they'd do. I'm not afraid for myself. Please don't think that I am. Giving myself up would be easy. But it isn't about me. It's my mother. That's how they operate. They punish not just you but those you leave behind. If I escape across the border, they'll get my mother. And I wouldn't be able to live with that."

My heart sank.

"Okay," I said, unwilling to give up just yet. "But maybe — maybe your mother can also escape?"

He put his glasses on, looked at me over them, and shook his head again.

I sensed anger rising inside me. "Our love must mean very little to you if you aren't willing to fight for it," I said. "A little obstacle thrown in your way and you're giving up already? I thought you were braver than that."

He glared at me. "You have no idea what bravery is, Vera. You don't know anything."

That hurt me. I stood up and began to put my clothes on.

"Maybe not," I admitted. "Maybe I don't know what bravery is. But I'd like to find out. Which is more than I can say about you."

9

The Russian embassy was hosting a New Year's party, and I invited Song to come with me. It wasn't a goodwill gesture on my part, I'm ashamed to admit it, for I knew that if I didn't invite her, Comrade Park would accompany me.

December 31, 1994, turned out to be a bitterly cold day in Pyongyang. The weather reflected my mood. The embassy was an unassuming three-storey building fronted with white colonnades and festooned with balloons. In the foyer, a man in a tuxedo helped us to remove our coats. After the dorm, the embassy seemed like a magical palace, with its marble staircases, gilded mirrors, and polished floors. Children were racing around, playing tag. A few men stood drinking at the door to the reception hall. At least fifty people had gathered there, sitting on chairs or leaning against the walls. Many held glasses of champagne and chatted in hushed voices among themselves. A grand piano stood in one corner, on which a man was playing a popular song, sung by a woman wearing a black evening gown, cut low over her heavy breasts. On an antique-looking pedestal desk in the opposite corner stood a large silver platter loaded with canapés of smoked salmon and cheese.

I scanned the room for my father, and spotted him sitting alone on a chaise longue.

"Vera." He rose to greet us. "You look lovely tonight."

I was wearing my mother's old dress—blue with gold trim on the shoulders, the only piece of her clothing I'd brought with me to Pyongyang. She'd left it to me with the rest of her wardrobe, but I'd never worn any of her clothes until now. I didn't know exactly what had compelled me to bring the dress with me from Moscow. Perhaps, on some subconscious level, I'd imagined that in that way she'd be coming there with me, or that the dress would somehow protect me, or at least look after me. It fitted a bit tight around my stomach, but that didn't matter to me because as I moved in it I caught whiffs of my mother's scent—her hair, her skin, her perfume.

"Comrade Song, always a pleasure," my father said, shaking her hand. "Can I get you something to drink?"

"Champagne," Song said.

He moved to the bar to fetch our drinks.

We sat on the chaise longue.

I gazed around the room, trying to see if there were people I knew. Two men in the corner were North Korean, wearing military uniforms. They sat stiffly side by side, watching the crowd, glum-faced and narrow-eyed. It was disconcerting to find them there, among the festivities. They seemed somehow incongruous with the holiday cheer, with the music, the lights, and the food.

My father came back with flutes of champagne and handed them to us. I began to sip slowly, worried that on an empty stomach the alcohol might hit me fast.

The music stopped, everyone applauded. Someone began to make a speech. I leaned over to him and whispered, "We need to talk."

He made no acknowledgement that he'd heard me, as he clinked glasses with Song.

There was another speech after that, and another. One of the North Koreans came up to the piano and raised his glass. He launched into a toast, something about the undying friendship between our two great nations and a five-year plan. Then he stamped his feet and shouted, "Long live Kim Jong Il!" People emptied their glasses, and in the Russian tradition everyone cried, "Hurrah!"

When the man at the piano resumed playing, my father excused himself. I was watching him disappear into the crowd when Song said, "Let's eat," and, without waiting for my response, rose quickly and moved to the canapés.

I wasn't hungry. The alcohol was making me nauseous. I drank too fast, after all, and had a light buzz. I was also growing exasperated with my father. Had he not heard what

I said? Where had he gone to, anyway? Just then I saw him approach the man at the piano, lean over, and say something to him. At once the man switched to playing the tango. A few couples stepped to the middle of the floor and began to dance. My father walked over to me with an outstretched arm.

"Let's dance," he said.

Unlike my father, I wasn't a good dancer at all, and had to concentrate on my steps in the crowded room as he led me around the floor.

"How are you, my darling?" he asked me.

"I have so much to tell you, I think I might burst!"

"I know."

"You know?"

"I know it's been hard. But your work has been worth it. It keeps you busy. Please tell me that at least your work is going well."

"It is," I said, gathering strength. It was now or never. "But listen, I have something to tell you. It's very important to me."

He pressed his cheek to me and turned me around, holding on to my wrist.

"What is it?"

"I've fallen in love," I said simply. "With a North Korean. His name is Shin. He works in the Botanical Gardens with me in the orchid greenhouse. He's my supervisor, and, well—Oh, Daddy, we've been lovers for more than a month now. I love him and he loves me. He means the world to—"

"Stop talking!" he hissed.

The shock of his words made me stop dancing. He pulled me along.

"Don't say anything else, I beg you," he said through his teeth. "You are mad. This is not love you speak of. It's madness. That's exactly what it is."

He looked around the room and I saw in his face that he was frightened. His eyes were wide and clouded over with dread. He looked like a wild animal that had been chased after, that had been haunted by some terrible malice that was certain to bring him to death.

I looked over his shoulder at Song, who was stuffing herself with canapés and watching us with awe. She stuck two thumbs in the air to show me what she thought of our tango. I forced myself to stretch out my hand and wave to her, to let her know in my turn that everything was great over here, and that she should continue to enjoy herself.

My father said, "You have no idea what you got yourself into. None. It's a dangerous game you're playing, little girl."

I took exception to his words.

"I'm sorry I've disappointed you, Father. Clearly, love is not something you think I should have. But I couldn't help it." I'd switched back to pleading. "Please believe me that I could not. I didn't want to fall in love. But it just happened, and it has changed everything. Now I need your help."

There, I'd said it.

The music stopped.

We separated and stood staring at each other, the space between us like a gulf.

"Encore!" someone cried. "Another tango. An Argentinian this time."

The woman singer brought a glass of champagne to the man at the piano. He emptied it in one go, placed it

on the floor beside him, shook his hands out, and began
to play again.

My father put his hands on my waist and steered me
forward.

"Listen to me carefully now. I'm only going to say this
once. You don't know what you're doing. You're being played.
This—this lover of yours is a pretender. How can you be so
naive?" He grabbed my arm roughly and spun me around
the floor. "Let me guess. You're going to beg me to help him
to get across the border." He glared at me. "Am I right?"

I blinked.

"Oh, I could strangle you right now, Vera! I think I really
could! It happens all the time. Everyone knows it. This
is exactly the sort of dirty tricks the North Korean intelligence play."

"What tricks?" I could only whisper.

"Honey traps. Attractive agents seducing targets to get
information they want. In your case—well, let me see,
there are rumours that the Russians are supporting the
opposition. The North Koreans suspect there's a smuggling network across the border with China and that
the Russians might be involved. Enter Vera Mishkina,
a twenty-one-year old botany student, who comes on
an exchange to Pyongyang. Her father is an embalmer
who knows people in the government. So, before long,
Vera is going to fall in love with a North Korean and ask
her father to help her lover escape. Her gullible, loving
father, his heart warmed by Vera's passionate pleas, has
contacts in the Russian embassy, so surely he should be
able to help—What was his name again? Not a real one,
certainly—Shin?"

"It isn't like that," I said, my heart breaking into a million pieces. Big, salty tears were flowing down my face. "He said he wouldn't leave without his mother. He didn't ask me for anything. It was my idea that you should help him!"

"Of course it was," my father said bitterly. "He's pretty good at his job."

"No." I shook my head stubbornly. "No. This is different. Shin and I — we are —"

But then I asked myself, what were we, really? Shin was a complete stranger to me. It was entirely possible that he was an agent, that he'd tricked me to get information from me. How my heart hurt inside my chest at that moment! I felt as though every one of my cells had burst. For a moment I didn't know where I was. I looked around the room, not understanding who all those people were. What were they doing there? Why were they dancing the tango and drinking champagne? How could the world still be here? How was I to survive that day?

Out of the corner of my eye, I saw Song making her way toward us.

"But he loves me," I said feebly. "He told me —"

"Good God, Vera," my father said in a tone of voice that ended our conversation. "I might've expected many things from you, but not this."

I'd realize later that, on that evening, more than anything else in the world, I'd wanted my father to be happy for me. I'd wanted him to tell me that everything would be okay. That he'd take care of everything and wouldn't let anything bad happen to me. Instead, he'd made it abundantly clear that he was disappointed in me.

I felt a hand on my shoulder and looked up to see Song.

"I'm not feeling so well at the moment," she said, doubling up. "My stomach hurts. It might be something I ate. Can we please go back to campus now, Comrade Vera? I really can't go on."

"Yes," I said. I saw no point in staying. I let go of my father and ran to the foyer.

In the car, on the way back to campus, Song said, "Has something upset you?"

I said, "Not at all."

"I can tell that something has, but you don't have to tell me your secrets. Anyway, I think my stomach problems may be tea-related. You know, the green tea I drink at the greenhouse, I think something's wrong with it."

IN THE DAYS that followed, Song drank only water. She poured it out of the sink into her cup and wouldn't put it down for a moment. Shin and I were thus reduced to communicating via books, which, after what my father had told me at the embassy's party, I actually welcomed. I simply didn't know how to be around him. He noticed the change in me. *What happened? You seem so far away.* It was true. I wasn't there. My hands might've been busy with compost, my eyes might have been looking into the microscope, but in my mind, I kept replaying my conversations with Shin. About his brother, about horses. I kept seeing our bodies, entwined, making love in his office. It was hard to believe that like a stupid insect I might've fallen so easily into his honey trap. It was inconceivable that Shin had played me, that he'd lied to me, that he'd pretended with me all along. He, whom I'd caressed so sweetly, kissed so softly, called such precious names. I could not understand how anyone could be capable of such cruelty, such trickery, such fraud.

A week after the conversation with my father, I could no longer be silent about it. I summoned what remained of my courage and left Shin a message in which I revealed what my father had told me. *Is it true that you've seduced me on purpose? Are you a spy?*

His answer came two days later and consisted of one word, *No.*

Did I believe him? I didn't know what to believe. Meanwhile, my body had changed to the point where I started to suspect that something was wrong with me. There was a new heaviness in my stomach, as if I'd swallowed a stone. I lost my appetite and suffered from bad migraines. I was frequently nauseous, violently sometimes. And I couldn't bike any longer, as it had become extremely uncomfortable for me to pedal, pressing against the narrow seat.

Then one day I was sitting at my work table, looking into a book, and all of a sudden my nose started to bleed. Big droplets of blood plopped on the white pages, staining them red.

I cried out, and Shin, who'd been working in the nearby aisle, ran over to me.

"I must take Comrade Vera to my office," he said to Song, pressing his sleeve to my nose. "You stay here and take care of the petri plates."

"But I don't know what to do," Song protested.

I said, "Please. You've watched me do it at least a thousand times. Tilt them slightly and pour in the melted agar. Let them cool before implanting seedlings. That's all there is to it, all right?"

"We don't have much time," Shin said as we entered his office. "Sit down and listen to me."

He closed the door, then brought out a cotton ball from the first aid kit and kneeled by me.

"Hold it under your nose. Keep your head up. You have to trust me."

"I don't know whom to trust."

"You have to trust me," he repeated. "I'm not a spy. When you see your father next time —" he began, but was interrupted by the three knocks on the door. Song stood watching us through the glass insert. "Tell him what I told you about the buildings with blue-painted roofs," he whispered, letting go of me.

THE NEXT TIME Song and I went to the bathhouse, I swam longer than usual in the pool. Floating in the cool water on my back made me feel better, as if the stone in my stomach had dissolved. I'd always loved swimming, but now swimming too felt different. It was as though I'd finally understood that we all had come out of the water and that into the water we all would return. When I was submerged, I felt cleansed, purified. It was as though by some curious osmosis all badness was leaking out of me. I could've drifted on my back in that pool for hours, if it weren't for Song. Of course, she was there, sitting on the edge and glancing pointedly at her watch every time our eyes met. Other bathers will be coming in soon, Comrade Vera. Please come out of the pool. Everyone's bathing time in North Korea was strictly rationed, like food.

When I finally came out of the pool, she handed me a towel, and while I was drying myself, she stared at my nakedness openly, boldly, without turning away.

"Comrade Vera," she said in a new, odd tone of voice. "I'm concerned about your health. You have not menstruated for two months. Don't you find that odd?"

I was aghast. Wrapping the towel around my waist, I cried, "What? Are you my blood keeper now?"

She smiled, brought her lips to my ear, and whispered, "Yes."

I stood still. And slowly, very slowly, I began to understand everything. Why hadn't the possibility of pregnancy crossed my mind? Because Shin said he had protection, because I trusted him, because — Oh, I could've died right there and then! Catching my reflection in a fogged-up mirror, I saw the telltale belly bulge. Pregnant! Yes, of course, I was pregnant. All of my physical symptoms made sense.

Song said, "By my calculation, you're two months in. You've started to show already, but can hide it under your clothes still. When they find out — and believe me, they will — they'll make you stay and have your baby here. The baby will be North Korean and they won't let you take it home."

My lips trembled. I was about to faint.

Song must've expected my reaction, because she put her arms out quickly to steady me and began to help me dress.

"It looks like a pretty bad situation for you. But don't worry. I won't tell anyone. Yet. Talk to your father. Make him get you out of here. As fast as he can."

SONG KNEW EVERYTHING. She knew it was Shin. She also knew about the sleeping drugs I'd put in her tea.

"I watched you two do it," she told me, grinning lasciviously, making me blush. It was such a reversal from the shy, reserved Song I'd known that I had a hard time wrapping my head around it. But then, how could anyone ever know the truth about another person? Or be privy to their innermost thoughts?

"Did you sleep then?" I asked her. "While Shin and I — met?"

"Sometimes. But most of the time I pretended. I'd wait until you went into his office and then sneak up on you."

I asked her why she hadn't reported us, and she said she was a romantic at heart. Besides, she'd betrayed so many people already in high school and at the university that she wanted "to take a break." But whatever her motives were, I couldn't question them for too long. The agony of waiting another two weeks until I could see my father again was unbearable, but things couldn't be helped. Meanwhile, to keep up appearances with Shin in the greenhouse, I left a message for him with my news in the *Manual of Cultivated Orchids*. His response read:

> Sometimes, botanists say, two plants attach to each other. One plant embeds in the tissues of another and feeds of its molecules. Their combination is said to be obligate, in that, if the plants separate, they can no longer live on their own.

It frustrated me no end. All the speaking in riddles was starting to grate on my nerves. Was he happy that I was pregnant? Did it change anything for him? If my father could help him, would he now be willing to risk crossing over to China, to escape to freedom to be with me?

I wrote back:

> *I'm carrying your child now. Does it matter to you? I'm going to leave here soon. My father would never leave me here. Of this I'm certain, no matter how upset he might be with me. Will you come with me to Moscow? If my father found a way to help you?*

He replied with:

> *I won't leave without my mother. But I love you. I love you. I do. Remember to tell your father about the buildings with the blue roofs.*

THE FOLLOWING WEEK, in the Red Lantern, Song passed a handwritten note to my father under the table. Yes, she did that for me. Perhaps she was telling the truth, after all. Perhaps she really was a romantic. I didn't know. I didn't care. All I wanted was to go home.

My father would tell me later that he was surprised by the pressure of Song's hand on his knee but had the presence of mind not to react to it. When his reply came two weeks later, passed back under the table to Song, it was like light after darkness. It made everything in me alive again.

> *I am shocked but not surprised by your news, Verka. Of course I will help you. Flying you out of Pyongyang, however, is not an option. There will be questions, perhaps a physical exam. We'll work something else out. I'm certain of it. As far as your friend goes, I can't promise you*

*anything. The information about the buildings with blue
roofs in the Gardens is very helpful indeed. Stay strong
and take care. Everything will be okay.*

Two weeks later, it was March already, and we were
having cold noodles again. My father seemed far away,
absent-minded. He'd touched none of his food. I also
noticed that he kept looking down at his watch.

"Are you in a rush, Professor Viktor?" Comrade Park
asked him.

"What?" My father looked up at him. "No. I'm just—I've
been thinking about something that happened at work."

"We won't ask." Comrade Park held his hands up in a
gesture of surrender. "We know better, unless of course
you want to tell us about it yourself."

"It's nothing. It isn't important. Some technical issues,
that's all."

"I see." Comrade Park turned to me. "Well, I've been
led to believe that another trip to the country is coming up
in a couple of weeks, and that you've volunteered for it. I
applaud your dedication and sincerely wish you good luck."

Song and I looked at each other.

"What are you talking about?" Song asked.

"Haven't you heard?" my father said quickly. "I'm sure
Vera mentioned it last time. She said that a team was being
organized in the Botanical Gardens. People were sign-
ing up. Vera has applied for permission to go, and so, as I
understand it, has Comrade Shin."

I felt my father's foot kicking me under the table.

"Yes, of course," I said. "We're so looking forward to
going, aren't we, Song?"

She refocused her eyes on me for a moment, and then slowly nodded her head.

My father looked at his watch again. And in the next moment I felt his hand on my knee. "For you I'll kill a bull," he whispered.

A fire alarm began to scream.

Everyone jumped to their feet and began running toward the exit.

Comrade Park dropped his chopsticks in the bowl. Then he got up, buttoned up his jacket, and motioned for us to follow him.

"We've got maybe two minutes," my father whispered into my ear as the panicked mob elbowed us toward the door. "Listen to me carefully — your life and the life of your child might depend on how well you do. I've arranged everything. In the north, a guide will take you and your friend across the river. A man will deliver a package to your friend at the greenhouse next week. Tell him to expect it. Everything will be explained in it."

The crowd propelled Song and Comrade Park farther up, separating them from us. Comrade Park turned his head this way and that, spotted me behind him, and began to muscle his way back.

"What about Shin's mother? She's old and in poor health —"

"Darling, I know all about it. My assistants will pick her up from the morgue."

"What?"

"The morgue. She'll have to die an unnatural death."

I stared at him, not understanding.

"On the day of your crossing, I'll fly back to Moscow

with the fresh crop of cadavers from the city's morgue. Your friend should take her body there."

"But — you don't mean —"

"She must pretend to be dead. A chemical powder and the instructions on how to prepare it, the dosage based on his mother's weight, and all other details will be in the package I'll send to him. He must do exactly as I say."

The alarm was silenced as suddenly as it had come on. Comrade Park reached us and grabbed me by the arm.

"There you are," he said gleefully. "What a funny thing to have happened today."

I TOLD SHIN about my father's plan. Everything was arranged. The only remaining question was whether Shin's mother would agree to play dead. For a while it appeared that she wouldn't and we feared that all hope was lost. She hesitated, but then Shin told her that it would be like falling asleep. A few hours later she'd wake up on a plane with a team of medical doctors from Russia attending to all her needs. Shin would join her later in Moscow, although it might take him a little while. According to Shin, his mother thought it over for two days and then said yes.

Shin had received my father's package. His mother would "die" the day before we went up north. In accordance with his mother's wishes, Shin would take her to the city's morgue. She'd always wanted to donate her body to science, especially to medicine. Her grandfather had been a medical doctor. Besides, it was her sacred duty to give back to her country after everything her country had given her.

The next day, the work brigade from the Botanical

Gardens would take a train to Chongjin. Comrade Shin would be among them, distressed by his mother's death but also determined to carry on with his work. From Chongjin, we'd be taken by trucks to a field camp near Musan. There, one night, shortly after a red flare would go up into the sky, a guide would meet us at a prearranged rendezvous point, and bring us to the Tumen River, where an inflatable dinghy would be waiting for us. We'd have to row it across to China, about a kilometre away. The border guards would be distracted five miles downstream, expecting smugglers. In fact, the red flare would be their signal to remain on high alert.

Once in China, we'd be met by another contact. He'd take us to a safe house in the village of Longjing, and then on to the town of Yanbian. There was a brothel there, run by a woman who'd shelter us for a good price. There, we'd get in touch with a Canadian missionary. He'd give us our passports and two tickets to the bus that would take us to Beijing. Two days after arriving in Beijing, we'd board the Trans-Siberian train to Moscow and that would be it. In less than a month's time, provided that everything unfolded as planned, I would be back in Moscow. With Shin.

The only problem now was Song. She wasn't impressed with our plan. Or, rather, she became frightened by what it meant for herself. If we escaped, she and her family might be punished. She wasn't prepared to take that risk. I hated blackmailing her, but I had no choice. I told her that if she reported us, I would not hesitate for a second to take her down with me. I'd lie and say it was her idea, that she'd thought it all up. I'd go even further and cite instances of her disrespect for the Kims. In the end, she'd agreed to keep quiet on the condition that she stayed behind in Pyongyang. If she didn't go with us up north to the country, she couldn't be blamed for our escape. She'd still be punished, of course, for her inattention, for having missed the signs of our discontent, but, most likely, she'd be spared the camps. To make her appear ill, Shin prepared a plant extract that made her cough up bloody phlegm. She was given antibiotics and advised against accompanying me on the field trip.

I forced myself not to worry about her fate because the time had come for me to look after myself. It was nevertheless with a heavy heart that I took leave of her on the morning of March 28.

She was lying on her bed in our room with her eyes closed. I packed the most precious of my belongings and then sat down on my bed.

She opened her eyes.

"I'll never forget what you did for me, Song," I said. "Thank you."

She smiled at me, but her smile quickly faded away.

"I wish you all the luck in the world, Vera," she said, for the first and last time calling me by just my name. "All the luck in the world."

SINCE SONG'S ILLNESS came on unexpectedly, no other minder was assigned to me. Comrade Shin had volunteered to be my translator for the duration of our trip.

As far as everyone else knew, Shin's mother had died. Her death did not come as a shock. She was old and had many health issues. Apparently, she'd suffered a heart attack.

Comrade Shin was upset by her death. But it was important for him to carry on. After all, that was what his mother would have wanted for him. To go on with his life.

THE TRAIN TO Chongjin took five hours, during which I actually missed Song. I'd grown so used to her company that it was strange to be alone. I sat in a compartment with five other women who played cards and ate sunflower seeds. They laughed among themselves, ignored me, and spat shells on the floor. After a while, unable to stand it any longer, I excused myself and went out to the corridor.

A man stood there, looking out at the scenery speeding by. He was smoking, and the stink of it made me sick to my stomach. I began to cough. My stomach lurched and I rushed to the bathroom to retch. It was mostly bile that came out, staining my teeth and leaving an acrid taste. As I was rinsing my mouth in the sink, there was a soft knock on the door.

It was Shin.

The space in the bathroom was so small, he had to push himself against me to squeeze in.

"Are you all right? I've been worried. How do you feel?"

"Not so good," I said. "I'm frightened. Those horrid women in our compartment. I miss Song. I—I don't think I can go through with it. I don't have any strength left."

"Look at me!" He took my face in his hands. "After everything we've been through? How can you say that?"

"No, I don't mean I won't do it. I don't have any choice. But it's just that I'm terrified of it. So terrified. What happens if we get caught?"

"I will protect you," he said firmly. "You can't think like

that. You must be strong, Vera. Right now is the time to be brave."

But to be brave was the last thing I wanted. I wanted to fall asleep.

"Only for a little while longer. Everything is ready now. We cross tomorrow night."

"Tomorrow?" I cried.

He put a hand over my mouth and kissed my forehead.

"Tomorrow or never. This is it."

We heard footsteps outside.

"I must go," he said, slipping a square of chocolate into my hand. "Eat this and listen. Tomorrow morning we'll walk past limestone caves. Remember it. That's the rendezvous point. It isn't far from the camp. At night, after the flare goes up, you'll have to get there using your flashlight. I'll wait for you there."

I nodded.

"But what if it doesn't go up? The flare, I mean."

"Then we wait until the next night. But I'm sure it will."

He kissed me, turned to the door, and stood still, listening for a few moments. Then, placing his hand on the lock, he turned back to me. "I love you," he said, and "Forgive me," and quickly stepped outside.

THE NIGHT BEFORE our crossing, I dreamt of my mother again. I was pushing her body in a wheelbarrow through the streets of Pyongyang. The streets were crowded, full of malnourished people in shabby clothes. They wandered aimlessly on the roads rather than walked on them, and after a while I understood that they were all dead. I wanted to hide my mother from them, by trying to pull a body bag over her head, but it kept sliding away, it was useless, her feet kept protruding, all bloated and black. As I cried out in horror and tried to cover her feet again, she opened her eyes and winked at me, letting me know that it was just a game. She was just acting, her expression said. There was no need to worry. She was only pretending to be dead.

I woke up in a cold sweat, and all day was haunted by my mother's winking face. By nightfall, I was exhausted. I had no energy left. My stomach was bloated, my muscles stiff after a full day of work. Five minutes after midnight, a red flare slithered up into the night sky. I climbed out of the tent, made my way to the bushes, and turned on the flashlight. I hardly know how I managed to make my way down to the caves in the darkness. Shin wasn't there, so I hid behind a tree, and stood still, clinging to it, trying to fight my fear and anxiety.

At last I heard a whistle, and in another moment there appeared a skeletal-looking man. Shin came up behind him. The three of us descended into a hollow, ran across a cornfield and down a dirt road. When we reached an old pickup truck, the man stopped. His metal-capped incisors gleamed grotesquely in the light of a lit match. Shin and I climbed in the back and held on to each other as the engine revved up.

After twenty minutes of bumping through the moonless landscape, the truck swerved to one side and came to a stop. The engine gave out with a burp. We jumped off and scrambled down a sandy embankment and farther along the river's edge. Reaching a thicket of tall grass, we saw an inflated dinghy with two oars. A yellow cone of the searchlight carved out the shape of the guard tower to the east.

I began to shake.

"Get in," our guide whispered, waving his arms frantically toward the dinghy. "Get in now and row across."

We stumbled into the icy water, holding hands. The bottom was slippery with silt and I faltered, catching my foot on an underwater root. Shin supported me under the elbow, preventing my fall. The water reached our knees, then our stomachs, dragging our legs downstream. At last we reached the dinghy and Shin helped me in.

I grabbed an oar and leaned into it. Shin did the same on the other side. The muscles in my arms felt as though they were going to tear, the small of my back was numb. I don't know how I found the strength to keep going, but the adrenalin must've kicked in. Sweating and straining and working together, we began to row across. Then my eyes caught something in the dark, some kind of movement, and in another moment a puddle of light spilled on Shin's face.

An ear-piercing scream came from the shore, somewhere behind me.

Then came a gunshot.

Shin lunged toward me.

"Swim," he shouted, pushing me forward. "Go home!"

Another shot came from the shore.

Shin's body shuddered. He swayed and plunged overboard.

I jumped after him and in another moment felt his hands around my waist. From under the water he was pushing me toward the far shore with all his strength. Then he found my hand, placed a ring on my wedding finger, pressed my palm, and let go.

I dived down to the bottom and began to swim across. I came up to the surface for oxygen, dived down, and swam, again and again.

I was a good swimmer. As long as I kept moving, I knew I would be okay. But the water was bitterly cold. Hypothermia would set in quickly. I didn't think I'd be able to make it. My body was worn out. I felt weak. But then, in the middle of that awful river, with the bullets swishing above me, I thought I felt my baby's kick, and something happened. Something shifted around me. It was as though some intangible force began to help me. Perhaps it was my mother, reaching out from the great beyond, pushing me forward, and pulling me by the hand toward the opposite shore.

At long last I found the bottom with the tips of my toes. I crawled out of the water and ran up the riverbank. My hands were bleeding from the glass shards the border guards had planted in the mud.

I made my way toward a tall, leafy tree and, stepping under its canopy, collapsed on the grass. A shadow moved out of the darkness and leaned over me. The last thing I remember was someone's hands wrapping me in a blanket and lifting me up.

10

And now, at the end my story, I must go back to its beginning. Namely, the State Institute of Cinematography, where my mother had studied Acting for Film and Television, and where a North Korean student named Dong-jun crossed paths with her in 1974. He'd come to study in Moscow one year earlier by direct order of Kim Il Sung.

Dong-jun was not only a handsome young man with apparent talents for the performing arts, he was also the son of the Second Minister of Transportation of DRKP. His mother was a forensic psychiatrist who provided expert assistance to the North Korean judicial system in child custody cases of convicted criminals. Since most criminals in North Korea were regular people who had "sinned" in some minor way against the Kims — forgotten to dust a portrait, say, or questioned a Party decree — Dong-jun's mother had come to know many regular families. She had also come to know real political dissidents and conscientious objectors to the regime. The family had returned to North Korea from Japan in 1965, where they played a prominent role in the "revolutionizing" of expatriate Koreans: Dong-jun's father had been the chair of the pro-Pyongyang Association of Korean Residents in Japan, where he worked to convince his countrymen to come back to their native land. He'd succeeded in many cases and been rewarded for his efforts with an important post in Pyongyang upon his return to the fatherland. And, oh, Dong-jun had a younger brother, who in 1974 was six years old. His name was Shin.

"What?" I interrupted my father, who'd been telling me the story. We were sitting in his study in our apartment in Moscow one evening, shortly after my return. My grandmother was knitting a scarf.

"Shin grew up as a typical North Korean child," my father went on, ignoring my outburst. "After all, he'd never lived in Japan. He was born and raised in Pyongyang, and, gentle by nature, he grew up to be a dutiful and loving son."

My father lifted the bottle of cognac off his desk and swished it around to see if my grandmother would have more. She put down her knitting and held a porcelain tea-cup toward him.

"Shin's father had always pushed his younger son to be the best student at school. He'd taught him to always follow the Party's instructions and quote passages from Kim Il Sung's works as often as he could. But his father had also taught him to think for himself. He told him stories about Japan and about Russia and about other countries around the world. He told him that North Korea wasn't the only place on earth that was good. He told him that all people were created equal even though they had different views about things. And he spoke of a future, of his vision of the united world. One day, he said, the world will be united. Everyone will be able to contact anyone else on earth. Soon, something will happen to remind people of their humanity. His face would light up with emotion and he'd hold his face between his hands and cry."

"How do you know all this?" I asked my father. "Did Shin tell you this? And when?"

"I've never met Shin," my father said, "but I did see him once. It must've been in early August last year, when I visited the Botanical Gardens. Before I wrote my letter to you. The letter they forced me to write."

My heart started to beat faster. I felt a strange tingling sensation in my limbs.

He moved to the window, parted the curtains, and looked outside, where the glowing star on the Spasskaya Tower cast red shadows on the night sky.

"Time passed," he continued. "It was 1973. Dong-jun

had just finished high school. He was eighteen. His father — remember, he was the Second Minister of Transportation — wrote a personal letter to Kim Il Sung. He requested humbly that his eldest son be allowed to go to Moscow to learn to be a movie star. He reminded the Great Leader of the beautiful boy with the voice of an angel who had performed for him at the Children's Palace twelve years ago. It had been Kim Il Sung's fiftieth birthday, and the boy had been his son. Perhaps the Great Leader remembered that he'd honoured Dong-jun greatly by letting him sit on his knee? The following day, their picture appeared on the front page of the Party's newspaper. It was such an honour. But now the boy was all grown up. He showed remarkable promise. He'd acted in many plays in his high school. He also played piano, excelled in tae kwon do, and spoke five languages, including Russian: his father had seen to that. But he still needed training. As such, the Second Minister hoped that Dong-jun would be given a chance to go to Moscow to study cinematic arts. The minister knew how much Kim Il Sung loved movies. Perhaps, having honoured his son so greatly once, Kim Il Sung in his infinite wisdom would honour him a second time?"

My father turned from the window to face my grandmother and me.

"Kim Il Sung thought about the Second Minister's request for ten long months. He ran the Second Minister's proposal by his own son, Kim Jong Il. After all, Kim Jong Il also loved movies, and, as his father's heir apparent, stood to benefit from Dong-jun's future career the most. In the end, the Kims decided to let Dong-jun go to Moscow. If he tried to do anything stupid, well, his family would pay a terrible price."

The front doorbell rang.

"Ah, as if on cue," my father said, stepping out into the hallway.

"Who's that?" I asked my grandmother.

"You'll see."

I held my breath, listening to every sound.

The front door opened and closed. A man's voice spoke to my father. Then I heard approaching footsteps. A man who looked remarkably like Shin, only twenty years older, appeared on the threshold. He looked around the room, as though deciding if he should enter. Then he bowed to my grandmother and, straightening his back, locked his eyes with me.

"My name is Dong-jun," he said, his eyes drifting to my stomach. "And you must be Vera. Your name has come to mean so very much to me. You've lived up to its promise. I owe a great debt to you."

He spoke perfect Russian, but it took me a moment to understand what he meant. Vera means "faith" in Russian, so he was implying that he'd had faith in me. But faith in what, exactly, and why he'd have it were mysteries to me.

"I'm confused," I said, reeling, my grief for Shin still fresh. "Please forgive me. You look like someone I know."

"My little brother," he said. "He owes a great debt to you too."

"Shall we have a toast, then?" My father brought out another glass and poured some cognac into it. "This may be the closest to a family reunion we'll ever get."

As I watched the two men and my grandmother clink

glasses, I was struck by the thought that they all knew each other well. Even my grandmother, who I'd been sure up to that evening didn't know anything about North Korea at all. As if overhearing my thoughts, she turned to me.

"Verochka, all in good time, my dear. Good friends must drink to their health first."

The three of them emptied their drinks. The two men chuckled, patting each other on the back. My father then settled into a chair, while Dong-jun perched on the arm of the sofa and said, "I met your mother in 1974. She was a beautiful lady, so strong in all respects. We struck up an easy friendship. Some thought it was romantic, but it was nothing like that. The wonderful thing about your mother was that she listened to me. Other students talked to me, but they never listened. I think you know what I mean.

"Soon after I came to Moscow, I began to organize my compatriots. My goal was to get other North Korean students who studied in Russia to launch an official protest against Kim Il Sung's regime. We were going to write an open letter to the North Korean parliament and publish it in the *Moscow Times*. It was my parents' plan, you see. They'd sent me to Moscow, hoping I might be able to trigger reforms. They'd thought that if the international community learned of what was really going on inside North Korea, about the purges, the tortures, the famine, then they would be more likely to support a coup. It was impossible to oppose Kim internally: everyone reported to the secret police. This is how it is still. People who spy on their neighbours are rewarded with clothing and food. Those who are perceived to transgress get sent to labour camps, or worse. Whole families disappear. So, our protest had to come from the outside.

"My parents were born in Japan, after their own parents moved there in search of better work in the 1910s. The whole of Korea, as you probably know, was annexed to Japan until 1945. So, many Koreans went there to look for a better life. My paternal grandfather prospered in Osaka because he'd made wise investments in food imports. My father, meanwhile, became active in the socialist movement in the 1950s, after the Korean War. He began to attend socialist meetings and to support Kim Il Sung. At one of those meetings he met my mother, who was a medical student back then. My parents were young and idealistic and, like many others of their generation, politically naive. They resented the Americans because of the atomic bombs, and thought the Japanese were corrupted by greed. They joined the Communists. Eventually, alongside thousands of other misled Koreans, they came back to their native land. In the summer of 1965, they crossed the Sea of Japan with all of their belongings and made their way to Pyongyang. But in Pyongyang, things looked appallingly different from what they were used to seeing in Japan. If their living conditions were not exactly horrible — after all, both of my parents were high up in the Party's ranks by then — they were a far cry from what they were used to. There wasn't enough food in the shops. They had to give up countless hours of volunteer labour on Sundays and chastise themselves for insufficient vigilance every week. Far worse was the climate of fear and Kim Il Sung's personality cult. They recalled the lifestyle they'd had in Japan fondly, and longed to go back, but it was too late.

Their choice now was to fit in and join in with the revolution or to be shipped off to a labour camp.

"My parents made a wise decision and joined the cause. That is to say, on the surface they joined it, but behind closed doors they bided their time. They felt betrayed and disappointed by the Party, but also refused to give up. They began to talk in whispers to like-minded people. Slowly, they began to organize. Year by year, and because of my mother's profession, they were able to put together a network of dissidents. But they had to be very careful. It was a dangerous game. The regime had eyes on everyone. Every single North Korean — man, woman, and child — was on its payroll. Before long, my parents realized that the only way to make something happen was to sacrifice themselves. When they sent me to Moscow to start the protest against Kim Il Sung, they knew that they'd be arrested, but they also believed that their sacrifice would not be in vain. They believed that the reforms I'd trigger might lead to their release. And if they died before that happened, so be it. There were millions of other innocent people languishing in the vast North Korean gulag."

Dong-jun fell silent and looked at his hands.

"But you didn't complete your mission," I said. "You didn't launch the big protest."

"No," he said. "But I did try, with your mother's help. She was a passionate woman. A good actor must be a passionate person who likes the idea that they could change the world. Your mother was like that. She was brave. She had many friends in Moscow — artists and writers, journalists and diplomats. She helped me get in touch with other North Koreans who studied in Moscow or worked as

officials in the embassy. She organized meetings. We had
to be careful about whom we approached, but most people
we contacted were willing to help. Their experiences in the
USSR had changed the way they saw Kim Il Sung.

"Within a year, we were a core group of twelve dissent-
ers — 'the disciples,' your mother had called us. We began
to compose our letter of protest. We decided to apply for
Soviet asylum, as your mother had found a lawyer who was
willing to help us. The Soviet authorities would grant us asylum on humanitarian grounds, the lawyer told us, because
the relations with Pyongyang had begun to strain by then.

"I corresponded with my parents via encoded letters
to keep them informed. My letters were full of highly
descriptive passages praising Russian cuisine. I'd write
about what I'd sampled in Moscow and suggest that my
mother try making it in Pyongyang. In turn, she sent me
Korean recipes to share with my Russian friends. In this
way, based on a previously agreed-upon cipher, I was able
to keep them up to date."

"I still remember," my grandmother said. "You asked
me for the recipe for rolled fish fillets with chanterelle
mushrooms one day."

"Yes. And my mother responded with the recipe for
Korean dumplings for you. I still remember it, word for
word. 'In a large mixing bowl, combine ground pork, beef
and tofu, kimchee, bean sprouts, scallions, garlic, and
ginger juice. Then add oyster sauce, sesame oil, crushed
sesame seeds, and salt. To assemble the dumplings, follow
these five easy steps.'" He looked at me. "Sounds perfectly
innocent, doesn't it? Yet this recipe spells out geographic
co-ordinates of known labour camps."

"But what happened?" I asked him. "Why did you fail with the protest?"

"We were betrayed. In retrospect, I should've known better and been less eager. Eagerness makes you blind. But it's always easy to see things the right way in hindsight. At the time, I was only able to see what I wanted to see in everyone."

How true, I thought. I too had seen only what I wanted to see in everyone in Pyongyang.

"The traitor was a Russian poet in love with your mother, one of her contacts in the art world. I don't remember now how he'd come to be a part of our network, or how he was going to help us in any case. Perhaps he knew an editor at the *Moscow Times*. He threatened to expose us to the North Koreans unless your mother slept with him. He said he'd write an anonymous letter and mail it to the North Korean embassy. Your mother refused, not believing he'd be capable of such a low thing. But he did, as it turned out, follow up on his threat.

"Soon after, I received a phone call, asking me to come to the North Korean embassy for an interview. Something was the matter with my father, the caller informed me. I smelled a rat right away. I knew from my mother's letters that everything was okay at home, so I told them I had a cold. I promised I'd come to the embassy when I recovered in a week's time or so. I knew I had to go into hiding. Your mother had found a safe house for me. It was a dacha of one of her friends, just outside Moscow, twenty minutes away by train.

"I packed my few belongings quickly and left my room in the dorm that same afternoon. It was a warm evening in mid-autumn. I still remember the leaves that glowed like miniature pumpkins on the trees. As I was approaching Belorusskaya metro station, a black car pulled up to the curb. I didn't think much of it and continued walking, until three North Korean agents jumped out and forced me inside. I was drugged and lost consciousness. When I woke up, I was in the embassy. They interrogated me. I played dumb. I faked flu-like symptoms and complained about them mistreating me. I threatened to report them to my father. I was a good actor and played my part well. The agents began to doubt themselves. They brought me food and medicine. We were on the second floor. I asked to go to the bathroom, hoping there would be a window, which I knew I would be able to break from the inside. To my relief, there was one: a hazy pane with no bars.

"I jumped up on the sill and kicked out the window. I was fit and strong and knew tae kwon do. The glass shattered. I curled myself into a ball, pulled my sweater over my head, and jumped outside. I landed and rolled on the ground. It hurt. I sprained my ankle, but somehow was able to run. In no time I reached the gates of the embassy, sprang up its iron bars like a cat, and was climbing over the spiky ends when they started shooting.

"I jumped down the other side, ran as fast as I could to the nearest metro station, and melted into the crowd. I knew I was very lucky and also that I'd be hunted for the rest of my life. Many people know about the kidnapping of Japanese by North Korean agents, but they also seek out and kidnap North Koreans who defect."

He turned to my father, who was sitting at his desk with his arms folded across his chest.

My father said, "This is why I wrote to you, Verka. When I came to Pyongyang, they threatened to harm you. And because of what happened to Dong-jun in Moscow, I knew they'd be able to do that. You'd be walking in broad daylight one day on the street in Moscow and a car would swerve and hit you. Or you'd drown in a swimming pool by accident. I couldn't take that chance."

I was astonished. "Could they do that right here in Moscow?"

"Oh yes. Remember a few years ago that mysterious illness in St. Petersburg? There are powerful drugs out there, my darling, that leave no trace in the bodies of their victims because these drugs decompose. A person can get scratched with, say, the tip of an umbrella on which poison has been placed. I couldn't take the chance that they'd harm you in Moscow," he repeated. "What would you have done?"

"Wait," I said. "Wait a minute. Are you saying that you thought I'd be safer in Pyongyang? That seems absurd. Why?"

"Verochka," my grandmother said. "Your father had made the right decision, the only decision he could've made. Don't blame him for anything now. It's unfair. You don't know the whole story yet."

"Well, tell it to me, then!" I cried in frustration. "Tell me everything right now!"

Dong-jun stood up.

"I beg your patience. It is a lot to take. But to untangle the threads of this complicated story, you must understand where the threads came from in the first place."

"I'll go make some tea," my grandmother said, putting

her knitting aside. "I think there are cookies." She flung the tartan blanket off her knees and rose from her rocking chair. On the way out of the room, she patted Dong-jun's shoulder. "You go on, dear. I won't be a minute. Go on."

He watched her disappear into the kitchen, and then said, "After I escaped from the embassy, I came straight to your parents' apartment. They were married by then and your father had just started working at the Mausoleum. All three of us agreed that it wouldn't be safe for me to stay in Moscow a moment longer. We didn't know which of our friends to trust. Your father had relatives in the city of Tula, about two hundred kilometres to the southeast, and that was where I went. He also arranged my new documents — a transit pass, a Soviet passport, and reference letters to prospective employers.

"In Tula, I rented a room in a communal apartment and found a job at a factory that made cars. The work didn't please me, but I was alive. I wished I could join a theatre troupe and continue acting, but I had to lie low. If people asked me where I was from, I told them I was born in China but moved with my parents to Russia when I was five years old. My parents were dead now, I'd tell them, and for all that I knew, it was true. Every day I thought about my family and wondered what had happened to them. Every night I dreamt about them, especially Shin.

"I lived in Tula for ten years, slowly building the foundation for my future work. In the eyes of the world, I disappeared. I hoped the North Koreans would forget all about me. I read a lot during this period, many books on political theory. I had time to think about what direction I wanted my life to take. In a way it was like being in prison, where you had time to reflect on what you did. Except that I wasn't a proper criminal even, because I had failed at what I'd set out to do.

"I realized I couldn't give up my struggle. If nothing else, the thoughts of my parents drove me on. I couldn't bear the thought that their lives were sacrificed in vain. I had to do right by them. So I began to write down my ideas and to devise new ways to resist the regime. Every once in a while a contact from your parents would come to Tula to check up on me. That was how I learned of the fate of our network in Moscow, which all but fell apart after I fled. Many people were kidnapped and flown back to North Korea, charged with high treason upon landing, and shot near the airport. Others disappeared and were never heard from again. But one lucky person made it to Siberia, pretended to be a Chinese migrant, and was hired by a logging company in the Far East.

"I knew that person well. He was one of the original disciples. Your parents knew him too. He began to make contacts with the Chinese who lived on the border with North Korea, and managed to organize a small trading network. Soon, information from North Korea would be exchanged for vodka or gold watches, and in return the Chinese would get ginseng or snakes.

"Many of my friend's clandestine traders hated Kim Il Sung's regime. They saw that even in the poorest regions in China life was much better than what they were used to in the fatherland. It didn't take much to persuade them that things needed to change. Not only might private business be allowed if Kim Il Sung's regime was overthrown and a new, better government took over, but also the

Koreas might become one country again. It's important to remember that everyone in Korea, whether they live in the North or in the South, believe they are one nation and wish to reunite.

"Thus, before long, my friend managed to establish nighttime crossing points at the Tumen River for political refugees. We began to raise money and to channel it out of Russia to our Chinese guides."

"Where did the money come from?" I asked him.

"From our supporters in Russia, like your parents, and from many others around the world. Some were journalists who interviewed North Korean defectors in the South and wrote articles about them in the West. Human rights organizations sent money as well. Christian missionaries helped us out also — Canadians, mostly, Swedish and Dutch. We also received a lot of help from the Americans." He paused. "I can't tell you any more than that, I'm afraid."

My grandmother entered the study carrying a large silver tray, on which jingled a platter of cookies, four teacups, and a teapot. She placed the tray on my father's desk, shuffled back to her chair, and took her time settling back in.

"Don't pour it yet," she said to my father. "Good tea, like a good story, needs time to brew."

Dong-jun said, "Through a defector smuggled out of North Korea, I learned my parents' fate. As I feared, they were arrested, tried for treason, and executed by firing squad. Nobody knew, however, what happened to my little brother, except that he'd become a ward of the state."

I felt anger rising in me. "Your parents sacrificed themselves because they believed in what they did, but what about Shin? What right did they have to sacrifice him?"

Dong-jun held my gaze for a few moments and then looked away, as if he was ashamed of his own emotion, as if it was all too much to take.

"I can't speak for my parents, or for what reasons they might've had for what they did. I can only speak for myself and tell you that I don't blame them for anything. I won't judge them. I don't think anyone should."

He stood up, thrust his hands in his pockets, and began to pace around the room.

"You see, my parents knew what would happen to them if their plan worked. They knew that the secret police would come to arrest them the moment we published our protest. They also knew what would happen to their thirteen-year-old son. Shin turned thirteen while I was in Moscow. He was finishing middle school. He'd excelled in all subjects and proven himself to be a loyal Young Communist. He attended all political meetings and recited passages from Kim Il Sung's books. He was also handsome and physically strong, and had been singled out by the Ministry of Internal Security as a candidate for the elite training spy school."

"Spy school?" I cried out, unable to help myself.

"None of which would have saved him from being arrested. If his parents were found to be enemies of the state, he would be an enemy of the state too. But my mother was a psychologist who made recommendations in child custody cases for the government. She knew how the system worked. In all political cases, when parents are arrested, their children are arrested too, unless" — he raised his finger — "unless their child was the one who had turned his parents in. Do you understand what I'm telling you, Vera? Do you understand that in the twisted world of North Korea a child who betrays his parents is hailed as a hero for the regime?"

"Is this what happened?" I managed to whisper. "Did Shin turn his parents in?"

"He did. My parents made sure of it. Everything had been arranged beforehand between the four of us. Everyone had a job to do. On the day of my abduction in Moscow, which also happened to be two days before the disciples were going to publish the letter of protest in the *Moscow Times*, Shin wrote his own letter to the secret police in Pyongyang, in which he spelled out his parents' 'crimes.' The next day my parents were arrested. Shin, meanwhile, was granted his wish. His wish, as specified in his letter, was to redeem his parents' guilt. Which meant he'd be sent to spy school, and which also meant that after graduation he'd continue my parents' work if I failed."

"Opposing Kim?"

"Yes. Twenty years later, it's 1994. Shin is a captain in army intelligence, working in Division 19. Kim Il Sung's declining health is on everyone's mind. What will happen after he dies? Will there be a transfer of power? Will it be Kim Jong Il? It looks like it might. Meanwhile, the country is in shambles. The Russians have turned off financial aid. They used to supply natural gas and industrial materials to North Korea, but now things aren't the same. The Cold War is over, and so, it appears, is Soviet help. South Korea is getting stronger. Economically, it's even stronger now than Japan. And while the Party is ratcheting up military spending, regular people are starving in the countryside.

"The Americans are picking up 'chatter' coming out of the Russian embassy in Pyongyang. There's a doctor, they hear, in Kim Il Sung's inner circle. They think something may be in the works."

"What doctor?"

"You've met him," my father said. "Remember the officer at the New Year's party? He gave a speech."

I strained to remember what he looked like, but that day — that day was when I told everything to my father. I couldn't possibly have paid attention to anything else.

My father said, "They called him 'the blood keeper' because he drew Kim Il Sung's blood every week. He analyzed it for chemical markers, looking for signs of disease. He was a good doctor, an expert; he knew everything about human blood. How many grams of albumin per litre, for example, was normal, or cholesterol, or triglycerides. When the muscles of the human heart are damaged due to a blocked artery, certain proteins leak into the bloodstream and indicate disease. Proteins like troponin, or a special kind of hemoglobin called A1C. So, the blood keeper knew before anyone else that the Great Leader had serious problems with his heart. He was such a good biochemist; some people believed he could predict the exact time of Kim Il Sung's death. Furthermore, he was expected to become a part of Kim Il Sung's embalming team, but North Korean intelligence had suspected he might also be part of an opposition group — a group of people in Kim Il Sung's inner circle who were going to try to take control of the Party after his death."

"A coup?"

"Yes, which was why the exact state of Kim Il Sung's

health was very important, as was the possible time of his death. But the blood keeper miscalculated, or perhaps— well, one can never tell with death. In any case, in July of last year, Kim Il Sung died unexpectedly of an apparent heart attack."

My father paused to pour our tea.

"And?" I asked, eager to hear the rest.

"And nothing happened," my father said. "Kim Jong Il took over the Party's leadership. There was no coup, or, rather, I should say there was no coup that we know of. Meanwhile, some suspected opposition leaders also died, unexpectedly, in their sleep. The oddest thing was that those people were cremated, but then they—returned."

"Returned?" I leaned forward in my chair. "What do you mean?"

"They reappeared alive in China, in South Korea, or in other parts of the world. It seemed they'd returned from the dead."

And then I saw it.

"Like Shin's mother, you mean?"

"Yes. But not his real mother, because you know now that Shin's real mother was dead. The mother Shin had told you about while you were in Pyongyang. She was to be smuggled out of the country after faking her death."

My baby woke up and kicked me.

"Who did Shin bring to the morgue, then?"

"No one," my father said. "She was a fake, a fiction, cre- ated by North Korean intelligence to go after the person who helped people fake their own death. The person I betrayed, the blood keeper. I gave him up in exchange for you. I knew what he'd been up to all along. He smuggled people out of North Korea by giving them drugs to make them appear dead."

Dong-jun said, "After five years in Tula, I was able to get a message to Shin. I told him that I was alive in Russia and asked him to wait. We had to be patient, I told him, if we wanted to reunite."

"Enter Professor Viktor and his twenty-one-year-old daughter," my grandmother said, sipping her tea.

"Indeed," my father said. "Shortly after landing in Pyongyang, I was faced with an ultimatum: do as we say, or else. If you don't, we'll hurt your daughter in Moscow. We have the means. But if you call her here, we promise that everything will be all right. We won't touch her. We guarantee it. Nothing bad will happen to her. She'll live in Pyongyang as an exchange student and work in the Botanical Gardens, that's it."

His body stiffened. He came near me and took my hand.

"You must brace yourself now, darling, because the worst is yet to come. The North Koreans came up with a special operation to get to the bottom of 'the returned.' Because of my position as the embalmer, they thought they'd use me. They suspected the blood keeper was involved, and so they needed me to get close to him. They knew I wouldn't help them of my own volition, so they came up with a sinister plan. Shin the spy became Shin the botanist. Song was in on everything from the start. Both of them worked in Division 19. He wooed you. She watched you and recorded your menstrual cycles to predict your most fertile days. To give him the best chance to make you pregnant, I'm very sorry to say. Because of your pregnancy, you became vulnerable and I became the pawn once again. It was clever of them. They knew I was going to do anything, anything possible, to bring you and your baby home. I'll have to bear the burden of it for the rest of my life."

My heart felt empty. I couldn't feel my legs. It was as if all at once my entire body shrivelled up and withered away.

"When Shin started to work in the Botanical Gardens," my father went on, "he noticed the buildings with the blue roofs. Whatever was going on in there was so secret that even he, with his security clearance, was denied access. There, as he told you, narcotics were manufactured for distribution to the West. And Russia was one of the main consumers of those. The Russian government was concerned but needed evidence to launch an official complaint. The North Koreans denied everything and labelled the drug containers with American stamps. Before I left for Pyongyang, I was summoned to the Kremlin. They asked me to see what I could dig up."

Dong-jun said, "I talked to your father and we agreed that it was our chance. The Russians would help to get someone out of North Korea in exchange for information about the drugs. Your father was to wait in Pyongyang for a message from a person who mentioned the buildings with blue roofs. The person who'd give him that message would be my brother and that person turned out to be—"

"My Shin," I said, relieved that the pieces of the elaborate puzzle were finally starting to fall into place.

"But if the North Koreans were after the blood keeper, as you say, and you gave him up in exchange for me, then why wouldn't they let me get out of Pyongyang the same way I got there? To fly out a plane?"

"They staged your escape across the river so they could follow you to the Chinese side. To figure out the supply routes and the safe houses for the defectors, to uncover the network Dong-jun's friend ran. All with the tacit agreement of the Chinese government, of course."

"Do you mean that the people who helped me on the other side, the people who took me to Beijing—" I gasped in horror. "Did I give them away?"

"No," Dong-jun said. "We expected the raid and were ready for it. None of our people were caught."

I gathered my thoughts quickly, trying to keep track of everything. As I did so, I realized that I'd been delaying asking the one question I most wanted the answer to.

I placed my hands on my stomach.

"But what about Shin? If he was one of their agents? Why was he shot?"

"He wasn't," my grandmother said. "They used rubber bullets. He pretended again."

"Do you mean to tell me that Shin is alive?"

"Yes," Dong-jun said.

"Where is he? In North Korea? What will happen to him?"

"He got out, the day after you. Beyond that—I don't know."

"Let's see that ring." My grandmother nodded toward my hands. "He gave it to you."

I slid the ring off my finger and passed it to Dong-jun.

He inspected it closely, and then brought out a penknife. He flicked the blade open and began to pry the ruby off.

"What are you doing?" I cried.

"Vera, be quiet," my grandmother shushed me.

Dong-jun passed the ring to my father, who brought out a pair of surgical tweezers from a drawer in his desk. He used them to extract something from under the ruby and placed it under the microscope.

"Microfilm," he said with satisfaction. "With the photographs we need. But I see something else also. It looks like some markings are etched on the metal inside. Co-ordinates of some kind, I think. Latitude and longitude." He copied them on a piece of paper and passed it to me. "Do the numbers mean anything to you?"

I shook my head no.

Dong-jun came over to look over my shoulder.

"I think I know what it might be."

He strode to a bookshelf and brought down a leather tome. *Atlas of the World*. Placing it on my father's desk, he opened it to the table of contents, and slid his finger down the page. Meanwhile, in the corner, my grandmother dipped another cookie in her cup of tea and smiled at me.

"The co-ordinates are in Canada." Dong-jun turned the book toward me. "A perfect place for a horse ranch. My brother will wait for you there. After the birth of your baby, when things settle down, the two of you can go there to live with him."

I sat there for a long time without speaking, listening to my baby's heartbeat. I thought about that doctor, the blood keeper, whom my father had betrayed to save our lives. The blood keeper had been saving people's lives too, by making them die. Not die for real. To die for a little while. The way all of us die every day, every minute, shedding bits of ourselves, like skin.

"Shin's assignment was to make pretend-love to you," Dong-jun said. "But in the end, his heart became true."

My grandmother said, "Everyone returns, Verochka. The living, the dying, and the dead."

And that was how I knew it. I knew that one day Lenin's body would be returned too. That one day he would be buried, next to his beloved sister, in St. Petersburg, where he'd always wanted his body to be.

Then I asked myself: but who was my blood keeper, really? Song? Shin? My father? My son?

I was sure it was all of us.

Everyone.

I am the specimen of love.

AUTHOR'S NOTE

I'm greatly indebted to the following works for inspiring several stories in this collection: A. S. Byatt's *Angels & Insects* (Vintage, 1995), Edgar Allan Poe's "Mesmeric Revelation" (*Columbian Magazine*, 1844) and "The Facts in the Case of M. Valdermar" (*The American Review*, 1845), Michael Pollan's "The Intelligent Plant" (*The New Yorker*, December 23, 2013), "Barbara Demick's *Nothing to Envy: Ordinary Lives in North Korea* (Spiegel & Grau, 2010), Andrei Lankov's *North of the DMZ: Essays on Daily Life in North Korea* (McFarland & Company, 2010), Chol-hwan Kang's *The Aquariums of Pyongyang* (Basic Books, 2005), Ilya Zbarsky and Samuel Hutchinson's *Lenin's Embalmer* (Harvill Press, 1999), Helen-Louise Hunter's *Kim Il-song's North Korea* (Praeger, 1999), Helmut Bechtel's *Manual of Cultivated Orchid Species* (Blandford Press, 1986), Jack Kramer's *Orchids, Flowers of Romance and Mystery* (H. N. Abrams, 1975), Tom and Marion Sheehan's *Orchid Genera Illustrated* (Van Nostrand Reinhold, 1979), Robert L. Dressier's *The Orchids: Natural History and Classification* (Harvard University Press, 1981), and Charles Darwin's *Fertilisation of Orchids* (John Murray, 1862).

ACKNOWLEDGEMENTS

No writer is a single strand of DNA. She needs a second strand to become a double helix. During the five years of writing this collection, the following were my second strands:

Comrade Zsuzsi Gartner, without whom these stories would have never been written; Janice Zawerbny, whose masterful editing made all the difference in the world; Sarah MacLachlan and everyone at the House of Anansi, whose confidence and enthusiasm sustained me; and my agent, Monica Pacheco, who rolled the ball and got a strike.

The Optional Residency MFA Program in Creative Writing at UBC, especially my supportive and generous early readers: Krista Foss, Jean van Loon, Nola Poirier, Trevor Corkum, Paul Aarntzen, Rosemary Nixon, Jessica Block, Katherin Edwards, Shawn Stibbards, Kirsten Madsen, Gudrun Will, Jacqueline Windh, Sioux Browning, Wayne Grady, Peter Levitt, and Annabel Lyon.

The Department of Molecular Biology and Biochemistry at Simon Fraser University, especially Bruce Brandhorst, Don Sinclair, and Jenny Lum, and all of my students, past and present, who have taught me everything I know about DNA.

My faithful friends: Kasia Jaronczyk, Paul Cowley and Claudia Zambrano, Nabyl Merbouh, Annette Stenning, Olga Arlitt, Monica Syrzycka, Joe Lee, Mackenzie Caulfield, Ivy Chung, Cathy Kilik, Kat Zambo, and Heather McCutcheon.

My "'mazing" family: Natalya Kovalyova (mamochka) and Vladimir Kovalyov (papochka); Dashka, Nikolai, and Jared Lorio; George and Linda Wicks; Corey-equals-everything Wicks and Melissa Linden.

Ingrid Northwood, the dearest friend I will ever have in this world.

And above all, Maia and Nadine, the keepers of my double helix.

IRINA KOVALYOVA has a master's degree in chemistry from Brown University, a doctoral degree in microbiology from Queen's University, and an MFA in creative writing from UBC. She is currently a senior lecturer in the Department of Molecular Biology and Biochemistry at Simon Fraser University. She has previously interned for NASA and worked for two years as a forensic analyst in New York City. She was born in Russia and currently lives in Vancouver.

CPSIA information can be obtained at www.ICGtesting.com
Printed in the USA
LVOW08s0018230316

480234LV00002B/2/P